# Sismo

# Sismo

**Marcia Biederman**

**Walker and Company**
**New York**

First published in the United States of America in 1993
by Walker Publishing Company, Inc.

Published simultaneously in Canada by Thomas Allen & Son
Canada, Limited, Markham, Ontario

Library of Congress Cataloging-in-Publication Data
Biederman, Marcia
Sismo / Marcia Biederman.
p.    cm.
ISBN 0-8027-3243-7
I. Title.
PS3552.I344S57    1993
813'.54—dc20        93-1866
CIP

Printed in the United States of America
2  4  6  8  10  9  7  5  3  1

*For Michael*

# Acknowledgments

Many thanks to Sergio and Mario Puga and the other volunteers at the Centro Cultural Tepito who took time out from their crucial work to talk to me. Thanks also to the young people who guided me through the operations of the Parque México shelter: Alicia Álvarez, Manuel Alejandro Martínez, Jesús Hurtado Ramos, and Alejandro Bernard Alonzo. Elena Colmenares' book, *Terremoto: Septiembre Rojo*, provided an invaluable hour-by-hour record of the events that followed September 19, 1985, in Mexico City. Lt. John Gasperin and Officer Paul Spennrath of the New York Police Department's Movie and TV Unit were helpful as well as entertaining.

# Sismo

$\triangledown$

# 1

BRIAN FOWLER CHECKED the trap he'd laid on top of the cheap veneer dresser in room 1102: a brown leather wallet stuffed with traveler's checks and 5,000-peso notes. The chambermaid in 517 had passed the test yesterday, so shortly after breakfast Fowler asked for a room change. The young girl with long braids cleaned this part of the hotel, the one who flirted with the desk clerk. She had an intelligent look about her. Fowler expected to find something missing.

He checked through the wallet once more before closing the drawer. This time, he remembered to pull out his tourist visa, stamped with all the official Mexican seals and made out of the kind of paper you could sneeze in. It's what Americans got for trips of six months or less, business or pleasure.

This hotel had stained carpets, fiberglass drapes, and wastebaskets made of used insecticide cans. Fowler was down here with his silk suits, Italian shirts, and designer luggage. He was here on business.

The housekeeping staff would go off duty soon, so he had to work fast. He took the water glass from the bathroom washstand and smashed it on the tile floor. Then he phoned the desk. It took ten rings for someone to answer. He always kept count.

"This is 1102," Fowler said in Spanish. "Can you send someone up with a mop? There's glass all over the bathroom floor."

"1102?" The clerk sounded skeptical. "Are you the gentleman from the United States?" In Spanish, Fowler had only a hint of an accent. They never could believe it, especially, for some reason, over the phone.

The elevator made three wheezy stops on the way down. At the ground floor it disgorged Fowler along with several bantamweight men dressed in dark pants and light pleat-front shirts. Mexicans, all of them. That was good. One held the arm of a woman cinched into a brocaded dress. Fowler took a good look at her. Trans Rio was interested only in commercial hotels. Not that kind of commerce. He hoped she was a wife.

The American from last night, Jim Rigg, was in the lobby bar again. Fowler took the stool to Rigg's right. Through the glass doors of the bar, he had a good view of the reservation desk and the two uniformed clerks. The one that the chambermaid with braids liked was reading a book.

If Trans Rio bought this place, they could do plenty of payroll trimming. Fowler would remind them when he made his report.

Rigg didn't want to go to the movies. He said he'd lost track of American films since he'd been down here. He was going to stay put in the bar.

"I hear this film is pretty good," said Fowler, who'd seen it three times. "Connie Oland's in it." He loved mentioning her name to men. He hoped Rigg would say something obscene.

But Rigg had scarcely heard of her. "The India Maria, she's the star down here. And I don't go to her movies, 'cause I don't speak Spanish."

Rigg yelled for the gray-haired bartender. *Joven*, boy, *traeme otra cerveza*. Fowler laughed so hard that bourbon dribbled into the deep cleft in his chin. Rigg only knew the disrespectful forms. He got a kick out of Rigg. Rigg made him miss Texas. Already, after only two weeks.

He'd taken Rigg for a tourist at first, and that bothered him. Trans Rio wanted to steer clear of the recreational trade. But after one drink together, he knew the guy had been in the country awhile—the way he called this town "Mexico" instead of "Mexico City," like the package-tour people did. Turned out he had a business in Monterrey. Said he'd spent the whole day today checking on one of his factories.

"Apparel," he said in answer to Fowler's question. "And I don't even look Jewish, do I?"

"Are you?"

"*Hell*, no."

Fowler saw the girl with braids stop by the desk to talk to the clerk. The clerk took his nose out of the book, and they horsed around, grabbing hands. Eventually, the message about the broken glass seemed to be communicated. She walked away in the direction of the elevator.

Rigg was inviting him to spend the evening with some hookers.

"You mean here? They come over here?" Fowler thought of the woman on the elevator. Hookers would be a major problem. Trans Rio wouldn't like that.

"Nah, back there in one of those little bedbug hotels, off the main drag." He jerked a thumb. "The Hotel Mina, and there's another one, I forget its name. The one with the big shamrock. That's why I like to say here. For the location. It's no Villa Real, that's for damn sure. Hell, I could afford to stay at the Villa Real anytime I wanted. But what's there to do over there except play golf?"

Fowler agreed about the Villa Real, ignoring Rigg's unspoken question about his own reasons for checking into this dump: He never let anyone know he was scouting for acquisitions. He declined about the whores.

"You don't know what you're missing. Some of them are just beautiful. Young. *Really* young," said Rigg, a smile spreading over his middle-aged skin. "And I've got rubbers from the States. Trojans. The ones the government sells down here ain't worth piss."

"I'll pass," said Fowler. It was a shame this guy wouldn't go to the Connie Oland movie. He'd be the perfect companion.

"You married?"

"Not for too much longer. My lawyer's working on it."

"One of those lengthy settlements, huh? I've been down that road myself. Just never let her know how much you've got." An idea seemed to dawn over Rigg, and he congratulated himself by taking a swig. "You're a smart boy. Stay in dung heaps like this, and she'll never catch on."

Fowler smiled the obligatory sheepish smile. Rigg was warm, but not as warm as he thought.

"She's trying to bleed you dry, huh? I know the type. Why don't these broads work if they want to go shopping all day?"

"Actually, she does work," Fowler said, silently thanking God he'd never have to hear about it again. "Something up your alley, in fact. Writes about clothing for a trade magazine. Covers it, I should say, and I guess I should call it apparel." He could hardly believe himself, still jumping through the hoops. The wife was always a stickler for jargon.

"You can call it shit, because that's what it is. That's what I manufacture anyhow." Rigg was working on a fresh beer. He laughed through the foam on his mustache. "She ever write about my company? I do a very big volume with the discount chains." Fowler asked for the name. Rigg said something that sounded like "Hymie Togs."

"*J-A-I-M-E* Togs," said Rigg. "That's my first name, James. You say it 'Hymie.' Hell, I don't need to tell you. How is it you speak the lingo so good?"

Fowler looked at his watch. The chambermaid should have finished by now. "I lived here for a few years when I was a kid. My father was transferred here for a while."

Rigg shook his head, enjoying his joke. "See, I was born to go into apparel. Hymie Togs. I fit right in with the Jews."

Fowler threw some change on the bar and went up to his room. At first he thought one of the traveler's checks was missing, but it was just the sweat of excitement on his hands making the notes stick together. He checked the bathroom, which now smelled of some violent disinfectant. She'd missed a few splinters of glass.

His copy of the *Mexico City News* was on the nightstand,

topping a stack of six or seven Spanish-language papers. He forced himself to leaf though it again, scanning every headline. Nope. Nothing about the death of a movie star's grandfather, not in the international section and not in Doris Pike's idiot column. Her topic for today: Impossible to find a decent English muffin anywhere in Mexico's Federal District.

He decided to take a second look at some of the other papers. Nothing in *Excelsior* or *El Universal*. He'd ignored *La Jornada* and *Unomásuno* today; they were left-wing papers, an unlikely place for the news to run. Still, they occasionally ran wire-service stories. He gave them a quick skim. Nothing.

The *News* had the most reliable listings of show times for American movies, so he turned to that again. The film was playing at one of those colossal movie houses out near the parkside end of Reforma. It would take forty-five minutes to get there, but Fowler didn't mind. He looked forward to escaping from the Guerrero district.

Anyhow, he wouldn't miss this screening for the world. He wanted to see the movie in a theater full of Mexican boys who'd howl and catcall when the leading lady removed her blouse. He wanted to see Connie Oland humiliated because she wanted to see him destroyed.

Fowler slipped his jacket on and patted the butter-soft leather, feeling for his agenda book. He felt he should make some notes about this hotel. There'd been so many of them over the past few weeks, all blending together.

But this was the best. He'd advise Trans Rio to buy it. It was ugly but clean, and the help was honest. Just what Trans Rio sent him to look for—a businessman's hotel with no pimps, no tourists, and no amenities.

A place like this ran itself. Fowler made a note in his agenda: "Hotel Suizo-Americano. Buy it."

Trans Rio should have done stuff like this in the first place. They never should have gotten into that luxury residential hotel line. You wouldn't have the grandfather of some hysterical movie star staying here. You wouldn't have grand juries investigating an accident the old guy brought on himself.

Back in the lobby, he checked the bar through the glass doors. Rigg was still drinking his head off. Fowler tried to catch his eye, hoping he'd change his mind about the movie, but the garment manufacturer was staring into the glassware rack.

He left the key at the desk. The chambermaid's boyfriend put down his book and produced some halting English, wishing Fowler a nice evening. Fowler rattled off a quick response in Spanish. He never liked to serve as anyone's free Berlitz lesson. The kid was impressed.

"I would like to know language like you do, sir." Fowler was running late, but he didn't mind listening to a little fawning. "My problem is, I don't get to practice. The tourists don't come here or to the Toronto."

"You work at the Toronto, too? What's that like?" Fowler was headed there tomorrow. It was under the same ownership. He hoped to make a package deal.

The kid shrugged. "*Económico,* like this. Nothing much." It sounded hopeful. "With English, I could get a job in the fine hotels. The Maria Isabel–Sheraton or maybe even the Villa Real."

"What's your name?"

"Juan Antonio Mendoza."

Fowler glanced at the book the clerk had been reading. "Student?"

"Yes. UNAM. Law."

Fowler gave him a little wave good-bye with his left hand, letting him see his gold watch. The kid gave it a good stare. Juan Antonio Mendoza, studying on the job. If Trans Rio took over the hotel, a certain law student would get his wish: He wouldn't be working here anymore.

Outside, the traffic on Guerrero Street was the usual jalopy race. Volkswagen Beetles nipped at Fowler's ankles as he crossed the street. Once on the other side, he started hailing cabs, but they all rushed by, full already. Busy for a Tuesday night.

The smell of lard wafted over from the corner, where a

solemn young man was frying tiny coins of meat on his portable *hamburguesa* stand. Two young girls wearing flimsy synthetic cardigans waited expectantly.

Fowler thought of his wife, maybe because of those sweaters. She'd been down here with him once, three years ago, in '82. It didn't take her more than a day or two to fix on some kind of industry buzzword for Mexican clothes, "low end" or "popularly priced," something like that. She had actually started talking like that at the breakfast table.

Fowler wondered what would happen if the Oland grandfather died and he was indicted. Could it affect the divorce proceedings somehow, entitle his wife to a bigger settlement? He let his hand drop, suddenly feeling the chill in the September air.

Something made him look up at the framework sign jutting from the roof of the fifteen-story hotel. Mexico's weak electrical current pumped through the plain block letters, setting them off dramatically against the sky; the Guerrero district was short on streetlights.

Fowler took out his notebook again to read what he'd written: *Hotel Suizo-Americano. Buy it.* Give or take a few burnt-out letters, the sign above him said Hotel Lara. The Suizo-Americano had been last week.

A bunch of teenagers in black vinyl jackets rushed by him, brandishing two-by-fours. They ran up to a car stopped at a traffic light. There was the sound of a blow, then windshield glass tinkled into the street. A gang. Nobody paid much attention.

Was Trans Rio serious, sending him to look at hotels here and in those other godforsaken districts on his itinerary— Taxqueña, Postal? Or were they just trying to get him out of the way?

Brian Fowler put away his notebook and waved at the taxis. He had to stop making mistakes.

The movie was all he hoped it would be. The cavernous moviehouse was jammed with young people. Halfway through the film, when Connie Oland stripped down to her bra and panties, Fowler twisted his head around. He'd memorized where some of the couples were concentrated. As always, the boys with dates oinked the loudest.

But the elation didn't last. Bored with the movie, or too unschooled to read the Spanish subtitles, the audience churned between seats and refreshment stand, returning with cheap candy and plastic bags full of noncarbonated soda. Fowler, his stomach already suffering the consequences of a Hotel Lara dinner, reeled from the smell. He left before the film was over.

The men's room off the lobby was another olfactory assault, and Fowler had no small change for the old gent selling sheets of toilet paper. He moved on.

He was in a solidly middle-class district, yet the first bar he came across was squalid enough for Guerrero. Too dispirited to hunt further, he ordered a drink and went to the john.

No old gent here. Instead, squares of newspaper hung on a hook by the flyspecked toilet. Better than nothing, Fowler supposed.

The square he selected carried a brief UPI story in its entirety. Connie Oland's grandfather had died as a result of a hotel accident. She'd called a press conference about it. She had cried. She had spoken about the need to regulate care of the elderly. She had worn an emerald green blouse and a tailored black suit. Word was expected soon from the investigating grand jury.

The dateline on the story was two days old. Just as Fowler had anticipated, Trans Rio hadn't bothered to call. But he'd get a call soon. He was going to be indicted.

$$\bigtriangledown$$

# 2

FOWLER STARTED THE next day with a hot shower. Maybe not quite as hot as the shower that had killed Connie Oland's grandfather.

He couldn't say the death surprised him. The old man had been burned pretty badly. The housekeeper who found him quit the next day—that's how gruesome it was. None of the employees were equipped to deal with medical situations. They weren't supposed to be. That was the idea behind La Ermita. It was a luxury residential hotel, the finest in Texas, for healthy old people with healthy assets.

Anyone else would have scooted out of that shower as soon as they felt the temperature. This sensory loss the Oland guy was experiencing, that was something he and his doctor should have revealed on his initial application. Sick old people belonged in nursing homes, not at La Ermita.

And the way he developed those infections after the burns. This Kenneth Oland was not a healthy old man, no matter how much tournament tennis he played.

Fowler turned off his own shower and grabbed a towel.

At the sink, he thought about his secretary, the one who'd given him hell about the accident right before he fired her. It was going to look very bad if she decided to testify. All those complaints from the guests about the hot-water temperature had gone through her first. As if the thermostat on a boiler could be fixed in the blink of an eye. Those things have gotten damned complicated. High tech. Electronic. Trans Rio couldn't just call up a plumber. Trans Rio got bids on everything. It owed that to its shareholders.

Fowler hoped to God that Trans Rio thought of some way to buy off that secretary. They'd claimed they would, if it came to that. To protect him, they said. Maybe.

Fowler pumped some aerosol shaving cream into his palm. He had to crouch to center his face in the mirror: the handmade wooden medicine chest was hung at Mexican height. A pair of blue eyes under nearly invisible eyebrows looked back as he slathered cream over his broad cheeks and chin. Stone cut, that's how his wife used to describe his features. Now she'd probably say low end.

That secretary had liked this face for a time. Fowler had noticed that; he'd even considered using it. Trouble was, she liked Connie Oland even better, always dropping her typing and running to the window when that slut came to visit Gramps. Connie Oland could buy her off with a flash of her capped-tooth smile.

The jurors were going to be another problem, thought Fowler, dropping a fresh blade into his razor. They'd probably sneak their autograph books into court.

He was completely dressed and half packed before the telephone next to the bed rang.

"Ready with your call to the United States." Fowler checked his travel alarm clock. It had taken the operator thirty-five minutes. A nation of sloths.

By ten o'clock he was on the sidewalk with his suitcases, waiting for the bellboy to find him a taxi. Rigg came out of the hotel, looking a bit unsteady. He told Fowler he'd hit the jackpot at one of the bedbug hotels, found himself a young one. He asked Fowler where he was headed.

"Balderas," said Fowler. "International telegraph office." He saw Rigg look at his bags. "Then off to Acapulco for a bit." In fact, he was headed south, to Taxqueña and the Hotel Toronto. But there was no need to tell Rigg.

"Good old Aca. Attaboy, get away from this stinking city."

The bellboy had finally succeeded in snagging a taxi. Fowler extended his hand for a good-bye shake, but Rigg asked if he could join him. He said there was a money wire waiting for him at Telégrafos Internacionales, and he might as well get it.

Fowler let him hop in. Companionship was fine, as long as it ended at the telegraph office.

The taxi crawled down Reforma behind a solid slab of buses, three abreast and all of them defecating diesel fumes.

"Smog's not *too* bad yet," said Rigg. "It'll probably settle in a little later." Some of the pedestrians hurrying by on the crowded sidewalks already had handkerchiefs clapped to their mouths. But not as many as usual.

"The air here's going to kill me," said Rigg, who'd lit up a cigarette. "You've got the right idea. Acapulco. I think I'll head that way myself, once I fix up things here. It's going to take a month of fixing at least."

"Production problems?"

"Production, mechanical, labor." He shook his head. "Labor," he repeated. "Everything runs a lot smoother in Monterrey. You ever pass by the garment center here, on San Antonio Abad?"

"Can't say I have."

"You ought to take a look. Anytime of the day or night, the damn Mexicans are picketing all over the street."

That could be a problem at the hotels, too. Fowler wondered if he should mention it to Trans Rio in his report. If they expected a report. Now that Kenneth Oland was dead, they'd probably drop the whole charade. They'd keep Fowler on the payroll until the trial was over. Then they'd trim him.

"I don't know what the hell these people down here want," Rigg was saying. "They don't want to work, that's for sure. Bunch of Communists. Monterrey, that's beautiful. But you can take this town and shove it, far as I'm concerned. The whole city's fucked up."

Everyone's car horn was going now. If it hadn't been for the suitcases, Fowler would have gotten out and walked.

Rigg said he was going to pick up funds that were wired to him weekly from his Texas headquarters in Harlingen.

"Forgot about it last week, so they've got a whole pile waiting for me. Isn't it something the way the peso's taking a dive? My greenbacks are going twice as far, just about. Yesterday, the Lara gave me four hundred pesos to the dollar. Pretty damn good."

"The banks give four-twenty-five."

"I've got no patience for banks," said Rigg with a wave of his cigarette. He brightened. "Hey, didja hear how one of these presidents down here, Echev-what's-his-name, got the Nobel Prize for chemistry?"

"Echeverría?"

"That's the one."

"No, I didn't hear," said Fowler, genuinely surprised.

"That's right. The Nobel for chemistry. For turning the peso into shit."

If Fowler had been in the mood for laughing, he would have laughed.

Finally they were pulling up to Balderas 7. Fowler checked his watch. He remarked that it had taken twenty minutes to go ten blocks.

"What did I tell you?" Rigg wouldn't have set any speed records himself, the way he got out of the cab. "This city is fucked. Incredibly fucked up."

Fowler let Rigg get ahead of him in line. There was, indeed, quite a pile of pesos waiting for the garment manufacturer; Fowler watched surreptitiously as it was counted out. They said their good-byes, and Fowler showed his tourist visa to the clerk.

He'd expected confusion, and there was some, because his money had been wired just that morning, and the bureaucrats had yet to finish recording it in all their little logbooks. In the end, 170,000 pesos in large bills were passed to him over the counter.

They'd been wired an hour earlier from a personal bank account at Citizens National Bank of Texas—so personal an account that even his ex-wife didn't know about it. Rigg had the right idea. Never let them know just how much you're worth, and they can't suck it all out.

With amazingly little trouble, Fowler found a taxi to take him to Taxqueña. The plan was to drop his bags at the Toronto, then cab back to the center of town. A few hours would be enough to pick up some of the standard things he got for himself in Mexico: leather goods, silver, Kahlúa. Might as well get some bargains, he figured. He'd be needing to save money for legal expenses.

He knew he had to get the shopping done right away. The call would come soon. In fact, a message might already be waiting for him at the Toronto. Trans Rio had his itinerary. They knew where to find him.

Damned if he was going to be the one to phone them after they'd neglected to tell him that little piece of news about Kenneth Oland's death. Anyway, these days he couldn't be sure they'd be accepting collect calls from him.

The Toronto was an institutional-looking affair of yellow and gray mortar, broader and squatter than the Lara and situated on a nicely tended lawn. The surrounding area was middle-class or aspiring to be. Boxlike homes stood behind steel gates and "beware of the dog" signs.

It was a poor man's version of the city's truly tony areas. Sprinkled between the homes were various commercial concerns. A toy company's lot was covered with huge grinning plastic ducks and mammoth beach balls. Pink and turquoise bathroom fixtures, many of them upside down or on their sides, formed a plumbing distributor's al fresco display.

This was the south-central edge of the city, the farthest reach of one of the Metro subway lines. The hotel lay a few kilometers to the east of the Real Thing, the fashionable Coyoacán district, and just below the southern fringe of the Churubusco Country Club. But the Toronto was no luxury spa. It drew most of its business from the nearby Central Camionera del Sur, the big interstate bus terminal that served points south.

Still, Fowler thought, as he presented his tourist visa and filled out the registration card, Trans Rio could get a little more per room here than at the Lara. The current owners were charging the same for both hotels, but the current owners were jerks.

Again, he wondered why he was looking out for Trans Rio.

He checked in to the Toronto and left for the Pink Zone, returning just before midnight with bundles under his arms: watches, cologne, a silver jewelry case, an onyx chess set to lay out when guests came. If the bartender over at the Villa Real hadn't reminded him about the packages, he would have left the whole kit and caboodle in town. He was that blitzed.

"You've got to help me out," he told the night desk clerk. "I need my key, but I forgot what room I'm in."

"Mr. Fowler!"

Fowler squinted until the clerk came into focus. It was Juan Antonio Whatzizname. The bookworm from the Lara. Fowler made a grunt of recognition.

"At your orders until seven A.M.," said the kid, in the servile Mexican manner that never failed to inspire Fowler's contempt. Big with booze, Fowler noticed again how short the kid was. Skinny, too. A good breeze would knock him over. Fowler felt tempted to lift him by the scruff of the neck.

The kid snapped to attention. He made a great show of searching for Fowler's name on the register. Once the room number had been discovered, he searched for it in the pigeonholes behind him, mumbling numbers as he went. Finally he produced the key with a flourish that should have had a drumroll under it.

Fowler had an eager hand extended, but Juan Antonio Mendoza was frowning at the key.

"This is a very bad room, 1032," he said. "I'll change it for you."

"Don't bother," said Fowler. "I'm crucified. I just want to get to sleep."

"Crucified!" the kid chortled an appreciation of the

foreigner's mastery of street slang. It made him all the more eager to switch the rooms. Already he was scribbling in the registration book.

"Here." Fowler finally had the key in his hand. "You'll like this better. Lower, but a nice room." He adopted a confidential tone. "They've had mildew problems in 1032."

The elevator took centuries to rise two floors. Maybe the kid had switched the room because you couldn't get to the tenth floor until next week. Fowler threw off his jacket, kicked off his shoes, and collapsed on the nearest of the two double beds.

There was a knock. When it turned into pounding, Fowler somehow hoisted himself off the bed and opened the door.

It was Juan Antonio Mendoza, laden like a pack animal.

"Here are your suitcases. They were left in 1032."

"Thanks. Just put them down right here, that's fine." Fowler kept his hand on the doorknob.

"And your packages. You forgot them just now at the desk."

"Just drop them. I'll see to them in the morning."

"_And_ your wallet." The kid looked very satisfied with himself, producing the brown billfold—the one Fowler used on the chambermaid bait. "It was out in the open up in 1032. You should hide it, you know. People steal."

"Terrible thought." Fowler grabbed it and began squeezing the door closed.

No sooner had it clicked than the kid knocked again.

"I almost forgot," he told Fowler's glaring face. "A telegram came for you. The day staff put it in the other room."

Fowler waited until the kid's steps had receded down the hall before he tore it open. It was from the court in Dallas. He had to be back in the States by September 20, two days from now. He'd been indicted. Criminally negligent manslaughter.

A monotonous sound awoke Fowler. Through half-closed eyes he saw his closet door flapping on its hinges. At first it moved gently, as if to a ghostly lullaby.

But this was a special lullaby, direct from the Ring of Fire. Within seconds, the door slammed into a wall and turned into shrapnel.

A quake.

By the time Fowler pulled himself into sitting position, the hotel was in full motion, rocking as if it were trying to detach itself from its moorings. The windows were exploding, dozens at once, and there was a steady popping noise, like firecrackers, as the electrical wiring pulled apart.

Fowler swung his feet over the edge of the bed as the Toronto began its crash landing. The walls above were pounding down in thunder claps, and Fowler fell to the tilting floor, hotly pursued by the bureaus, chairs, and fallen mirrors that were rushing toward the vortex.

He was on his back, slanted back like a TV viewer in a recliner, watching quite a show. The ceiling was beginning to pull loose.

Then the room's two beds came hurtling toward him. He winced as they cleared his body and slammed together over him. Broken glass rained under the beds, pelting his ribs.

The ceiling collapsed, banging violently onto the beds before releasing a bomb of plaster dust. Then, as if that had been the grand finale, everything was still.

The worst part for Fowler was the dust. If only he could have coughed it out of his lungs, but he was pinned tightly under the sagging bedsprings. He paid dearly for the few coughs he managed. The coils speared into his chest and sides.

At first he was calm, waiting. He didn't mind, really, that he couldn't move. He wanted nothing to move. His dread was that it would start up again. This was peace.

But his body refused to be peaceful. Everything inside him was rebelling against the dust. Some saliva formed in his mouth, and the dust became heavier against the lining of his cheeks. Mud formation. His chest tightened, and he wheezed like an asthmatic.

His body was becoming alien to him. It was a factory of involuntary responses, running at full capacity without need for his supervision. He could no longer feel his limbs. He wondered if they'd been crushed beyond use. Nothing seemed alive to him but his chest and head, fighting the dust with their useless fluids.

Even the tears started.

The darkness was impenetrable. He stared into it, unsure whether his eyes were opened or closed, or whether he'd been blinded. His mouth gave up its battle against the dust, and the wheezing seemed to subside. The factory had shut down. Nothing to do but wait.

He heard a rasping sound and wondered if it was coming from deep inside himself. The death rattle. It sounded distant, maybe because he was already hovering overhead.

He heard it again. Leather against rock. Footsteps. Close.

He tried to call out, but his tongue and teeth were packed in silt. The bedsprings tightened against his ribs as he inhaled for the effort. There was a fairy tale he'd read as a child. Iron Henry, about a man with metal bands around his heart. It was horrible stuff for kids, nightmare fodder. He was Iron Henry now.

The footsteps moved away and returned, moved away and returned. After each retreat, they came back more tentatively.

He remembered an exercise from a long-ago gym class. First you concentrated on your toes. You had to start with the toes. You tensed them completely, then you made them relax. One by one.

The footsteps were leaving. It was his mouth he needed, but he forced himself to go on.

He made his ankles relax, then his calves. He heard a muffled yell, as if through three walls. He was on his fingers now. Still the yelling. He could hear the words this time: "Is anybody there?" His palms, his wrists, his forearms.

The final test in this exercise was the back of the tongue. To relax that was to relax completely. Fowler forced the tension out of his forehead, the mask of his face, his jaw. . . .

"Help!" The English word came ripping out of him. He'd meant to use Spanish, but it had come on its own.

Rock ground against rock, first dully, then louder.

"*Tranquilo, tranquilo*," said a voice. "I'm coming."

Twice more, Fowler had to call out. The rescuer was tunneling toward him and needed to know his exact position. Finally, hands grabbed Fowler's shoulders and began tugging. The bedsprings held their relentless grip, but Fowler, his Spanish returned, begged the man to keep pulling. As the coils ripped his hair, he bit his lips to prevent himself from screaming.

His belt was caught, but by now his elbows were free and he could work his way out.

"Back out. I'll crawl after you," he told his savior, still invisible in the darkness. The man agreed in a broken voice. Fowler could hear him weeping.

When they emerged from their mortar cave into the light, Fowler saw what he'd begun to sense—that his rescuer was Juan Antonio Mendoza. They sat together on the rubble for a while, embracing. This was not to Fowler's taste, but he was shocked and shaking, and needed to hold on to something at any rate. And he knew that he'd offend the Mexican if he pulled away. His adolescence in the country had taught him more than the language.

Finally, it was time to stand and walk down the mountain of rubble that once was the Hotel Toronto. Fowler reached the neat little lawn—still there, amazingly, and not swallowed into the earth's bowels—and some women charged up to him, offering him water.

He sipped it and looked up at the hotel. The walls had collapsed, leaving the floors stacked like a very short order of pancakes. Drapes and electrical tubing protruded between the layers. Only a few bottom floors had escaped pulverization. If he hadn't switched rooms . . .

The ladies had left to minister to others. People in bathrobes and pajamas were sitting on the grass, shrieking and crying. There were soldiers on the scene. Men were climbing over the debris.

Fowler could hear faraway sirens. But around him, the

Taxqueña district looked calm and untouched. It was as if the Hotel Toronto had been singled out for pinpoint bombardment.

Absently, he'd been rubbing his hands down his chest and sides, where the bedsprings had pushed hardest.

"Do you need a doctor?"

It was the voice he'd welcomed so when he was pinned under the rubble. But, now, it filled him with revulsion. There'd been a witness to his helplessness.

"I went off shift at seven," Juan Antonio said. "I'd walked only two blocks when it happened." He told how he'd run back to the hotel to check on his coworkers. Already he'd pulled two corpses out of the wreckage.

"Then I thought of you. Thank God I'd put you on the third floor. The first room they put you in—" He was in tears now. Mechanically, Fowler thanked him, feeling nothing. He'd been through enough; he didn't want to hear about the corpses. He watched the kid join the men on the heap. One, he noticed, had a pickax. One pickax for about a dozen men.

Fowler noticed for the first time that he had no shoes. He had to get to a hotel and clean up. The Villa Real might be a good choice, if that was still standing.

He walked out to Tlalpan and flagged a taxi, feeling positively embarrassed about his appearance. Things seemed relatively calm, except for the fact that the traffic lights were out. Maybe the Toronto had somehow been on the epicenter of a minor earth tremor. That would be just his luck.

But as the taxi traveled north on Tlalpan, Fowler saw that this had been something major indeed. People were streaming through the streets, crying and wringing their hands, and the ambulances and Red Cross vans sped crazily across the intersections. Here and there were fallen buildings; others stood leaning into the street. Many of those still erect were disfigured by huge scabs of missing masonry.

There was a traffic tie-up near the Victoria Plaza station of the Metro. A traveling circus had set up its striped tent in the neighborhood. Now rescuers were dragging bodies out of a fallen paper factory and setting them under the big top.

The cab driver twisted around to face his passenger.

"*Qué desmadre hizo este sismo, no?*" he said. What a bitch of an earthquake.

Fowler remembered that he'd have to pay the man. Instinctively, he patted his pocket, almost shedding tears of joy when he felt his wallet.

But it was only the brown one, the one he used on the chambermaids. His tourist visa, his credit cards, and most of his cash were buried in the rubble of the Toronto. He was carrying a few traveler's checks and some Mexican bills. In cash, he had barely enough to pay the driver, whose eyes, he now noticed, were watching him in the rearview mirror.

"You said you want the Villa Real?" the driver prompted. Like most taxis in the city, this one had no meter, and Fowler, in his shock, had neglected to negotiate the price.

He told the man to drive on. They entered the Centro, the ruined heart of the city, where building after building had plummeted to the ground, and the sound of sirens was incessant.

"Keep going?" asked the driver. "Just to here is four thousand pesos."

Twice the usual amount. "Fine," said Fowler, who had no intention of paying it. Let the driver complain; the police seemed otherwise occupied. Fowler could see how to play this bitch of an earthquake.

# 3

CONNIE OLAND HADN'T even set foot from her trailer on Manhattan's East Sixth Street when the cop, guarding the sawhorses marked "Police Line" got his first question.

"What's going on? Are they making a movie?"

Tourists, thought the cop, looking at the eager young couple in matching windbreakers. He nodded and got the expected smiles. With perhaps an extra smile from the woman because the cop, whose name was William Bermudez, was lean and darkly handsome.

The second question came from an angry resident, first of the day. Bermudez had braced himself for trouble from the moment the door to the brownstone flew open. Out came a red-faced man. He went huffing and puffing down the street until he was nose-to-nose with the cop.

"When the hell are they going to get out of here?" demanded the man. "Where are we supposed to park?" The man swept his hand toward the equipment vans and the actors' trailers, abruptly curtailing the gesture before it encompassed the blue-and-white police car lettered MOVIE AND TV UNIT over the stripe on the side. "How long do they expect us to live with this? They're hogging all the parking spaces on the whole goddamn street. Look at this one. You could fit five cars in that space, easy."

Bermudez followed the index finger to Connie Oland's trailer. It was her private one and pretty much an elephant. The other actors had those compact jobs that were rented out of Long Island City. Connie Oland needed a tanker because she was carting her own hairdresser and stylist around, the planning officer said. The planning officer was probably the only cop in the NYPD who knew what a stylist was.

"It's their first day filming here," said Bermudez. "First day for this particular company."

The man sputtered scorn. "I could care less what company it is. They going to be shooting at night?"

"Maybe," said Bermudez. The real answer was, positively. Bermudez liked that. He'd asked to do an extra tour out here. He needed the overtime.

The resident's corduroy jacket made angry friction noises. "Night shooting again! I can't believe it."

Elsewhere in this neighborhood, a drug deal was probably going down, someone was probably getting mugged, and a squatter was probably hauling water up six flights of stairs to an apartment in a condemned building. Here, this man was worried about night shooting. East Sixth was a mix. The production companies liked the old low buildings with the eyebrow trim over the windows, good for period pictures. The local populace wasn't quite so quaint. Around here, you had your skinheads and your Indian restaurants, your artists and your street people. But more and more lately you had professional types like this red-faced guy, sitting at home at ten in the morning in his stiff new jacket and shiny leather shoes.

"Do you have any idea what it's like to try to sleep with those lights glaring in your windows?" he asked Bermudez.

Civilians did that to cops in this unit—they asked questions that seemed personal. It had taken Bermudez a while to get used to that. For years he had passed through the streets with a magnetic force around him, repelling some people, attracting others. He had grown accustomed to averted eyes, scornful glances, faces pleading for help. Respect and disrespect were equally familiar, but this indifferent form of address was something foreign to him at first, like the discovery that English had an informal "you" form. He responded to the personal question in the impersonal way he'd learned. He shifted weight, rubbed his scar, re-crossed his arms, lowered his head so that his cap brim shielded his eyes. He could have been any cop.

The man seemed satisfied and moved on. That satisfied Bermudez.

"You'll be like a human information booth," the lieutenant had told him, "it's like permanent parade duty." The interview had been held on a warm autumn day like this one, almost exactly one year ago. The unit had a waiting list a mile long—there was no shortage of cops looking for decent hours, clean work, and removal from danger—but they'd called Bermudez in for a talk twenty-four hours after he'd put in his request.

There'd been dogs howling outside the open window; the Movie and TV Unit shared quarters with the K-9 Corps in Flushing Meadows–Corona Park, site of the 1964 World's Fair. The lieutenant had mopped his brow and glanced nervously at the dogs on the lawn and beyond at the hulking metal globe sculpture left over from the fair. The lieutenant had been kind, moist, slightly embarrassed, mumbling his way through the questions, using antiquated terms or civilian language to discuss police work as if he, too, were a remnant from the day of the Johnson Wax Pavilion and the GM Futurama.

"I'm going to tell you everything about this unit. The good, the bad, and the ugly," he said to Bermudez. It was a habit of his to use movie titles in his conversation. His eyes followed Bermudez's gaze to the wall and the photographs of himself posing awkwardly with television and film stars.

Someone on East Sixth wanted something from the human information booth. It was one of the many local women who wore black from head to foot, including on the eyelids: the downtown Manhattan regional costume. She moved toward Bermudez as if in her sleep.

"When are they going to take that snow shit off my windows?" she asked, pulling at her bangs. "It got hot the other day. I might want to put my air conditioner back in.

All I got for cooperating is a hundred bucks off my rent. It's not worth it."

"Take it up with your landlord," said Bermudez. The thought of that seemed to exhaust her further. She meandered away.

About the only people without any questions were the autograph critters. A bunch of them were standing ready on the sidewalk outside her trailer, lined up neatly as usual. Either they did it by taking numbers or there was a code of professional courtesy for social rejects. Bermudez recognized most of them from previous patrols. No matter how secret a schedule was kept, they always knew where every film, TV program, commercial, and music video was shooting.

Bermudez walked over to them, feeling the weight of the gun on his hip, like a vestigial organ.

"No autographs till they're all finished here," he said. "It might be four or five hours." As if you could discourage anyone in this group. As if they didn't already know the rules. As if they weren't going to try to break them anyway.

"Yes, Officer, sir," said one of them. It was the middle-aged woman, the one the cops called Anne Frank because she stood with the others all day but never asked for any autographs. She just wrote down the names of the celebrities she'd seen in a grubby notebook.

The others waggled their heads in insincere agreement. Bermudez was always surprised that their eyes were in the same place as other people's and not suspended on green stalks growing out of their foreheads. One pair of eyes in particular caught his attention. It belonged to a young guy standing behind Anne Frank. Nothing special about him. Medium height, medium build, dark sweatshirt with the Hard Rock Cafe logo, jeans, sneakers. An average, inconspicuous guy—which is exactly why he stood out from the rest.

He was holding a little autograph book, the type that said "Autographs" on it, ordinarily purchased by elementary school girls shortly before the last day of school. Bermudez glanced at it for a moment. All the others except this guy

and Anne Frank were clutching photographs of Connie
Oland. No manila envelopes for this bunch; they were
always ready to shove the photo and a pen under the star's
nose the minute the trailer door opened. For the older celebs,
the ones who'd been very big once but were now doing
laxative commercials, the autograph hounds lugged around
whole piles of photos from different decades. Some of the
stars would spend time leafing through them, usually choos-
ing to sign one from the Pleistocene era.

"Let me see what you got there," said Bermudez, and the
skinny old man who wore a heavy sweater and shorts in all
kinds of weather proudly handed over his Connie Oland
glossy.

"Not bad," said Bermudez.

"Isn't she just the most beautiful thing you ever saw?"
said the old man.

"And so nice, too!" chimed in another of the regulars, a
tall, round-shouldered girl with an unfortunate skin condition. Bermudez knew what "nice" meant to these people. It
meant that the star didn't spit on them.

He took a good look at the photo. Connie Oland was a
great-looking babe, no doubt about it. The pictures she made
weren't exactly his style—romantic stuff, usually, with a lot
of talk—but he'd been dragged to a few on dates, and this
actress certainly looked fine. Moved well, too. There was one
scene he remembered in particular. She played a woman who
was always fighting with her stepson until one day she shut
up all of a sudden and switched on the stereo and started
dancing. And the teenage boy was surprised, and they started
dancing, and everything was okay between them after that.
Then the whole movie changed into a different story about
the husband's midlife crisis, and Bermudez went to the
lobby to buy some Jordan Almonds.

She'd been in the papers a lot lately, something about her
grandfather and a lawsuit. Bermudez hadn't seen her in the
flesh yet, and he was looking forward to it. Not that there
was likely to be a lot of flesh showing on East Sixth.

Production companies used this location for the historical pictures. She'd probably come out wearing a bustle or something.

"What's this?" Bermudez asked. There was a second photo under Connie Oland's of a furry fabric monster.

"The Muppets are doing exteriors in Midtown at four." The man in the shorts took back his photos and glanced anxiously at his watch. That left Bermudez wondering about two things: how a Muppet signed an autograph, and how this group always got hold of the shooting schedule.

Could be there was a leak in the Movie and TV Unit. Could be these nutcakes pooled the nickels they got from scavenging for empty soda bottles and paid off an officer for information. Bermudez was almost able to believe it, that some cop was using them as a Christmas Club.

He took another sidelong glance at the autograph-book man, the novice. He was bored, tapping his foot on the pavement and shifting the position of his arms. For the others, even the waiting seemed pleasurable.

The resident who wanted the snow shit removed from her window was right. It was a warm day for September, warm enough for Bermudez to do without his jacket. He didn't care for it. The NYPD used hip-length jackets, not the waist-length ones that Bermudez would have preferred. The costume designers had made a mistake about that in the cop drama that was shooting in Midtown a week ago. Bermudez liked it when he got to patrol those things even though it got a little tedious to explain to the locals about the real cops and the fake cops when they asked questions about why the entire police force was running around in their neighborhood. Technical advisors, that's what those police shows needed. The unit's former CO was a technical adviser now, out in Burbank.

"This job has nothing to do with glamour," the planning officer had said when he came in to finish up the interview. "You won't meet any of the actors. The most I meet is an AD—assistant director—and that's usually to have an argument about why they can't shoot a car chase on Sixth Avenue at rush hour."

The planning officer had banged his fist on the desk with every one of these final words: Don't get into this if you think it's related to show business.

Since then, Bermudez had seldom seen the man when his nose wasn't buried in a copy of *Back Stage* or *Show Business*. "Just checking to see if Madonna's coming here to do a soda commercial," he'd say. "I gotta know these things. By the time the film commission gets around to telling me, it's too late to dig up the personnel." The planning officer often talked about the ex-CO who'd gone Hollywood. He was burned about it, envious, more green than blue you might say.

A patrol car came cruising down the street. It crept past Bermudez, stopped, backed up. A window rolled down and a broad, ruddy face rubbernecked out.

"Yo, Bermudez." The cop at the wheel was grinning. Bermudez didn't recognize the face behind the grin. But he was used to that. There'd been two big news conferences, and the brass at One Police Plaza liked to fill up the folding chairs with a cross-section of cops, sort of like the bunch of soldiers you followed in a war movie. This cop with the grin would have been the family-man GI in the war movie, the one who carried pictures of his kids around.

Bermudez went over to shake the hand that was stretched out to him. He read the name on the badge: Kenna. Irish, or maybe Polish or Italian. Bermudez never paid much attention to the distinctions; he wasn't like Vecchio, always slotting everybody into their ethnic groups with a sneer and a slur. Vecchio would be by later, checking up, Bermudez remembered. Claimed to be an expert on the subject of ethnicity. He said he could smell it a mile away. He was one of the sergeants in the Movie and TV Unit. He was the one who thought Bermudez was Dominican.

Kenna's partner gave Bermudez a smile and a little salute. Another stranger.

"I heard you got transferred here, but I didn't believe it." Kenna was swiveling his head around, taking in the film-equipment trucks, the trailers, and the techies who were bustling around now, setting up the lights.

"Yeah? Well, believe it," said Bermudez.

Everyone had expected him to ask for a promotion to detective. He remembered the reporter's puzzled face after the final question of the news conference, the one after the second incident. He couldn't recall now which reporter it was; there'd been so many, even more than at the first conference a year and a half before.

He'd loved the first one, sunning himself in the video lights and the strobes. It had been a fluke, really. Richard Maubry, a previously undistinguished skell, had embarked on one of his customary jags of knocking over retail establishments in Brooklyn and Queens, as was his wont between jail terms. What made this string of robberies remarkable is that Maubry managed to shoot three cops in the process. One died of his wounds as Maubry continued his shopping spree. The tabloids brought out the seventy-two-point type and started braying.

Bermudez at that time had owned a share of a video rental store on Metropolitan Avenue. He was practically a silent partner with two friends who managed it. They at least drew a salary; Bermudez was taking a loss on it. He dropped in one off-duty evening to take home a couple of tapes and go through the books. Maubry, apparently uninformed of the store's financial problems, had picked that night to rob it at gunpoint. Bermudez put down his tapes and pulled his two-inch-barrel .38 out of his ankle holster. The shootout had lasted a long fifteen minutes. Bermudez started out behind the counter, then zigzagged over to the Thrillers/Adventure section. Maubry darted out from Horror and ducked behind Comedy. Final inventory: a flesh wound in the neck for Bermudez, 15 percent of the stock and displays in shreds, and a shattered leg for Maubry.

Luckily, no customers had been in the store. There were

never any customers in the store. All the laurels Bermudez got from the brass and the press didn't change one basic fact—you couldn't make a dime off that lousy location. They asked him what he wanted. He wanted to stay at his current command, the Three-Four, in uniform. They seemed to like that; they wrote headlines about loyalty. He let it go at that. The real reason was the old police academy recruiting poster that he'd read a thousand times as he hung on a subway pole, shuttling between his family's apartment in Red Hook, Brooklyn, and his early-morning job at a midtown luncheonette. It had a photograph of uniformed cops, bunched up real close, but one guy's head was just a shaded patch inside a dotted outline. imagine yourself here, it said, and Bermudez imagined it hard as he pulled the coffee spigot and smeared bagels with cream cheese. Sometimes cops would come into the luncheonette, and the people in suits and bow-tie blouses would stop crowding up on one another; maybe because the whole business of beating out other people to the crullers and bear claws and blueberry muffins seemed silly in the presence of a gun and a nightstick.

By his twenty-first birthday, Bermudez had his face inside the dotted line. By the time of the second news conference, the faces of most of the cops he worked with were beginning to seem like shaded patches. They had half-screens in front of their faces, and he kept wondering what they were hiding. Betrayal? Deception? Greed? The fanfare was even bigger the second time around. But it didn't matter anymore. His fifteen-minute partner, Griswold, was dead by then.

Even this family man, Kenna, stopping for a chat while he was on patrol—who could be sure what he was doing to keep up the payments on the house in Kew Gardens or Rockaway or Sunnyside?

"Jeezum Rice, Bermudez," he said. "You're wasting yourself here. You used to be a cowboy. A frigging cowboy. You ought to be out there rounding up the scuzzballs." That bit of fatherly advice said, he drove off. Bermudez had noticed that Kenna's partner was sucking coffee through the lid of a plastic-foam cup, on duty. The scuzzballs had nothing to fear from those two.

East Sixth was now a tangle of wires and equipment. Bermudez pulled the police barricades farther into the street and stepped out to make sure the traffic flowed around them. The AD wanted to plunk something next to Connie Oland's van, so Bermudez signaled to the autograph seekers with a jerk of his thumb, and they moved a few feet away. Meanwhile the AD stepped into the trailer, probably to give the star an indication of when she'd need to be ready.

The autograph critters kept their antennae quiet as the AD leaned into the trailer door. Like Bermudez, they could sense when filming was going to begin, and it wasn't time yet. Only the normal guy with the grade-school autograph book looked ready to pounce, every muscle tense as he stared at the half-open door. What we've got going here is an apprenticeship, Bermudez thought. He wondered if the autograph nuts passed through the same stages he had: enthusiasm, disillusionment, adjustment. And what should he call the latest stage, the one he had entered shortly after hearing about the technical-advising ex-CO? Restlessness. Or maybe dementia.

The cars flowed smoothly around the police barricades until a green sedan jumped the curb across the street and parked on the sidewalk fronting one of the Indian restaurants.

"You look cold."

It was Sergeant Vecchio in an unmarked car. In a war movie he would've been the officer who got fragged. He left his door hanging open into the street as he strutted over, causing traffic to slow as it maneuvered between the door and the blue NYPD sawhorses.

"Put on your jacket. We've got three guys calling in sick already." A point-to-point radio was crackling on Vecchio's gunbelt. Bermudez wondered why he had it on. The Movie and TV Unit answered radio calls only when filming was at a standstill. Which happened once in a while, now that more companies were faking New York scenes up in Toronto. It was cheaper to make movies there, and you could throw some garbage on the street and—boom—instant Big Apple. Except for the free police assistance. New York was the only city in the world to offer that.

"Caldwell makes it in tomorrow morning, you're off this assignment," Vecchio said. "We need you in Bay Ridge. There's going to be a rock group making a commercial. Could be bad. There's a high school nearby, and we think the news leaked out already."

"What rock group?"

"What the hell do I know? Maybe your kind of music. Salsa. What's that mean, anyway? Sass?" Vecchio had complained several times to the Police Benevolent Association about the unit being "overrun" with minority hires. "Everything under control here, Bermudez?" Vecchio asked, changing topics without taking a breath.

"A couple of pissed-off tenants, that's all."

"I don't know why you were put here. We got a music video filming in Spanish Harlem. We could have used you up there. I don't know how you do it, Bermudez, all these soft assignments. If I didn't know better, I might say it was favoritism. I might say it was the same thing that got you all those medals and all that press when you were just doing the same job a hundred other cops do every day."

"You got a call to answer?" Bermudez could hear murmurs coming through the radio.

"Don't be a wise guy." Vecchio switched the radio off. "So happens I like to tune in to what's going on in this city. You ought to watch the way you talk to your superiors. I betcha Broadbent don't talk that way to his sergeants, and he's a real cop, not one of you affirmative-action jobs."

Vecchio made a point of worshiping other hero cops, "other" in the sense that they weren't Bermudez. His hero these days was Detective Broadbent of the One-Oh-Nine, a precinct that patrolled a section of Queens not far from the Movie and TV Unit headquarters. Broadbent had just cleared the Salad Bar Murder. A Korean greengrocer had been murdered. At first everyone was tying it to a black–Korean conflict that had been flaring all over the city. But the killer turned out to be a Korean. It was a personal thing, but the guy was crafty. He used the ethnic hostilities to throw investigators off his trail.

Before the case was solved, Vecchio used to go around saying that Koreans who opened up high-priced stores in black neighborhoods were begging for trouble. Afterwards, he claimed to have been a few steps ahead of Detective Broadbent.

"They're going to give Broadbent the full treatment at headquarters, and I bet he don't ask for no cushy job afterwards. That guy's a real cop," said Sergeant Vecchio, who had spent the last ten years of his career in the Movie and TV Unit.

A UPS truck pulled to a stop, unable to negotiate around Vecchio's door. It took only a nanosecond for the car horns to hit upon a strong choral sound.

Without turning, Bermudez sensed a new energy on the movie set. "Better close your car door, Sergeant," he said, "or this picture's going to go over budget right here when the director buys a blowtorch and rips it off."

Vecchio muttered something a bit stronger than "Jeezum Rice," sauntered to the car, and peeled off. Traffic resumed normalcy.

Lights bathed the sidewalk, and the actors, the cop, and the autograph seekers got ready to take their places. The unknown performers chatted as the AD walked to Connie Oland's trailer and knocked. The door opened, and the star appeared. Bermudez briefly felt himself microwaved from the core out as he glimpsed high-density blond hair and dangerous eyes before turning his attention to the autograph seekers. It was Anne Frank's cue to leave, which she did after quickly jotting the famous name in her notebook. The others dutifully stayed in place, though their upper bodies were pulled forward, like moths to a klieg light.

The new man, the apprentice, displayed a little native

ability finally; he was straining to see her just as hard as the old pros. Possibly because he was younger and in better health, he seemed to be the most eager, although while the others looked transfixed—almost high on something—he seemed agonized, little knots chasing down his neck.

Okay, they were all going to behave themselves and wait until the filming was over. Nobody broke ranks and asked for an autograph.

Some residents had gathered in front of the Indian restaurant opposite, their hands on their hips. Bermudez watched them warily as the director boomed instructions through the PA system. The locals on East Sixth had been known to disrupt filming by hooting and yelling. After all, this was the neighborhood where the residents celebrated the opening of a Gap store (guaranteed to drive up rents) by painting its windows black.

This time, though, they were calm, interested. They were watching Connie Oland work.

All except the woman in black, the one who'd complained about the snow shit. Bermudez spotted her among the group with their backs to the restaurant. She hustled out into the street, not walking in her sleep this time, and waved her stick arms in the air.

"Get out of our neighborhood," she yelled, in a voice that boiled up all the way from her black leather boots. "No more fucking filming."

Everything stopped dead on the set, and everybody waited for the cop to come over and nab her, but he was running in the opposite direction, toward the man who had been holding the teenybop autograph book. The book was in the gutter now, and the man was up in Connie Oland's face, screaming about how her boyfriend was in the KGB and she needed him to protect her, gripping a knife and bringing his arm up and back for the plunge.

It was a simple matter for Bermudez to wrestle him to the ground and cuff him.

It was the kind of thing, as Vecchio would say, that a

hundred cops did every day. But you couldn't explain that to the *New York Post* photographer who was there to get a few snaps of Connie Oland.

Turned out there'd been a major earthquake in Mexico while all this was going on. That gobbled up most of the evening news programs and the front pages the next morning. Still, there was room inside the tabloids for a juicy local story.

"Hero Cop III," the headlines said. Bermudez finally cried that night, for a dead policeman named Griswold.

▽

## 4

THE SERGEANT IN charge of NYPD public affairs phoned at ten o'clock the next morning. Bermudez had been up for hours, cutting things short when the relatives called to congratulate, ducking out to buy eggs and onions at the Korean bodega, rattling around the apartment unsure what to do with himself; he was that used to a steady day tour now. Someone else was going to Bay Ridge.

"You got a news conference at eight in the Grand Ballroom of the Waldorf-Astoria," said Sgt. Janice Melton. There was a bored edge to her steely voice. She'd preferred it when he was a beginner and she could issue orders about sound bites.

"The Waldorf-Astoria?" He didn't like it.

"Wear some wet-look goop on your hair, but nothing too punked out." She rapped out these commands as if they were instructions for surrounding a building. "Connie Oland'll be there. She's staying there. Here's the spin: She's the damsel in distress, you're her white knight."

"I gotta do this and something at headquarters, too?"

"Nothing else. This is it. And Bermudez?"

"Yeah?"

"Remember to smile this time."

He was hungry. It had taken the white knight four hours at Central Booking to put through paperwork on the perp, and another hour to help detectives from the Ninth locate the girl who'd screamed just before the knife flashed. A hot dog from a Sabrett pushcart had been yesterday's dinner—not an unusual occurrence, since the kitchen in this apartment was so small that the cleaning lady mopped it standing outside. He decided to give it a try again, stacking bowls and plates over a counter the size of a compact disc to product an omelet and a plate of fried *plátanos maduros*.

He ate in the dining area at his new table, which was shaped like a refrigerator crate with angry, dark veins of wood grain. It was part of a furniture set he purchased at a Long Island shopping mall from a store called This End Up. The idea was to sell indestructibility to families with male children. Bermudez liked it because lately he kicked the furniture so much.

The coast was clear as Bermudez walked the four blocks to his car. He liked the new neighborhood better than ever for being a mile away from Red Hook where at this moment some enterprising reporter might be snooping around his old building. Nobody stopped to bother him.

In the Chinese take-out restaurants that were metastasizing all over the neighborhood, young men wearing martial-arts headbands raked noodles over hot cooktops. The door to a Latin record store opened, and a Julio Jaramillo number from the fifties seeped out. This was Fifth Avenue, Brooklyn—no relation to its glittering namesake in Manhattan, twelve subway stops and 200 tax brackets away.

Burmudez got into his car. He needed to see Ernesto. The FDR was brutal, but traffic thinned out considerably on the Bruckner, and it was a clear shot down Castle Hill Avenue to the Salk Towers housing project. The Bronx was like Vermont up here, minus the cows; it had depopulated so long ago that wildflowers were springing up in the vacant lots. The cop parked and took his garment bag off a rear-door hook.

Salk Towers loomed over a landscape that was part pastoral, part ashcan school. This clot of concrete high rises had all the architectural finesse of a Lincoln Logs structure. It was as practical and disheartening as any other housing project in New York, but with one important difference—the people who lived here owned their apartments in a co-op arrangement. This and a few other projects in the city had been built under an old state law, back when the local government offered subsidies for buildings that didn't quite meet the glamour standards of a Battery Park City or a Trump Tower.

Ernesto Acosta had bought his one-bedroom here for $3,000. That was two years ago; he'd been on the waiting list for seven. Occasionally he poked fun at himself for being a homeowner, just as if he'd laid out 150 grand for a Cape Cod in Pelham. Salk Towers was as bourgeois as an ex–Young Lord would go.

Bermudez roused the snoozing doorman and told him to phone 12C and say who was coming. Then he shuffled around in the lobby awhile before pushing the elevator button. He always gave Ernesto a little time to stash away the illegal substances.

Upstairs, the homeowner was waiting on his doormat.

"Why they calling you that movie star's white knight, man?" he greeted Bermudez. "What's this white crap? Don't you tell 'em you're Latino?"

Bermudez followed Ernesto's skinny shoulder blades into the apartment, making his entrance on a jazz chord. Ernesto seemed incapable of surviving without his stereo gasping in the background, like a heart-lung machine connected to him by invisible tubing.

Bermudez made a quick assessment of the seating options in the dining room–living room combo while Ernesto padded on rubber flip-flops into the kitchen. The sole chair in the room was piled high with papers and file folders that apparently had overflowed from the dining room table. Bermudez eyeballed some of the documents. "We, the undersigned," one began. No matter where Ernesto lived, he quickly turned his neighbors into the undersigned.

There was also a draft of a proposal for a fund-raiser to benefit the Mexican earthquake victims, but it had been crossed out with a big $X$. What Mexicans New York had—and there weren't many—lived mostly in Brooklyn and Queens. They were outside Ernesto's solidarity market.

Bermudez decided to settle for one of the larger floor cushions, scooting back on it so that his spine rested between a poster of Che Guevara and a thumbtacked collage of Ruben Blades album covers. A Puerto Rican flag that had surely taken steroids was suspended from the ceiling like a canopy. Already Bermudez was breathing to a different tempo. The jerky beat of the streets relaxed into a *bomba*. Here were shoes in a corner, open books on a coffee table, doodles on a pad near the telephone, evidence of a life spent at home.

"Have a drink, Officer." Ernesto flopped down on the Oriental-Woolworth's rug and opened his arms to produce a jug of cheap red wine, a glass, and a mottled plastic tumbler that Bermudez remembered from the bathroom.

Bermudez checked his watch before reaching for the glass. Nothing escaped Ernesto, who already had a few drops of Famiglia Cribari glistening in his beard.

"Clocking the booze again?"

"It breaks down slower than you think. There's a formula—"

"None of the other cops worry about it."

"That's them."

"Booze and donuts. Ain't that what they live on? With maybe a little police brutality for dessert?"

"That's them. This is me."

"Where you parked, Willie?"

Bermudez told him.

"In that case," said Ernesto, talking from behind his tent of shoulder-length hair as he poured out some wine, "I'd say driving while intoxicated is probably the least of your problems. We had maybe a dozen auto thefts in that block the last two weeks. We got a committee working on the problem."

Ernesto had a committee working on everything, except maybe cleaning this apartment. Though he might have been waiting for the dustballs to grow so big that they could sign up for a task force.

"Have a talk with the precinct about it," Bermudez suggested.

"Me? Talk to the fucking cops?" Ernesto pointed to the garment bag that Bermudez had slung over a box of books. "What's that? You going to a prom?"

"Worse. A news conference at the Waldorf. Eight o'clock."

"The Waldorf? Just 'cause some asshole had a Jones for some actress and wanted to carve her up? You know how many women of color are sliced and diced every day of the week? The Waldorf, right. The pinhead police are using the taxpayers' bucks for the Waldorf."

"It's Connie Oland's money. She's staying there. If I do this, I don't have to do a ceremony at headquarters."

"She rent your tux, too?"

"That's no tux in there. It's my uniform."

Ernesto choked on some wine. "You gonna leave here in cop drag?" he croaked between coughs. "What if the neighbors see?"

"Shouldn't be any big deal around here. They'll think you're a suspect."

"Long as they don't think we were socializing." Ernesto was only half joking. "There goes my reputation, there goes my credibility."

"There goes your grant money."

"Yeah! No! Who cares? Leave it to you to drag the whole thing down to money."

It always went like this, ever since their first meeting. That happened on Broadway. Ernesto was selling T-shirts in front of Macy's; Bermudez was arresting him. The big retailers had pressured the department into doing one of those futile sweeps of unlicensed street merchants. Contradictions of capitalism, Ernesto called it, the free-enterprisers restraining free trade. Bermudez learned all those phrases and more as he took Ernesto in to be booked.

They saw each other again when the case went to court. Bermudez gave his testimony, then watched the show as Ernesto, acting as his own counsel, argued that the T-shirts were a form of protected free speech because they were printed with political slogans. The judge bought it. One of the T-shirts had been introduced as evidence. Bermudez bought that.

He and Ernesto went for coffee. The subject of Ernesto's previous felony convictions came up, and Bermudez discovered that he'd collared an ex–Young Lord.

"You heard of us?" Ernesto had been obviously pleased.

"Like Latino Black Panthers."

"We were into community organizing, like the Panthers. We were never into violence. That was a crock. Media distortion."

"I've heard of the Young Lords a lot of times."

"So the young Latinos talk about us. That's great. We're kind of role models, huh?"

"I heard about you from the older cops," Bermudez said, picking up the check, the first of many he would pick up. "They hated your guts."

They began by seeing each other only when one of them was in the mood for a verbal Nintendo game.

Then Griswold got killed, and Bermudez discovered that the only person he wanted to talk about it with was Ernesto.

It was shortly after he'd been assigned to the command in Washington Heights. The first couple of years it was fine. Drug dealers were always a factor. Then they became *the* factor. The neighborhood became the trading center for a mutant form of cocaine called crack. Cars with out-of-town license plates started cruising the streets, looking for connections. The papers said crack was starting to fan out through the whole city now. But not then, not when Bermudez was working the midnight tour. Most of the deals—and the violence—were coming down in a small slice of upper Manhattan.

His partner of three years couldn't take it, transferred out. He'd just had two weeks with a new one, Griswold, a tough black guy with a silly-looking gap between his front teeth, when a call comes in from a guy on West 151st Street who says he's been threatened with a gun. He also says someone's selling drugs on the ground floor of his building.

The complainant seems a little out of it—not drugged, just a little crazy. Bermudez and Griswold decide to check it out anyway. They call for backup, and the cops patrolling the adjacent sector come over. Kelleher and Ianelli, their names are. One of them is going to watch the front door while the other guards the back. Bermudez has heard some things about Kelleher and Ianelli, but he doesn't believe every rumor he hears. These are good guys.

The complainant named the dealer as Trinidad Someone, so when Bermudez and Griswold knock down the door and barge in with their guns drawn, they expect to find a male Hispanic. But Trinidad is one of those girl-or-boy names, and what they find is a young pregnant woman with a little kid tugging on her arm.

Bermudez puts her under arrest, but she jerks her thumb toward the back of the apartment and says, wait a minute, I've got another baby in the bedroom back there. So they follow her down the hall, and there's a crib there all right, with a tangle of blankets, which may or may not be covering a baby. The light's not so good here, it's hard to tell.

And she reaches into the crib, and a feeling comes over Bermudez, but he doesn't act on it because she's pregnant and he can hear her kid crying down the hall. She pulls out a gun and blasts Griswold with it, and Griswold squeezes off one shot with his own gun before falling to the floor.

She's wounded, and she slumps back and drops the gun, so there's really nothing Bermudez can do but handcuff her, and it turns out she only has a flesh wound. Griswold's wound, that's something else entirely. That turns out to be fatal.

Kelleher and Ianelli hear the gunshots and come running through the front door. Both of them, through the front. One of them was supposed to be guarding the back. Those things that Bermudez heard—that these two let drug dealers escape because they're really only interested in tossing the apartments to steal money and drugs—well, they don't seem to be just rumors anymore. These cops aren't good guys after all. After this, Bermudez isn't sure who the bad guys are. Most of all, he isn't sure he's really a cop. A cop wouldn't just stand there and let his partner get shot. He couldn't even grieve right, he didn't even have that. He'd hardly known the guy. Sometimes he couldn't even remember what Griswold looked like alive. Talking to the widow had been bad. He couldn't cry with her. It all seemed like a stupid joke.

Bermudez breezed through all the interviews with the DA's office, leaving out the part about the back door. That wasn't hard. The hard thing was looking out into the audience and seeing Kelleher and Ianelli at the commendation ceremony and not being able to kill them. A few weeks later he started filling out his application for the Movie and TV Unit. And he started visiting Ernesto more regularly.

They'd finished off the entire Cribari family and Ernesto had blown the tune to "De Colores" on the empty jug before Bermudez noticed what was playing on the turntable.

"The Last Poets," Ernesto said. "From the sixties. Political poetry."

"They're shitting on George Washington and the flag and everything else."

Ernesto cracked a wicked smile. "I put it on specially for you, 'cause I knew how much you'd like it." Then he turned serious, the crow's feet deepening around his eyes as if to remind Bermudez of the difference in their generations. "When you going to get past being bummed? When you going to rise up angry?"

Bermudez stretched. "Time to put on the uniform."

"Why you even going to this freak show tonight?"

Bermudez unzipped the garment bag. "Because my Aunt Norma wants Connie Oland's autograph. If she's still handing them out."

He made it to the Waldorf in record time, arguing with himself the whole way. Ernesto always had that effect. Bermudez wasn't sure if it was good for him or not.

## 5

SGT. JANICE MELTON, NYPD principal spokesperson, was
waiting for him in the lobby. She wore a pink suit so crisp
that it might have been 50 percent rayon, 50 percent Kevlar.

"We're on the third floor," Melton said. "You'll take five
questions, we'll cut it short, then Miss Oland will join you
for a brief photo op."

A good way for the police to really stick things to the
firefighters, Bermudez thought, would be to give them
Sergeant Melton.

"I've got to hang around while she takes questions?"

"She won't. Her press agent prepared a statement. Very
grateful for your quick thinking, feels safe in New York with
the NYPD on the job. Nice statement. I wrote part of it. The
beginning's good, anyhow. Then they went off on a tangent."

There were no folding chairs this time, no section marked
MOS, for Members of the Service. Instead, you had a cavern
that could seat 1,500 for dinner, a crystal chandelier and two
tiers ringing the walls, like something out of Lincoln Center.
All this for a small corps of newshounds looking kind of
lonely as they huddled together in front of the built-in stage.
The cops weren't in the audience this time, they were
patrolling.

The Grand Ballroom was a security nightmare, flanked to
the east and west by foyers, each of which communicated
with the ballroom and the lobby via half a dozen doors.
Added to that were entrances to the kitchen. A lot of people
wouldn't have picked this room as the coziest place to be,

the day after some schiz tried to turn their face into lemon zest. But for Connie Oland everything was under control. Uniforms decorated every door, and the foyers were thick with trench coats. The department was doing it up.

Sergeant Melton hustled Bermudez over to the microphone-studded podium, rapped out an introduction, and selected one of the waving hands. Up popped a woman in a mixed garment message—pinstripes and cleavage in combo. Bermudez was rattled. This must be an entertainment reporter. The crime-beat gals wore blouses under their jackets.

But the questions were the same old ones, and Bermudez delivered the same old answers. I was just doing my duty, the way everyone on the force is expected to do.

You should have asked Griswold, he thought. Right before Griswold died trying to stop drugs you should have asked him what the other New York police officers were doing.

"Are you a fan of Connie Oland?"

The question came from a man with a downtown-nightclub haircut and a sly smile on his face. Melton moved closer to Bermudez, telegraphing "no." He knew the drill. He was supposed to stand in the midst of this NYPD–Hollywood joint venture and say that movie stars weren't special. He was supposed to say the police were here to protect everyone.

"I think she's more a fan of mine at the moment." He heard it at the same moment the press did; the words hadn't formed in his mind first. The reporters laughed and scribbled in their skinny notebooks.

Now, heads were turning toward a certain door, and the camera strobes and video lights really got going, as if recovering from a brownout. Photographers who had grouped in front of the podium now dived for the side of the room as Connie Oland marched up. She walked quickly, not stopping to pose—a new Miss America who'd decided to grab her crown and dash down the runway to catch a train.

Bermudez stepped to one side and prepared for the handshake, but instead she was all over him, her arms around his shoulders, soft skin, lips, and silky hair brushed against his face. She kissed him, and pleasure and resentment arrived at the scene simultaneously. It was how he felt when a cat stepped on him as he slept.

Now her head was turned toward one of the cameras, one with the logo of a major network, still pressed against his. "My hero!" she said. The photogs went to town, and an enormous surge of candlepower was released, the kind of light you were supposed to see in those near-death experiences.

A moment later she had released him and was huddling with someone in her entourage, a stocky man in a brown suit. "The statement," Bermudez heard her mumble. "My grandfather?"

The brown-suited man came forward. "Thank you," he told the reporters. "Miss Oland is sorry she can't take questions, but it's been a very long day for her. Details are in the statement. Feel free to call me if you have questions."

Bermudez heard only half of this. He was watching Connie Oland as she swept out of the ballroom, surrounded by a circle of attendants. She never once looked back at him.

The press was half gone by now. Melton, too, had crackled away.

"So," Bermudez said to the brown-suited man.

"So," said the man. Bermudez followed him as he stepped off the podium.

"Miss Oland's staying here? This hotel?"

"She is." The man was looking at his watch. Bermudez was looking at him. A press agent, huh? He could have easily been mistaken for one of those guys in the glass booths at the Coney Island arcades who gave out change for the video games.

"What's her room number?"

"That's confidential."

"What's her room number?"

"Uh, 4212, in the Towers."

All it took was a small movement of the hips, a shift of weight toward the gun side. That's all it ever took.

The forty-second floor was at the top of the building. Bermudez went up there, nodding to the cops guarding the private entryway and the private lobby. They thought he had an invitation. It was natural to think so.

Bermudez knocked on the door of the suite. Sure enough, a Gold's Gym type stuck his head out of 4210. He was a hell of an ugly customer, with the kind of face most people couldn't achieve without pulling a nylon stocking over their heads.

"I'm Bermudez. She's expecting me."

The bodyguard nodded and drew back into the room. He must have been hired sometime that morning.

Bermudez counted to himself, allowing fifteen seconds for the bodyguard to walk to the door connecting with the adjoining room, five seconds for the announcement, twenty seconds for the mistress to bawl out the slave. . . .

"Through here." An arm that could have worn a cummerbund as a bracelet was signaling to him.

He crossed through a foyer into a living room, where Connie Oland rose from a little candy box of a couch and told Piltdown man to leave them alone.

Bermudez ignored her outstretched hand. The time for the handshake had passed. He picked out a chair to lounge on, as far from her aura as possible.

Because she was beautiful, of course. He'd seen that in the glimpse he'd gotten yesterday and the extreme close-up downstairs, but the full impact was hitting him only now, like a slow-acting pill that was finally kicking in. But he was fighting the effects, diverting his glance from her church painting of a face, with its promise of terrifying miracles, to concentrate on the banal worldliness of her black turtleneck and long flannel skirt.

At the news conference he'd felt fleeting annoyance at her lack of ornament. Now, however, he saw how the turtleneck draped over her full, slightly low-slung breasts, and how the skirt fell into the valley between the shallow curve of her belly and the beginning rise of her thighs, and he decided that this particular version of the outfit could qualify for a new patent.

"You didn't like the kiss," she said.

It wasn't a question. He felt no need to comment.

She fingered some threads in the brocade upholstery near her knee. He laced his fingers together behind his head and tilted his chin up, keeping her in his field of vision. There was something special about the way she carried herself, even sitting down. He thought of that movie scene he liked—her, dancing with the stepson.

Maybe it was that memory working tricks on him, but faint music seemed to be playing somewhere. Bermudez looked around but couldn't locate the source. No stereos in here, just a TV peeking out from the half-open doors of a console. The music stopped, and a voice murmured softly like an obscene caller. He figured that a radio must be on in one of the other rooms leading off this one. No doubt this suite stretched out past the Pan Am Building and into Grand Central.

The actress got to her feet and walked to a window behind the couch.

"You didn't want to be there, I saw that right away," she said.

Bermudez looked up and saw her reflection superimposed on the Manhattan skyline. She was clutching her elbows. "It was a stupid publicity bit. I need the publicity."

"Right," he said. "You need publicity. Nobody ever heard of you."

"It's not what you think. There's a special—"

She was going to tell him about a new movie she had coming out, or a Broadway show she was going to be in, or something like that, and suddenly all the juice failed in that electromagnetic field she'd been throwing around him. Everyone in New York had a hustle, and hers had to do with being beautiful and famous, but he was up on his feet now, and she was turning to look at him.

"Next time you need to kiss an orphan, lady, call the Fresh Air Fund."

He figured that the wooly mammoth next door wouldn't mind if he bypassed customs this time and exited through

the usual door, but before he could fling it open, she'd ducked
under his arm and turned to confront him. She pulled a piece
of paper out of her skirt pocket and waved it in his face.

He scanned the top margin—arty letters all crammed
together spelling out the name of a PR agency, but her finger
tapped something on the bottom, and he took it and read:

> The threat against Miss Oland's life came at a par-
> ticularly difficult time for her personally. The man who
> has been indicted by a Texas grand jury in connection
> with the death of Miss Oland's grandfather failed to
> appear at his arraignment in Dallas this morning. Brian
> Fowler, a manager for Trans Rio Hotels, had been trav-
> eling on business in Mexico where communications
> have been impeded since yesterday's earthquake.
>
> After flying to Dallas this morning to await Mr.
> Fowler's appearance, Miss Oland returned to New York
> to thank Officer Bermudez for his heroism.

"That," she said when he'd finished reading. "*That's* why
I need publicity. Not for myself. Not for some asinine
picture."

"Sorry about the jet lag I caused you. Hey, here's an idea.
If you really want to thank me, give me your frequent-flyer
miles for the trip."

Her eyes connected with his, almost with a click.

"You don't want to listen to me, do you?"

She had a voice like an organ, so that she sounded like
she was sighing and talking at the same time. Something
about it made Bermudez ashamed, but he didn't show it.
Instead, he propped his back against the door he'd planned
to exit from and folded his arms.

"Explain it to me. How's this press release going to help
you? I don't think they follow Page Six of the *Post* in Mexico."

"But they read the wire services in Dallas, where a certain
DA thinks he may already have gotten all the mileage he wants
out of his connection with me. Sure, he'd like to keep it up,
but only if I foot the bills and keep the publicity machines

greased. You should have heard him this morning."

Bermudez watched as she pulled at the brim of an imaginary hat and spread her feet apart. She seemed transformed, heavier, as if somebody had waved a wand over her. "We'd love to go after him, ma'am," she said in a perfect Texas drawl, "but we're so danged busy as it is. Fact is, I've been busier lately than a cat come to shit on a marble slab."

She snapped back to normal, if you could call her usual appearance normal. "Extortion, plain and simple," she said.

"So. So the guy didn't show. So you hire a private detective to run down to Mexico and scare him up." Bermudez made a show of looking around the suite. "You must have enough bread to swing it."

"Hired!" said Connie Oland.

"Pardon?"

She strolled over to a cabinet he'd taken for the kind of table where women put on makeup. A push of a button revealed rows of bottles with expensive labels. She pulled out two wineglasses and proceeded to fill them.

"You've got the job. Let's drink to it."

Bermudez maintained his position at the door.

"Lady, with all due respect, may I asked you if it's escaped your notice that I'm already employed?"

"Oh, I'm well aware of that." She pushed the bar doors closed with a knee and walked over to him carrying the wineglasses. "New York Police Department. A patrolman, is that the correct title? But your ambitions are much bigger than that."

Different, anyway. She was on the right track.

She extended one glass toward him. "Excuse me if I'm getting awfully personal, but you were the one who got things off on that note, you know."

"Me?"

"You. So now you might as well have some wine to go along with all my *bread,* as you put it."

She was back on the couch she'd been on when he first came in. He felt silly standing there with the wine, so he flopped down on the little snub-nosed sofa across from it. A love seat, he guessed they called it.

"I've got this ambition written all over my face, huh?"

"More in the way you stand. Actors have to study things like that."

"Yeah? Well, you've got to hit the books a little harder. For starters, I'm not a detective."

She shrugged. "But you're a special cop, aren't you? A hero cop."

"That's what the press release says."

"That's what I saw when you saved me from those two crazy people."

"One crazy person."

"There was an accomplice, too. The woman who yelled at the film crew and created a distraction."

"She wasn't in on it. She was just your garden-variety East Village weirdo. She yelled because she wants the production companies out of the area. A lot of the neighborhood people do."

The movie star was listening the way you'd listen to a broadcast about a hurricane coming in.

Bermudez had planned to run through this quickly, but instead he found himself slowing down. "She probably lives in a sixth-floor walk-up where the water's off half the time, but she likes it because it's Manhattan, and because she removed all the old linoleum from the floor with her own footlong fingernails so now it looks just like a SoHo loft."

Connie Oland—Connie, as he found that he was beginning to think of her—wore a small smile that could have been sold at Tiffany's.

William tried some of the wine. It was so much lighter than the swill he'd had at Ernesto's that he could hardly taste it.

"Anyhow," he continued, "she puts up with all the inconveniences, but the night shooting's been interfering with her shut-eye, so she goes over the edge a bit and starts screaming. The guy who lunged at you was waiting for an opportunity. From the second you came out of the trailer he had his eyes on you. Never on the street. I was watching. Why would he do that if he was waiting for her to come in on cue?"

Connie raised her glass. "See. I told you that you could do detective work. The actual detectives assigned to the case seem convinced that the two were working in concert."

"Sure they are. They'll blow a couple of days finding out that she's never been south of Secaucus and this is his first trip out of Tuscaloosa, and they'll file a lot of reports, and they'll come to see it my way."

"So when are you going to start for Mexico? Your Spanish is bound to come in handy there. Isn't that right, Officer Bermudez?"

She pronounced it the way his mother did, Ber-moo-des. Most people made it sound like an island or an onion. So did he, as he'd done ever since the third grade when his family moved from Ponce to Red Hook, where he'd learned English by the sink-or-swim method. They said that kids just picked up new languages. That had been more or less true for him: He swam while his best friend Papo sank. The kid was slightly hearing impaired. None of the teachers noticed that, but they noticed he wasn't catching on to English. Bermudez had heard about Papo recently. He'd been living at Manhattan Psychiatric since adolescence, diagnosed as retarded.

He put his wineglass down and held his head in his hands, thinking about Papo and thinking about the way Vecchio ragged him about affirmative action. And he thought about how Connie Oland was here in this room with him, offering him a quick ticket to a new life. Destination Hollywood, with a stopover in Mexico. She was a major star, enormous. A word from her, and any technical-assistance job he wanted would be a cinch.

He wasn't about to say anything about it now. Hadn't she

just told him that she didn't like that Texas DA's attitude? She didn't like deals. People were just supposed to do things for her.

Getting the time off wasn't that big a problem. He had plenty of unused vacation time racked up, and nobody created a hassle with a hero cop. The crazed autograph hound would undoubtedly be tried, and he'd have to be there to testify. But the way the court calendars were crammed full, that could be months away.

He looked up at her and smiled. She was smiling back. And why not? She'd gotten what she wanted, and she thought she'd done it all with star power.

A reggae tune was whispering from somewhere.

"You got music on in another room?"

"Here," said Connie. She crossed over to the console he'd noticed before, opened the doors wide, and turned a knob on the television. So that's where they stuck the radio.

He took her hand and led her to the center of the room and started dancing. He was good, and he knew it, and he enjoyed having her watch for a while as he went solo. She joined in, and he felt like he'd risen out of his body and walked into a movie screen. He was halfway to California already.

Later, in the bedroom, she asked him to keep his uniform on while she undressed. Her skin was impossibly translucent; he could almost see the blue through it as she wrapped herself around him. When his shirt was off, she took his arm and held it around her waist.

"Look," she said, indicating the mirror behind her where his brown skin rested above her buttocks. *"Café con leche."*

He laughed admiringly as he pulled her down on top of himself. She was probably thinking about Mexico, and how she had that pesky earthquake licked.

▽

# 6

T HE MOST IMPORTANT thing was to find cash. That's what sent Fowler back to Guerrero, hoping the Lara was still standing with Jim Rigg in it.

Fowler was wounded now, because the debris on the streets had cut through his stockinged feet. When the Villa Real turned him away, he'd stumbled five or six blocks before a cab stopped. It took him to Guerrero for free, cramming him in with a family of five who'd lost their home in the earthquake and were going to stay with a relative. It was ghastly, all the shrieking and crying.

How refreshing to see Rigg, almost as Fowler had left him, but serving himself in the bar of the Lara. Fowler came in through the street entrance, stubbing an unprotected toe on the buckled sidewalk outside. The building to his back had come down, but the Lara looked intact.

"Bartender didn't show up," said Rigg, pouring with a shaking hand. "Doesn't matter to me, long as the bottles are okay. That's the first thing I thought of, after I stopped sliding from one end of the room to the other—is the bar okay? Turned out this was the best place to be, on the lobby level. There's a rip in my wall I don't like to look at."

He seemed to notice Fowler for the first time. "Anything for you? You look like shit." Their last meeting and Fowler's mythical departure for Acapulco seemed to have escaped Rigg's mind, shaken free in the temblor perhaps, or corroded by alcohol.

"Yeah. Well, I was buried alive in the Hotel Toronto. They pulled me out."

"Didn't anyone ever tell you to stand in the doorway?" said Rigg. He slapped Fowler on his tender shoulder. Fowler began with a laugh that broke into a sob. When it was over, Rigg was offering him a whiskey. Fowler accepted.

"The Lara wasn't hit too hard, but the electricity's out and so's the water," Rigg reported.

"The building in front didn't do so well," said Fowler. "A hardware store, wasn't it?"

"That's not out front. It's across the street here," said Rigg, pointing to the door from which Fowler had entered.

It happened sometimes, Fowler assured himself, these short circuits. He'd been using Spanish all day, so he'd forgotten the English expression "across the street" and translated the Spanish equivalent, "*en frente de*." The American expats who lived here had lapses like that all the time. They'd even adopted some false cognates into their everyday language. It didn't mean his brain had been permanently damaged by trauma.

His grammar was apparently good enough for Rigg, who was talking now about how he wanted Fowler to accompany him to the "bedbug hotel" on Mina Street, still juiced with electricity, and translate the television newscasts.

"Maybe they'll tell us when we can expect to be able to flush our goddamn toilets again. I've got to stay down here a few more days, because my factory got a little perturbed."

Since he was about to be pressed into service, Fowler decided this was a good time to ask for the loan. Rigg, after all, was his only resource. At the Villa Real, he'd discovered that all the phone lines to the United States were out. He'd expected trouble about his missing tourist visa, but they were more concerned about the other kind of Visa. With his credit cards gone and no way to verify his account numbers with the issuing banks, he got the boot. Couldn't say he wouldn't have run his own hotel the exact same way.

"Glad to help a buddy," said Rigg, digging into his pockets.

But he didn't look at all glad, and he came up with just forty dollars in pesos. "Maybe the news will tell us whether the telegraph service is okay," he said. So that was it. He was afraid his lifeline had been cut.

"Shame to leave the happy hour," Rigg said, lining up his empty glasses for someone to tend to later. "Everything's gratis today. Whole staff's running around on the street somewhere, seeing if their loved ones got made into cement sandwiches." Fowler limped with him to the door; Rigg had promised a cab if they could find one. In the dim lobby, they passed the unattended reservations desk. "Choose a key and stay for free," suggested Rigg. "No one will be the wiser."

Things were livelier at the Hotel Bailey on Mina Street. The walls had huge pocks of missing plaster, and faint chalky stripes on the floor showed the fresh trail of a broom. Otherwise, the quake seemed to have done little damage here. Though it would be hard to tell.

Three women were seated on a couch in the lobby under a big wall-mounted tin shamrock. Their eyes were glued to a nervous black-and-white television. Hookers, Fowler supposed, though at the moment they weren't painted or dressed for the part. He knew places like this. It wasn't an actual brothel, just a flophouse where streetwalkers were invited to bring a friend and stay awhile.

Rigg introduced him to the oldest of them, a woman named Chelo who, he said, "sort of runs the place." Her hard face could have been forty or fifty years old, but Fowler, noting few gray strands in her unclean hair, judged her to be a high-mileage thirty-five. She was cooperative enough, agreeing to brief him on the news they'd been watching all day. "Just TV-Thirteen," she said. "The Televisa news tower fell over. They think most of the announcers are dead."

She ticked off some of the headlines on her thick-skinned fingers: the Centro and the Colonia Roma had been hit hardest, the Centro Medico and Juárez Hospital had collapsed on hundreds of doctors and patients, gas-leak fires were spouting from the ground, a large number of water mains were broken. She finished and looked at Fowler expectantly, maybe even reflexively. These women were accustomed to payment for their services.

"What's she saying?" Rigg had settled into a discolored easy chair near the couch. "What about telegraphs?"

But Chelo knew nothing about them. Rigg resigned himself to watching the pictures on the television.

Fowler glanced at the screen. A newscaster was reading names of people who were being sought by their families. Chelo followed his eyes.

"That's been going on all day," she said, dismissing it with a wave of her hand as if it were the Jerry Lewis telethon. The girls, however, were listening raptly, as if waiting for the names of people they knew.

"Them?" mocked Chelo when Fowler asked. According to her, they knew no one in the city. They were hicks, from the provinces, new to the capital.

"I'm hoping they don't go home," she confided to Fowler in a whisper. "Someone told me the buses are running, but please don't let them know."

Fowler approached them.

"Who wants to earn five thousand pesos?" It would make a substantial dent in his meager loan from Rigg, but it was necessary.

One of the girls leaned forward eagerly, but the other pushed her back. "Not today," she said angrily. "This is a national tragedy."

"Not that," said Fowler, disgusted that such a thought would enter their minds, they looked so undesirable. "I need someone to get me shoes and some clothes." No one had seemed to notice the dust caking his face and hair or his unshod feet. Then again, the TV had shown naked people running on the sidewalks.

Both girls were eager to run the errand, though the one concerned about the national tragedy paused to comment on the news reports, which had resumed. There was a particularly gory story about rescuers sawing through corpses in order to reach survivors in a fallen building.

"*Hijo*," yelped the girl, with obvious relish.

Fowler chose her for the mission, figuring that her aggression would help her get the job done quickly. The shoes were the main thing. He had Chelo produce paper and pencil so that he could trace an outline of his feet.

"What the hell are they saying on TV?" Rigg called out.

"In a minute," promised Fowler, busy giving instructions about the clothes. "Not too much polyester," he said, counting out enough money for cheap domestic goods. At this rate, maybe he would have to sneak into a room at the Lara after all. "And don't get any shoes unless you think they'll fit. I have bigger feet than most Mexican men."

"Don't worry," said the girl, whose name—prophetically, he hoped—was Milagros, or Miracles. She said she knew a place in Tepito where people made shoes on the sly, as good as the ones in stores but manufactured secretly so as to avoid business taxes.

"Is Tepito standing?" asked Fowler. It abutted the Centro to the northeast—an ancient part of the city teeming with contrabandists, flea markets, and tenements full of poor, thieving families. He could hardly imagine it ruined, it was such a wreck to begin with.

"No way to find out but to go there," said Milagros. "They won't be reporting on Tepito." She gestured toward the television. "The bourgeois neighborhoods and the commercial areas, that's all they care about."

"Me, too," said Chelo. "That's what I care about. Where do you think we'll get customers if the hotel district is a complete disaster? Go over to Tepito with your communist ideas. You'll find plenty of communist company there."

The girl left an exhaust trail of cursing.

"Buddy boy, if you don't hush up, you'll miss it when they say about the telegraphs." Rigg looked tense and unhappy. There were no bars in places of this kind. They were strictly BYOB.

But both Fowler and Chelo had forgotten about Rigg for a

moment. On the small, fuzzy screen was "dramatic footage"—standard stuff for any two-bit local news program in the United States, but still fairly unusual in Mexico. It showed a crumbled building enveloped in flames, with three or four fire hoses trained on it. The building had been reduced to chunks of masonry, listing hard into the street, but Fowler could recognize it by the enormous Hotel sign on its roof, intact except for the *H*, and the insignia next to it: two script capital *Rs*, one of them reversed, supporting the outline of a crown.

"The Regis," said Chelo, clucking her tongue. "It's a little far, but we get some business from those hotels near the Alameda. The taxi drivers bring them."

"Is the airport all right? That's what I want to know," said Rigg. "If they can't wire me the money, I'll have to fly up to Monterrey and get it."

"The airport it is well," said the prostitute who had been sitting silently next to Milagros. Everyone was astounded by her English. "Planes are come today with money from—" The word failed her, but she circled her hand to indicate points abroad.

"There you go," said Rigg, rising. "We're okay now, Fowler. If the telegraph office is kaput, I'll just have to make a little trip up north before I clean up the mess at the factory. You're all set, too, buddy boy. You can go back home."

"Not without money or credit cards," murmured Fowler, who was thinking.

"There's gotta be a way. You're good for it. Go by the consulate tomorrow, and see if they can't fix you up. What do you say we celebrate with a drink at the Lara?"

Fowler said he'd wait for the girl to return with the clothes. He watched television some more—interviews with people who'd lost family members, shots of bodies being piled up in Red Cross vans. It turned dark, and Chelo turned on the dim overhead light. She had no water, but she offered to get some for him to wash in, for a price.

He sent her in search of it and stood in the doorway. Sirens still screamed, but they seemed muted by the darkness. On lightly trafficked Mina, life appeared almost normal. No buildings on this block had fallen, though there was one tall one with a V-shaped bulge in its middle. A cluster of people seemed to be setting up camp on the sidewalk, rigging tubing and plastic into tents, but Fowler assumed they were refugees from elsewhere.

The skyline looked different, mainly because some of the illuminated beer advertisements were extinguished. But the Latin American tower, the tallest building, was still erect. It wasn't visible from here, but Fowler had seen it on television, standing tall behind the remains of the Hotel Regis. As for the darkness, Mexico City had never been well lit. He always noticed that on night flights here. It was almost like landing in a field rather than in a city of eighteen million people.

A Red Cross van came yelping down Mina, and Fowler breathed relief as a helicopter passed overhead. He wanted things to be as chaotic as possible because he was going to disappear into the rubble. He'd decided that when he saw the films of the Regis. No one would imagine that anyone in that hotel had survived. And, except for the flames, the Toronto looked every bit as bad.

Fowler would wait a few minutes longer for the girl to return with the clothes. After that, he'd leave for another bedbug hotel in another part of the city—someplace that didn't require tourist cards for check-in. Not that he needed Brian Fowler's tourist card anymore. Brian Fowler had died in the earthquake. He couldn't be tried in Texas for manslaughter.

Bailey might be a good name, he thought, looking at the sign above the door where he was standing. No, that would be a clue, if they ever sent anyone after him. They might do that, once things settled down.

The girl was taking her time. Maybe she'd made off with his money. He'd been counting on her ties to Chelo and the hotel, but she seemed smart. With the prostitution business due for a downturn, she may have decided to split. Much as he wanted the shoes, he didn't want to stay much longer. It was bad enough that three people here had already seen his face. Had Rigg called him by name? The one who spoke English might have heard it.

Rigg, that was a problem. Rigg knew he was still alive. He could only pray that the garment factory problem would be straightened out fast and Rigg would fly back to Monterrey for good. What a dunce he'd been to go back to the Lara. Pure amateurism. Trans Rio knew he'd been staying there. It'd be a logical place to look for him. If the staff had been in, dozens of people would have known he was living. The bartender, the waiters . . . but they hadn't been there. They'd been home with their families.

Except for Juan Antonio Mendoza. He and Rigg were the two people who'd seen Fowler after the quake and knew who he was. Rigg would go back to Monterrey eventually. He'd have to figure out what to do about Mendoza. Money would shut him up. He had to get money.

The girl returned with two counterfeit designer shirts in unlikely shades of blue and some black socks that barely reached to Fowler's ankles. She'd located a highly acceptable pair of gray drawstring pants. Fowler changed in a dank bathroom off the lobby, first dabbing himself with water from the shallow basin that Chelo had produced.

He pulled two pairs of socks over his torn and bleeding blisters. The girl had gone overboard following his instructions, and the shoes were a size too big; they were shoes for somebody else. Fowler tightened the laces and scuttled off into the apocalyptic night.

$\triangledown$

# 7

WHEN DAWN CAME he was grateful. And by that time he was Tom Dixon.

He'd chosen the name for its pronunciation values while he lay trying to sleep in the public square. He selected Dixon for its closeness to Nixon, a name that most Mexicans could hear correctly and could pronounce in some form or another, which was more than they could do with Fowler. Tom sounded acceptable with the long Spanish o, and Thomas was close to Tomás. He'd be rid of that double vowel in Brian that Mexicans always mauled into a diphthong.

There were some amusing Mexican names he'd like to have tried pawning off as American, like Hanibal or Jesús, but those were just thoughts he had while trying to ignore the wailing adults and crying children coating the vast floor of the Zócalo in a solid layer.

Fowler sat up in the gray light and tried to massage the stiffness out of his limbs. His chest still ached from the cave-in.

"Those boys are tremendous, they never stop," said one of his neighbors, a paunchy man with a legion of small children. He was pointing to a fallen building west of the Zócalo that was swarming with volunteers. Many had covered their mouths with surgical-style masks that seemed to have been made of striped dishrags. The commercial structures on Avenida 16 de Septiembre had fared worse than the national monuments flanking the square. The National Cathedral, the presidential palace, and City Hall still loomed over the Zócalo, as dour and formidable as ever.

Fowler watched the activity around the rubble. Some of the volunteers had formed a kind of pebble brigade and were passing buckets of stone down to the sidewalk.

"Useless without heavy equipment," he mused aloud.

"You a foreigner?" asked the paunchy man.

Fowler felt vindicated. He'd decided against impersonating a Mexican, and he was right. The giveaway wasn't so much his slight accent and light hair—he could convince someone of this man's class that he was from another region or of Spanish descent. But the comment about heavy equipment, that was something that wouldn't have occurred to a Mexican.

"American," said Fowler. Anything else was too risky. He couldn't manage British English, and his scanty knowledge of Canada would collapse under questioning. "Tom Dixon," he volunteered. Might as well break it in.

"Nice vacation for a tourist," said the man. "Your friends won't believe it when you tell them about this, I bet." He spoke as though the news media didn't exist. "You'll go tell them, and everyone in the United States will know Mexico City is a complete *fracaso*."

That was something else Fowler never could have mimicked successfully: the perpetual national embarrassment. As an American, he just couldn't fathom it. He found it contemptible.

"I should help those boys, but I'm too old," said the man, all of whose children appeared to be under the age of five. "And I have to take care of the kids." Actually, his wife seemed solely in charge of that. She had taken them over to the sidewalk to relieve themselves, an idea that seemed to have struck all the mothers in the park simultaneously. Fowler didn't like to look.

"A big guy like you could probably move a lot of those slabs," said the man. "That one in the checked shirt, over there, he does the most." Even as they watched, the checked shirt began dragging something over to the waiting Red Cross van. His lack of urgency left little doubt as to what it was.

"The ones near the sidewalk are very weak," continued the commentator. "They keep sitting and resting." He spoke of them as if they were players on a soccer team.

Fowler had heard their scraping and cursing throughout the night. Those noises had been what kept him awake, afraid to sleep even when he'd grown accustomed to the cold ground and the sobbing around his elbows. There were people in that building, some of them probably still living, trapped for almost twenty-four hours now.

Maybe it had been stupid to spend the night in the Zócalo when there was enough cash in the brown wallet for a flophouse. But he couldn't stand the thought of sleeping within walls and a ceiling. A room could convert to a sepulcher. And money was needed for food.

He picked his way across the square, nearly tripping over a sleeping child as he suddenly lost his balance.

"*Algo pasó.*" Something happened. Every third person seemed to be saying it. Others shrugged. But he'd felt it all right: an earth tremor.

Brian Fowler had good cause for staying in Mexico City. He'd have to think of a reason why Tom Dixon would want to.

The newsstands around the Zócalo were up and running. One of the vendors was busy clipping copies of the blood-and-horror tabloids to the top of his kiosk. Even on dull days, they managed to serve up a steady stream of car-crash and drug-war gore. Now, they were in their glory. Fowler averted his eyes from the cover photos of mutilated bodies.

"How's business?" he asked the vendor, selecting *Excelsior* and the *Mexico City News* from nearly depleted piles. Both newspapers featured photos of the devastated Hotel Regis on page one, he noted with satisfaction.

"Not bad," said the vendor.

"Everybody's hungry to read the news, I guess."

"Or to sleep under it." The vendor indicated the crowds in the Zócalo. "The first deliveries came a few hours ago. They sold out in a flash. For covers."

"You've got a good location here," said Fowler, interested to see how new market niches were emerging.

"Not really. These people are going to be trouble. A lot of them lost their money when their houses fell down. You have to keep an eye on this bunch. They've been stealing like crazy."

In that case, use your profits from the stepped-up sales to hire some kid to watch for shrinkage. Fowler didn't bother saying this aloud. It was a rare Mexican who could figure out how to exploit an opportunity. But there was postquake money to be made, he was sure of that. He sat on the grass, reading the papers and plotting his next steps.

The *News* was the most important because the American media would use it as a source. They'd pick up stories from it; Fowler had been instructed about that by his wife. Even on that vacation here, her mind had stayed on the career ladder. "A good pickup sheet," she'd said about the *News*, checking it for stories about garment manufacturing. "Foreign papers are great for tips. Who will ever know you've stolen from them?" A born thief, that woman.

The *News* estimated the number of dead at five thousand, about triple *Excelsior*'s government-approved estimate. Their customary emphasis on American- and British-inhabited sections of the city provided plenty of horrifying data and alarming photos. The Colonia Roma, saturated with expats, had been rocked badly, but so had the adjacent Hipódromo de la Condesa, a quiet neighborhood of condominiums, tree-lined streets, and a heavy dose of foreign residents.

This was good. If anything, the damage would be exaggerated in the U.S. press. Fowler hoped that NBC and CBS were down here already with their cameras rolling.

But the short piece in *Excelsior* about hotels was a grave disappointment. Of 250 fallen buildings, an astoundingly high number were government owned. Hotels made a dismal showing, and the Toronto didn't appear in the list of the missing. The Versailles was gone, the Principado, the Diplomático—

only the centrally located had been reported so far.

Bad luck. If the Toronto had been reported, maybe no one would bother looking for him. Maybe they'd just ask the Mexican police to take a look.

Then again, the police and the army still seemed to have their hands full. Block after block, as Fowler made his way west, he saw cops and soldiers around the broken and leaning buildings, endearing themselves to the Mexican public in their usual way.

He passed a badly damaged building that had been cordoned off. "My mother is trapped in there," a man was screaming. Two soldiers were preventing him from entering. Others stood before the rope cordon, posing with their bayoneted rifles. No rescue effort seemed to be under way.

Not that the rest of the soldiers were idle. They'd lined up some dead bodies on the sidewalk, chalking *Muerto* next to them. Apparently, some other agency or armed service branch was responsible for pickup. The smell of decay was already thick in the smoggy air.

The Mexicans are really going to blow this one, thought Fowler. He'd enjoyed reading an approving editorial in *Excelsior* about the president's refusal to ask for foreign aid. You could always get a lot of humor out of *Excelsior* and out of President De La Madrid.

It was a dozen blocks down Madera, then another dozen north on Balderas, to the Lara, where Fowler was going to try to make contact with Juan Antonio Mendoza. He would ask the girl who'd run his errand last night to bring Mendoza over to the Hotel Bailey. The girl was all right; she didn't know who he was. It was Mendoza who'd seen him raised from the dead.

The hard part would be to buy Mendoza off. It was difficult to do such things with no money. Fowler had to pray the kid would accept a deferred payment plan. He had to contact Mendoza immediately, before he started bragging about his rescue of an American—if he hadn't started already.

As for the money, it shouldn't be too big a problem to get

hold of some seed capital. Withdrawals from his personal account would be noticed by his wife's lawyers, but there was a good chunk of cash in the "consulting" account she knew nothing about.

The papers said that the long-distance lines were still down, but there'd been no mention of the telegraph system. He'd stop at the international telegraph office first. It seemed like an eternity since he'd been there with Rigg.

Two dozen blocks was a long way to go for aching feet in shoes that didn't fit. So, when he reached a building where the soldiers were involved in a chat, Fowler sat on the sidewalk and swiftly undid his laces.

The bottoms of his outstretched feet matched perfectly against the soles of the shoes he'd spied. He put them on.

"For shame," a woman yelled at him. Fowler scrambled to his feet, smudging the chalked letters that spelled out *Muerto* as he did so. He left the discarded Tepito shoes next to the corpse. Let the woman put them on it if it bothered her so much. The dead didn't need a good fit.

Fowler walked away, more comfortable now. He cared nothing for these people's beliefs and traditions. Tradition had held them back. Tradition had given them garden tools for tackling an avalanche of concrete.

Fowler drummed his palms on the counter while the telegraph clerk pretended he could read the English words on the form.

"You're asking for money?" He pointed to the dollar sign preceding the entire amount contained in Fowler's "consulting" account.

"Right."

"I hope you aren't asking to have it wired here, Señor Fowler."

Fowler looked around nervously. This was the last time he intended to use his real name—his banker could scarcely respond to a telegram from Tom Dixon. He hoped no one had heard. The place was packed solid as a second-class bus.

The wait in line had delayed him much longer than he'd calculated. Any minute now, Rigg might walk in and ask him why he hadn't gone back home.

"The banks are closed. We have just had an earthquake," the clerk informed him. "We cannot pay out money here."

"But they'll open again."

"Maybe," shrugged the clerk. "In the meantime, we have orders not to accept money wires."

There was no time to think. Already, the pushy European behind Fowler was trying to displace him at the counter.

"I'll ask to have it sent to the post office." Fowler grabbed for a pencil stub and began crossing words out. "And predate this to the eighteenth, okay?"

"I can't do that."

Fowler was prepared. He held out all the brown-wallet cash. Not much, but enough to compensate for a simple modification on a telegraph.

The clerk leaned forward, and Fowler sensed a new intimacy between them. Good.

"I am happy to serve you in whatever way possible," the clerk confided. "But there is no way to change the date. It is locked into the equipment." The tone of regret told Fowler that it wasn't a question of raising the ante. It was over. He couldn't send a telegram dated a day after his death.

Chelo and the girls were still watching television at the Hotel Bailey.

He pulled Chelo aside. "They haven't found out that the buses are running?"

"They decided to stay. There's still plenty of business. The Maria Isabel–Sheraton went this way and that way—"she rocked on her tattered bedroom slippers to show him—"but it didn't fall. Just a few cracks."

"Tourists are still staying there?"

"Of course not. But the government is putting PEMEX workers there. They've come from the provinces to help with the rescue. We'll have plenty of customers. What are you doing here?"

Milagros didn't want to run over to the Lara for him, particularly after she learned how little he was offering.

"I'm busy watching this spectacle of government corruption," she said. "Look at this, the Nuevo Leon." Fowler had seen it already in the papers—a thirty-six-story apartment building crushed to pieces. It was in Tlatelolco, a government-owned housing project not far from the Hotel Bailey. Hundreds were feared dead. He hoped it wasn't going to upstage the Regis as a photo opportunity.

"That building was damaged in the 1980 quake," complained Milagros. "A thousand times, the residents asked the government to fix it."

"Earthquakes are an act of God," said Chelo.

Fowler left them to squabble while he haggled with the girl who had spoken to Rigg in English. She agreed to pop over to the Lara and look for Juan Antonio.

"Just say someone wants to see him on an urgent matter." As a test, he added, "Don't mention my name."

"I don't know it," said the girl, incurious, accustomed to male anonymity. One anxiety was gone.

But she returned alone. "They said he hasn't shown up for work. He sent his brother to tell them he's working with the Red Cross."

"Watch, the hotel will fire him," Milagros called out from the couch. "That's what you get for being a Good Samaritan."

Fowler hoped she was right. With Mendoza unemployed and at home, no one but Rigg would be left on the blazed trail. Even if Mendoza's absence were only temporary, it would give him more time to get hold of money. It would be better to deal with the kid with cash on hand.

Time was badly needed. With telegraphs out of the question, he'd have to send a letter to Citizens National Bank. For twenty pesos, Chelo dug into the depths of her reception desk and came up with a soiled piece of paper and a crumpled envelope. Predating it to September 18, Quake Day Minus 1, was a simple matter.

He bought the stamp at the main post office on Tacuba.

"Will there be any delays receiving mail from the States?" he asked the young woman who sold it to him.

"No, *señor*. One batch of mail was lost, but everything has returned to normal."

Fowler didn't know whether to believe it. The post office was smack-dab in the Centro and surrounded by wreckage. But the grandiose building looked the same as usual, dripping with stone carvings. Fowler wondered if it had been built in the days of Porfirio Díaz, the man they called the Dictator. Díaz put up some fine buildings.

Even without special delays, the letter would take about four days to reach Texas and three days back. Fowler had asked his banker to use an international express service, but he wasn't sure they'd deliver to a post office. Still, he had no choice; he had to get his mail here, addressed "General Delivery."

He hadn't done anything like it for years, not since his student vacations in Europe when some seasoned hitchhiker had told him it was quicker to use poste restante than to wait in the mail lines at American Express. He was about to seal and stamp his envelope when it occurred to him that he'd better see if the system was in effect here. Above one of the windows, *Lista de Correos* was painted in ornate letters, but that could be merely decorative at this point. Fowler approached and read a typed roster mounted in a glass case to the side of the window. A list of mail recipients followed each of three dates.

Someone had taken great pains to type out all the last names in capitals, but since almost all the general delivery users were foreigners lacking the Hispanic's matriarchal second surname, there'd been some confusion. Mary Jane Carlisle, for example, had been typed Mary JANE Carlisle.

Fowler took his letter to a ledge, unfolded it, and crossed out his own name above the *lista de correos* address. He replaced it with "Plano Associates," which is what he called his bogus consulting firm. It was, after all, the name under which he had the bank account. Brian Fowler couldn't have his name posted here for everyone to see, and Brian Fowler couldn't pick up mail. He was dead.

Of course, when the check arrived, there'd be the problem of cashing it without identification. He begged a sheet of paper from the man who'd sold him the stamp and started his letter all over again. This time, he asked to have the check made out in the name of the business. There'd still be problems cashing it, but it wouldn't leave tracks. Once he had a check for $15,000 in his hand, cooperation could be arranged.

Then again, cooperation might be more easily purchased at one of the money-changing houses than at a bank. Fowler had very little experience with them. He'd used some of the reputable *casas de cambio* in the Pink Zone to cash an occasional traveler's check. There were others in the poorer neighborhoods that might better serve his purposes, but they might not have too many pesos in their vaults at any one time.

He took up the pen again. "Please distribute the money as follows," he wrote. "Four checks for $500, three checks for $1,000 each, one check for $10,000." He could take the smaller checks to a bunch of places. They'd go through, and his credit would be good for the big one. "I don't want the whole amount in—" He racked his brains for the common English expression that he wanted. It was gone, the way he'd forgotten "across the street" when he was talking to Rigg. The hell with it. "I don't want it all at once," he wrote.

One lump sum, that was the expression. He remembered it later in the "family" restaurant on Tacuba where he'd decided to celebrate by having supper. Odd, how he forgot those things. It even sounded funny. "Lump."

While waiting for his soup, he fanned out his remaining peso notes—careful to keep them below the table because the place was jammed with customers. He began calculating how he could make them stretch for seven days.

He was doing that when the second earthquake hit.

▽

# 8

T HEY WERE GOING to send someone down to the lobby to get Bermudez. He didn't feel right hanging around the security guard, maybe because the guard was in uniform, and he was not, and it didn't feel right yet doing police work in plain clothes. Just like it didn't feel right being a New York cop in Dallas.

It was hot today, and damp—a tropical heat that he'd seldom felt on the mainland. The air-conditioning system in this building could have used more pep. Outside, the humidity had enveloped him like a mosquito net, reminding him of the small town outside Ponce where the New York Police Department supposed he was right now, using his accrued vacation time to visit a suddenly ailing grandmother.

He had no one to whom he could address these thoughts but Connie, who was staring at him out of the *People* cover on the lobby newsstand. She'd told him how she was giving out lots of interviews these days—unusual for her—provided the reporters let her mention her grandfather's case.

She was a sly one, Connie. He'd had a good couple of days with her in New York after that evening he'd agreed to be her errand boy. If he hadn't known she was an actress, he might have been fooled into thinking she cared something about him.

Not that it mattered. The only thing that mattered were those introductions she could wangle for him when the next crop of cop movies went into production. Technical director: William Bermudez. It was going to look great on the credits.

Touching that face and body on the magazine cover—that had been great too. He plucked a copy off the newsstand and flipped through it. There were some nice black-and-white informal shots inside. Connie cooking lasagna, Connie lounging around her Malibu beach house, Connie with that same half-smile on her lips that he himself had once produced . . .

"Police Officer Bermudez?"

He shoved the magazine back into the rack.

Trans Rio had sent a secretary to guide him past the security checkpoint, a very young and perky one. She did a lot of talking on the elevator ride up. How was his flight, she pretended to want to know, and how did he like Dallas? In New York, a kid who acted like she did was probably on uppers.

Dallas? All that he'd seen so far was the highway between the airport and his hotel, and between his hotel and here. The hotel room looked good: cable TV (which they didn't have yet in Brooklyn), built-in sunlamp, crazy little shoe-shine sponges on the night table. He reminded himself to try those sponges out later.

The elevator door opened directly across from glass doors lettered TRANS RIO. Time for Bermudez to cross the river.

"Here we are," announced the cheerful little secretary. Bermudez stepped out. She stayed on. The elevator door closed, and she was whisked away.

Inside the glass doors, the temperature plunged to meat-locker level. Bermudez's shirt began drying as he approached the reception desk, black and curved like a monumental boomerang. The receptionist ignored him. She was brushing her hair, and each time the brush passed through there was a crackle of static. Bermudez wondered if she was doing this to show off. It must have taken an awfully expensive air-conditioning system to suck the moisture out of this particular Dallas day.

She took his name, still brushing.

"Have a seat," she said. The hairbrush advanced over her bangs and a noise spat out at him like gunfire.

Bermudez settled into a low leather couch. Magazines were spread out on a coffee table: *Fortune, Money, Hotel Executive, Hotel World, Hotel Era.*

A third female appeared and ushered Bermudez to an office the size of a Central Park West apartment.

A man moved forward to shake his hand.

"Tad Gill," he said. Tad or Ted—Bermudez couldn't be sure because of the drawl. He knew the last name though. Bermudez had phoned the president's office for an appointment. This was the president.

Gill was medium height, fiftyish, jowly. There was a droopiness to the eyes that reminded Bermudez of Donald Duck comic strips where some of the people walking around in the background are actually dogs in suits. His tie had a fancy knot in it, and his oxfords had no need for those little shoeshine sponges.

Gill gestured toward a man seated on an armchair. Bermudez had missed him at first; his suit camouflaged him against the brown upholstery.

"L. P. Hammond," said Gill. "One of our attorneys."

Hammond raised himself slightly out of the chair, nodded, dropped back. He was tall and thin, only thirty-five or so but brittle looking, as though the fierce dehumidifying had drawn the juices out of him.

Gill motioned Bermudez to a chair while he himself retreated behind a desk so streamlined that Bermudez wasn't sure whether it was for writing on or for flying.

"Well," said Gill. "So you're going to help us track down the elusive Brian Fowler."

"I'm going to help Miss Oland track him down," Bermudez said.

"And us," Gill repeated. "It will be a great help to us."

"And the DA," contributed L. P. Hammond. Something in his knee creaked as he lifted it to cross his ankle over his opposite leg.

The woman who'd escorted Bermudez to the office appeared in the doorway.

"Coffee?" she asked.

"Later," said Gill.

Bermudez drew a notepad out of the inside pocket of his suit jacket. "I need to know Fowler's movements in Mexico City preceding the earthquake," he said.

"Later," said Gill.

That wasn't the way you talked to a New York cop. Bermudez scrambled to his feet. "You guys want to cooperate, you better cooperate," he said. "Or maybe you don't want one of your employees going on trial. Maybe things would come out. Maybe Fowler didn't do this single-handed."

The canine eyes were watching Bermudez. "Good," said Gill. "Very good. We like a feller with spunk."

Bermudez snapped his notepad closed. "You decide you want to tell me anything, I'll be back at the Bainbridge."

"Terrible choice," said the hotel chain president. "Lousy pool."

But L. P. Hammond was up on his stork legs now, restraining Bermudez with a touch on the arm. "We'll give you everything you want," he said, his unaccented voice breaking in on Gill's drawl like a radio announcer. "We just want a few things understood."

Reluctantly, Bermudez sat again.

A wave of cool air surged through the office. L. P. Hammond's chair creaked as he perched on it again. He cracked his knuckles.

"Your questions are well taken," said the lawyer.

"Great," said Bermudez. "But I didn't ask you for a report card. How about some answers instead?"

"You spoke of a trial," Hammond continued. "Mr. Fowler, if found, will almost certainly be placed on trial. It is likely to be well publicized. A celebrity is involved. The DA certainly wants a trial."

"How about you? You want a trial too? Seems to me if I was Fowler, I'd get a smart lawyer, and the smart lawyer would probably start telling me to throw the blame on higher-ups." He didn't trust these guys. The best thing for them, next to a dead Fowler, was a lost Fowler.

"He can try," Hammond agreed. "But I don't think he'd succeed in convincing a jury of that."

"Is that right?" said Bermudez. "The jury's going to believe that he made decisions about fixing a water heater all by himself?"

"Not only did he make that decision by himself, but he failed to inform us that a similar, less serious accident, had befallen another guest of ours one year previous," said Gill.

"That's why Fowler's facing manslaughter charges," said L. P. Hammond. "One incident, that might not have been all that bad. Two?" The fingertips of the long thin hands pressed together, as if the lawyer was saying last rites for Fowler.

"In that case," continued Gill, as if Hammond's speech had been a footnote, "the burn was not as severe. But the accident should have been reported. We demand that all accidents in our hotels be reported.

"Fowler knew the procedure," said Gill. "He filed other accident reports. Not that one." His lips curled back into a smile, revealing large, sharp teeth, like the blades of a paper shredder.

"Misguided penury," clucked Hammond.

"Fowler had some trouble meeting his budget," Gill translated. "So he decided to scrimp on needed repairs. He told his secretary so. She's willing to get up on the witness stand and testify to that. Testify to the fact that the guests were calling him to complain about the water temperature too. We were never informed of that in any way, shape, or form. And, by the way, that little girl was terminated by Fowler. For reasons we cannot quite determine."

"She's a great admirer of Miss Oland's," Hammond commented. "Reads about her in fan magazines and that kind of thing." He pronounced the words "fan magazines" carefully, as if afraid to release a bad smell.

"Very nice," said Bermudez. "Except it seems to me that Miss Oland's needs would be just as well served if the DA went after Fowler's superiors. It's just a case of somebody

taking the rap." He'd been over and over this with Connie.
She had a theory about it.

Hammond inclined his head toward the desk. Over to Gill.

"Let me tell you something about that DA," said Gill.
"He's the damned finest one we've had for a long time. I
would hate to see him voted out next year when his term's
up. Looks to be a tough race too." Gill stretched his hands
out before him, and his right sleeve hitched up over his wrist.
All he needed was a pen to write out some campaign
contribution checks.

"You left out another possibility," Hammond informed
Bermudez. "Trans Rio could be indicted. As a corporation."

Bermudez knew what this meant. "No trial."

"A fine perhaps," said the lawyer. "Could be a stiff one."

"In other words," said Gill, his gold watch gleaming,
"nothing." He opened a drawer in his desk and handed
Bermudez some pieces of paper printed in fancy computer
type. "Here's Fowler's Mexico City itinerary. There are notes
on the right-hand side about our conversations with him,
when they occurred, the content, all that kind of thing."

"You'll want the arrest warrant," said Hammond.

"I'm all set on that." Bermudez had already located the
courthouse on the map they'd given him at Hertz.

"I'll see you out," said Gill. As they walked toward the
hallway, Bermudez heard a strange snapping sound behind
him. He looked back to see Hammond trying to work a crick
out of his neck by rolling his head in circles.

Gill walked him back to the reception area. "Ber-mu-dez,"
the executive said, rolling the syllables under his jowls.
"What kind of name would that be?"

"Just one of those names an American citizen might have."

"New York," mused Gill. "Puerto Rican?"

"Right."

"How's your Mexican?"

"Pardon?"

"The way they jabber the language down there, can you
compren-day? It's not really Spanish, I understand."

In New York people said the same thing about Puerto Ricans.

They were at the glass door now, shaking hands.

"Oh, I went to a tutor for that," said Bermudez. "Had him explain all the differences to me."

"Is that a fact?"

"Good thing I did too. For a few dollars more, he taught me how to understand Texans."

The perky little secretary had been waiting for him by the elevator doors.

"Some security system," he remarked as they descended. "I get an escort both ways. Has there been a lot of crime in this building or something?"

She giggled. "Oh, no. It's just that they're trying to find things for me to do."

He let that one pass.

She said good-bye on the ground floor. But a moment later she was running after him, a copy of *People* in her hand.

"Here," she panted. "I just got this on the newsstand, this issue you were looking at before. I know I really shouldn't, but you know Connie Oland, don't you? Do you think you could get her to autograph this cover for me? If it isn't too much trouble. She could send it to me here, care of Mr. Gill."

He didn't need to be told that she used to have things to do in the field, at one of Trans Rio's residential hotels for the elderly. As Brian Fowler's secretary.

"I'll see what I can do about the autograph," he said, tucking the magazine under his arm. He figured that this girl had done some autographing of her own: those little initials that secretaries type at the bottom of memos. He didn't suppose she'd remember any memos from Fowler requisitioning service on a hot-water heater.

Maybe if Connie asked her to remember . . . But being a fan was one thing, and being employed was another. Bermudez had no need to ask her about the salary for her new job. He was sure it paid a lot better than her old one.

Connie had it right. It was get Fowler or get nobody.

# 9

WHEN HE CAME to, Fowler saw five white pillars framing cypress trees and evenly cut rectangles of cerulean blue sky. He was either in heaven or in one of those Maxfield Parrish prints his wife used to collect in the seventies before the taste became too common.

A hand nudged him, and a small olive-skinned face came into focus.

Damn, though Fowler. The Snoopy Brigade. The Spider Brigade was so much easier on the nerves.

Soon there were three of them, climbing all over him. "We've got hot coffee and beans today," they were yelling. "And eggs! The Spider Brigade never finds eggs."

Fowler picked one of the ten-year-olds off his bruised chest and slowly raised himself to sitting position. Blankets, sweaters, and raincoats were spread across the white stone floor of the Parque Mexico, but the people who had slept on them were gone—finished with their groaning and arguing and fucking, and everything else they did next to him in the dark. The sleeping pills had been well worth the 2,000 pesos he'd splurged on them. He hadn't heard a thing.

The children's brigades were a nuisance, but they were definitely useful. Fowler had a good thing going here. If you had to sleep out in the open—and ever since the second quake, a lot of people preferred sleeping that way—it was best to do it in a middle-class neighborhood.

He got the idea of coming here by reading the *News*. He was back to reading the papers almost as diligently as he did in the prequake days. Out of habit, he still looked for wire stories about Connie Oland, but celebrity gossip had been displaced by the notices of canceled events, endless human-interest stuff full of sentimental drivel about "heroic rescuers," and page after page of poorly reproduced snapshots of people who had disappeared on Black Thursday. Somehow there was still room for Doris Pike's column. It had returned on Saturday, full of italicized or Meaningfully Capitalized exclamations about the way her building had *rocked* and *swayed* during the earthquake, and how she had located some *wonderful* psychiatrists in the Pink Zone who were treating people for the Shock of It All.

The *News* had its uses. It told him that the banks had reopened, which would probably make things easier no matter where he went to cash his checks when they finally arrived. It said that international long distance would be disrupted for an indefinite period of time because the microwave dish on the communications building had fallen. Fowler was a little distressed about that. Now that his financial needs were squared away, he had no reason to call the States, but he'd been hoping that Trans Rio or the court would call down here and find out about the Hotel Toronto disaster. Still no word about the Toronto except in the most obscure local papers.

The *News* went in heavy for valiant-community-response stories, and among them were a number of articles about the unofficial shelter in Hipódromo de la Condesa. Probably a lot of reporters from the *News* lived in the neighborhood; the district was full of foreigners. The reporters wrote about the kids in the Parque Mexico who were helping the homeless with food and blankets. Made them sound cute as buttons. Made Fowler realize he could camp out here until his money came without spending barely a cent.

The kids saved special bits of food for him. They preferred him to most of the riffraff the earthquake had washed into their neighborhood. Not too many local people were sleeping in the Parque Mexico. This was the kind of place where people lived behind elaborate grillwork in pale stone houses—none of the Centro's hysterical reds and turquoises for the Condesa. The area had been shaken pretty badly by the quake. There had been some deaths. A number of penthouse condos had collapsed. But this was the type of neighborhood where dislocated people had someone to take them in.

Fowler had the kids to take him in, at least until the schools reopened. They loved "Meester Dixon." They loved every minute of the disaster, actually. They told Fowler how happy they were when the second quake hit—only 7.3 on the Richter scale compared to the initial quake's 7.8, but enough to bring some additional buildings down. The tremors were continuing. The kids could be in luck again.

"Where did the water for the coffee come from?" he asked them. The pipes had been badly damaged, and many sections of the city were still without water. Where water still ran out of taps, it often came out dark and dubious. All kinds of stuff was seeping in. More than usual, which was bad enough.

"We boiled it like the Red Cross told us," said one of the kids, evading a direct answer. No one liked to discuss the additional holes that were popping up in the pipes—neatly shaped, the way things were when they were made by tools. It was a common sight on the street these days to see boys crawling out of manholes.

"How many minutes did you boil it for?"

"Ten!" "Twenty!" "An hour!" Since they were all lying, Fowler decided to believe the one who said twenty. The Red Cross advised boiling it for ten, which was no use at all at this altitude, where water boiled so rapidly. Everyone was going to get sick, and the restaurant toilets around the park would look even worse than they did already.

"Meester Dixon, will you really take us to Disneylandia someday?" This from the boy who'd woken him up, a round-faced little runt whose parents had actually named him Sócrates.

"Sure, I'll take you on that ride in the giant teacups," said Fowler, who had to think of different variations every time this question was put to him—Sócrates didn't want to hear about Mickey Mouse anymore. Fowler thought he remembered the teacups from television commercials that had run during his youth. He had never been to Disneyland; he didn't particularly like children. But a little ingenuity bought him first-class treatment from the kids' brigades. A few days ago, when it had rained, everyone else got soaked all night. The kids brought him a big piece of plastic.

Even better, Sócrates had sneaked him into his parents' house yesterday for a quick shower and shave. Nice condo. A regular Disneylandia for adults. Fowler wondered when he'd ever be able to live like that again.

He was doing everything right now, he told himself. Okay, so he didn't have any money, but he'd found a nice unofficial shelter (there was no question of going to one of the official ones run by the government; even the poor were afraid of those) where kids with clean fingernails got him food. Annoying as they were, they took some of the ghastliness away, making it all seem a little like Boy Scout camp. Okay, so he'd made a mistake letting Rigg see him after his rescue, but Rigg would go back to Monterrey sooner or later. Okay, so it was too bad about Juan Antonio Mendoza knowing his name, but he'd fix it all up with an exchange of money—or, rather, the promise of money—for silence. Just as soon as Juan Antonio Mendoza came back to work at the Lara, which he hadn't done so far.

Fowler accepted a cup of coffee from one of the teenaged girls who were cooking in the corner of this amphitheater, or whatever you called the enormous white platform set among the park's palms and cypresses. It slept 100 or so these days. Everyone huddled together on the big concrete floor. The ground might have been softer, but there were no crawling insects here. At any rate, this is where the kids set out the blankets and coats they'd collected, and the earthquake victims tended to do what they were told, Fowler had noticed. They were *damnificados*, a word that meant only they'd been harmed or affected. But just as "one lump sum" sounded odd to Fowler's bilingual ears, so did *damnificados*. It sounded like a snatch of a horror movie title—something like *zombie*.

This place was only a pocket park, a sideshow to nearby Chapultepec, where half the city crowded in on Sundays. Still, it had really been "done up." The platform was incredibly elaborate, ringed by a low wall with pillars rising from it at intervals. In each corner was a concrete gazebo with a Moorish roof. At the entrance, a colossal naked woman sculpted of stone perpetually spilled water into a trough from jugs gripped in her armpits.

In the five days Fowler had been there, the fountain had been steadily losing water pressure. He took a look at it and saw three people bent over the side of the trough. He had a strong suspicion he'd just discovered the source of his coffee water.

One of the girls doing KP duty offered him a limp tortilla and cold scrambled eggs. He was not one to eat breakfast, much less after taking sleeping pills, but he took it and chewed dutifully. He needed his strength. He had to check on Juan Antonio Mendoza again. But he'd stop by the post office first. Maybe the money had come in early. It would be better to see Juan Antonio with the money in hand.

"Good-bye, Meester Dixon," the girls yelled as he headed toward the Juanacatlán station of the Metro.

There was something else he had to do today; he was going to have to move somewhere else, away from this Sesame Street where he'd become one of the featured players. A name change wasn't enough of a cover in a place where people lay together half naked, learning each other's smells and identifying marks. The arraignment had already been held. The hunt could be on. He had to be careful now.

The Metro no longer terrified him as it had at first. It had absorbed the earthquake well—rumor had it that Japanese officials were coming to study it as well as the unharmed

Petróleos Mexicanos installations. Amazing, thought Fowler, feeding the turnstile with a one-peso ticket. Mexico had something to teach Japan.

The Pino Suárez station was one spot that had gotten it, so he had to transfer to a northern line at Balderas, pushing his way through claustrophobic corridors. Everybody was back to work now; some of the men who slept next to him in the park clicked their briefcases closed in the morning and set off for the office. The piped-in music was back on in the Metro stations. Today's tune: "Mood Indigo."

The Metro station shops had reopened, and vendors again blocked the passageways with their painted bark, unfinished furniture, and clothes. One of the T-shirts was printed with the slogan, LA CRISIS ME VALE MIERDA. The economic crisis doesn't mean shit to me.

A good slogan for politicians like De La Madrid, Fowler reflected. He's got a $96 billion foreign debt and a $5 billion repair bill for the earthquake, but he spends a day or two sitting on his duff before asking for outside help. Some people were angry about that, but more of them were angry at the U.S. ambassador, John Gavin, for estimating the total dead at 20,000—twice what even the leftist papers were calculating. Gavin wasn't popular here. Fowler had always considered his appointment a mistake. People remembered how he used to do the Bacardi rum commercials.

They weren't talking about that in the *lonchería* on Mina Street when Fowler came in, defeated by his fruitless visit to the *lista de correos* window and nauseated by the restaurant's lard smell. Like everyone else, they were talking about the dogs, the canine search-and-rescue teams that had been flown in from various countries to detect survivors in the wreckage. The German and French teams aroused the most interest because they were said to hate one another to the point where cooperation was becoming impossible.

The men slopping up rice and beans at the *lonchería* counter were taking sides. Fans of the Germans pointed out that their team had rescued a dozen people and pulled out about seventy bodies from the American Airlines office, the National Purchasing Office, and a high school. The Francophiles weren't as quick to produce statistics, but they compensated by shouting and turning red under their straw rancher's hats.

Everyone shared a good laugh at the Israelis, who had sent a team of war-trained demolition and medical experts. They'd brought special balloons to lift the rubble, but the Mexican buildings had fallen in such a way that the balloons were ineffective.

"Maybe if we told those Jews there was money under the cement," someone suggested. He was rewarded by a burst of laughter. Fowler, settled on a counter stool and sipping a tepid Coke, smiled and thought of Rigg's joke about "Hymie Togs." Rigg. He sobered. But surely Rigg was back up north by now. That left just one problem.

Fowler nursed his Coke and waited for an opportunity to interrupt, but the men were still shouting about the dogs. At first he'd taken these guys to be a small splash from Guerrero's vast ocean of unemployed males—precisely the kind of men he'd come here to met. Now, however, he gathered that the man who told the Israeli joke was a PEMEX employee, one of the Petroleos Mexicanos oil workers who'd been called in from all over the country to clean up the mess. It seemed that this man worked nights, operating an earth mover at one of the wreckage sites. He said the dog teams, both French and German, were annoyed with the Mexican army for failing to halt traffic during their rescue missions. Apparently, their ultrasonic devices—and maybe the dogs' nostrils, too—required complete silence.

Everyone joined in on a hearty curse of the army. It seemed that the French and German resource teams could get away with a lot more criticism of Mexico than the U.S. ambassador could. They had not done Bacardi commercials.

Fowler wondered how long he could stand sitting with them. This was the rankest of the several restaurants he'd visited for the same purpose that had brought him here today.

It could have been the power of suggestion, but the smell emanating from the grill reminded him more and more of dog.

There was a lull, and he plunged into it, offering 2,000 pesos to anyone who would carry a message for him to the Hotel Lara, to a Juan Antonio Mendoza. Dealing with the hookers had been easier, but he was glad they were gone. Business never really picked up, Chelo told him right before she shuttered the Bailey and left to join a sister in Guadalajara. The girls, Milagros and the other one, had gone back to their home states.

Even with them gone, Fowler dreaded all of the Guerrero district, where he'd been forced to return again and again like an amateur murderer revisiting the scene of the crime. But he didn't have enough money to lure a messenger to the Lara from some other part of the city. It was a quick job here, just around the corner.

To his surprise, the PEMEX worker—already earning overtime, no doubt—was the first taker. Fowler suspected a trap, and as the minutes went by and the man failed to return, the suspicion grew stronger. The others stayed at the counter, poking spoons into oozing custards. Everyone seemed to be waiting. Fowler didn't like it.

The PEMEX man returned, red-faced with enthusiasm. "Just as I thought," he announced to everyone in general. "Some of the Frenchmen are staying there. Right over there in the Lara. I asked the desk clerk about it. Didn't I tell you?"

"The dogs, too?" someone asked.

"What do you think? You think dogs like that sleep in the street?"

Fowler couldn't quite take it in. He had sent the man to ask for Juan Antonio Mendoza—as unobtrusively as possible, he'd cautioned—and the man had evidently caused a scene in the hotel lobby. About the message, he knew he had no need to ask. It had been lost to Francophilia.

"My money," Fowler said, almost in a whisper.

"Oh, sorry." The PEMEX man pounded a fist into his own head, damning himself for being an idiot. The others stopped blathering. It was soon so quiet that a canine search team could have easily worked in peace.

The PEMEX man swept the straw ten-gallon hat off his head. Fowler watched, fascinated.

"This Señor Mendoza, you knew him well?"

"Not very well."

"I am glad. The hotel said that his brother came by to explain why he hadn't been to work. He was killed in the second earthquake. He was one of the rescuers in that building that collapsed, out on Tlalpan."

"Near the Metro station. General Anaya," someone added unnecessarily.

"A terrible thing, for a rescuer to be killed," someone else said.

"God's will," everyone said at once. About forty gallons' worth of straw hat was removed from head and held at breast.

Their attitude of piety gave Fowler a chance to slip out before they saw the joy in his face. He, too, was a believer. He always believed in celebrating. He rationed out a few thousand pesos and went to Sanborn's on Madero for a treat.

Sanborn's was like being home. Once you got past the historic blue-and-white-tiled exterior, you were in a completely false Mexican restaurant serving hamburgers, cheese sandwiches and the kind of bland, imitation tacos you would find, say, in Atlanta or New York. Even the waitresses dressed in crisp regional costumes seemed inauthentic, like Italian actresses playing Mexicans in a cheap movie.

Fowler had meant to dawdle over his hot dog and Nescafé, but he ended up wolfing them down. Instead of the usual crowds of tourists, a scant dozen foreigners were scattered over the dining room. Most were unaccompanied men, like himself, but much neater and cleaner. The *de rigueur* outfit seemed to be a nondescript jacket and slacks ensemble accessorized with a clip-on penholder. Obviously, these were the foreign experts who'd been shipped in from the industrialized world. Fowler, with his unshaven face and Tepito clothes, felt nonindustrialized, almost savage.

Two tables away from him sat one of the engineering types, unmistakably American. Fowler pushed back his chair and approached him, claiming a need to borrow mustard. But his real need went deeper than that. He was starved for a conversation in English, the language of work, purpose, development. And it was a test of sorts, to see if the man would shrink away from him.

"Here you go," said the man, extending the mustard bottle. Unfriendly. Or maybe just northeastern.

Fowler pointed to the photo ID card clipped to the man's shirt pocket. "Down here to clean up the mess?"

"Right," said the man, the frost in his voice thawing just a bit; he liked the subject. He lifted his coffee cup for a sip, and when he lowered it, his eyes had come alive over his long nose and knife-edge lips. He looked level at Fowler and said, "Explosives."

"So they're letting you go ahead," said Fowler. He'd read about all the delays. No sooner had the government asked the experts in than street protests were organized to oppose the dynamiting. The Mexicans would rather spend months hand-sifting the rubble for corpses and memories than blow the whole thing up and start building again.

"Not yet. But I bet they'll settle things pretty soon," said the man, raising his coffee cup again. "We're expensive. The meter's running."

It was running on Fowler, too. He mumbled his thanks for his mustard and retreated to his table. The demolitions man seemed incurious enough, but still, it had been foolish to risk so much exposure.

He paid the cashier and dived into the magazine racks beyond the dining area. Sanborn's counter boutiques and drugstore were nearly empty but for a handful of wealthy Mexicans who'd stopped by to fuel up on English-language computer books or Gucci handbags while their capital city fell apart around them. Fowler pulled a copy of *Time* off a rack. The Mexican earthquake had made the cover, and he was delighted to see a nicely cropped picture of the Hotel Regis mess inside.

But no mention of the Hotel Toronto, neither in *Time* nor in *Newsweek*. Fowler put both of them back. He shoved them in front of the copies of *People*, which this week featured Connie Oland on its cover.

▽

# 10

THE TRIP TO the courthouse was uneventful. Bermudez would have liked to swing by the place where Kennedy was shot, but instead he headed out of the city toward the suburb where Fowler's wife lived.

She'd said she wouldn't be home from work until six o'clock. Bermudez found a fast-food place in a shopping mall near her neighborhood. Next to the condiments counter was a rack full of thick stapled booklets labeled *Renter's Guide*. They were free, so Bermudez took one to kill time. He couldn't believe the deals they were offering around here. One month free, no security deposit, we welcome pets under forty pounds.

It was five past six by the time he remembered to look at his watch. Monica Fowler's directions took him to a small apartment complex, very much like the ones in the *Renter's Guide* photos. These weren't rentals, though. They were condos. He could tell that by the big Open House sign stuck into the front lawn.

"Just temporary,' she told him when she came to the door. "Just until this divorce thing gets sorted out."

She was tall and very thin with a good-looking made-up face. Her dark hair fell loose until about the top of her ear. Then some kind of shearing machine had taken over, clipping it close to the head. Bermudez was reminded of the hedges at the Brooklyn Botanical Garden. She wore a long white cardigan trimmed in red braid and a red knife-pleat skirt. She'd told him on the phone that she was in the fashion business. He had a few questions he would have liked to have asked her about pants cuffs, but it wouldn't have seemed professional.

They settled into the living room where she'd set out all kinds of crackers and hunks of cheese in colors he never would have thought of as edible.

"When is the last time you heard from your husband, Mrs. Fowler?"

"My *estranged* husband," she corrected him. "I haven't heard from him since we separated seven months ago. All communication between us goes through our lawyers. By mutual consent, I might add." The knife pleats shimmered as she shifted in her seat.

"If it turns out that he's checked out of the hotel where he last stayed, do you have any idea where in Mexico he might be?"

Monica Fowler crossed her hands on her knees. "I have no idea how he could stomach Mexico in the first place."

"You've been there with him?"

She rolled her eyes up. "God, yes. I proposed it to several magazines as a story. The Vacation from Hell. Nobody would touch it. Too much advertising revenue from the Mexican tourist council."

"Did he know anybody there? Business contacts, for instance."

"I believe most of his former classmates are in the business of getting political patronage jobs."

"Classmates?"

She told him about Fowler's adolescent years in Mexico. Bermudez took notes. The wife painted a vague picture of a fancy prep school attended by brats spawned by the executives of multinational corporations.

"Your husband speaks Spanish?"

"Not to me, I assure you." She wrinkled her nose in distaste. "He was somewhat helpful with our gardener. And a cleaning woman."

Bermudez had seen those phrase books for communication with the servants. Please take the garbage out. This is a vacuum cleaner.

"The earthquake was really powerful," Bermudez said, watching her face carefully. "I hate to say it, but—"

"He might be dead?" No tears welled up over the blue eyeliner. Instead, small taut lines seemed to break through the concealer around her mouth. "That would just be perfect. Do you know what that would mean to me? This! Forever!" She waved her hand around the apartment. It didn't look too bad to Bermudez; pretty large, in fact. It wouldn't have surprised him if the cutoff point for pets here was more than forty pounds.

"He doesn't even have title on the house," she spat. "Trans Rio bought it for us."

"Hmm," said Bermudez, shaking his head in sympathy. He knew that already. "How about life insurance?"

"Oh, I was the beneficiary in days of yore. Not now. He took care of that."

"It goes to a brother, a sister?" Bermudez prompted. He could check it out with them.

"The lung people," said Mrs. Fowler, clinching her upper and lower lipliner together in what was supposed to pass as a smile.

"Excuse me?"

"American Lung Association. His father died of lung cancer."

"I bet they appreciate that."

"I don't think they even know about it. Oh, don't get the idea that he's a saint or anything like that. He just enjoyed replacing my name with the name of an inanimate object."

The wife leaned over the fruit bowl and popped a grape into her mouth. "Look," she said, "Brian is absolutely no use to me dead. The only way I'm going to get back what I put into this miserable marriage is if I get a piece of everything he earns from now till doomsday. I want him found. Alive."

"I'm going to need a little help on that. Do you have any photographs?"

She rummaged through some drawers under a wall unit and came up with a three-ring photo album. She tossed it next to the cracker tray.

"I've got some coffee brewing in the kitchen," she said. Bermudez declined. "Well, I'm going to get some for myself. I can't get through those pictures without some caffeine for fortification."

She went out of the room on a gust of complaints about the way the apartment was laid out.

Bermudez helped himself to a photo preview. Most of the snapshots held by the album's little plastic sleeves were landscapes. Lots of beaches, lots of mountains, a big helping of sunsets. Finally he got to the people. Monica Fowler looked good in a bikini, but Bermudez was more interested in the blond man standing next to her. The same blond man sat with her at an outdoor restaurant table, dropped line off a fishing boat, climbed up a cliff on ropes. In most of the pictures, he and his wife were half of a foursome. They seemed to have vacationed in packs. Maybe they needed the other couple as a buffer.

He was a healthy-looking man, the kind of man who'd have no trouble taking out a large life-insurance policy. He'd been separated for seven months. For a lot of people, that wasn't enough time to get around to everything. Like changing the beneficiary on an insurance policy.

Bermudez had no doubt that Fowler and his wife couldn't stand each other. But what if he'd staged his own death to wriggle out of the indictment? There might be a big fringe benefit to that. His wife would collect on his insurance policy, and he could demand half, threatening to reappear if she didn't fork it over.

Mrs. Fowler came back with a cup of coffee on a saucer.

"Glad to see you're finally starting on the cheese," she said. She plunked herself next to Bermudez on the sofa. "Okay," she said, starting to open the album. "Memory lane."

"Before we start," said Bermudez. "I just want to clarify something. Have you been in touch with your husband since September nineteenth?"

The coffee cup clicked sharply on the saucer. "I told you already. I haven't talked to him since the separation."

"Would it refresh your memory if I told you that someone who knows you—someone very close to you—has given me different information on that point?"

"Who might that somebody be?"

"Somebody with the first name of Pam."

"Pam? Pam told you that?" She looked genuinely puzzled. "Why in the world would Pam tell you such a thing? I never gave her any reason to . . . it simply isn't true."

"Forget it," said Bermudez. He had what he wanted. "Let's look at the pictures."

"When did she talk to you? I can't believe she would say that."

Bermudez pulled the album toward him and started flipping through it. He found the picture of the two couples rock climbing and slid it out of the plastic.

"Pam," he said, tracing his finger under the words written on the back of the photo. "New Hampshire, '84. Me, Brian, Pam, and Barry," he read out. "Looks like a nice person, this Pam. I've never had the pleasure of meeting her."

He expected anger. Instead, Mrs. Fowler was lifting the coffee cup to her smiling lips. "Very clever," she said. "Maybe you will be able to find Brian after all. I must say I had my doubts."

Because my name is Bermudez, Bermudez thought. And you despise Mexico.

They looked through the photos. She offered to give Bermudez all of them, but he only needed a few.

"Stay for a liqueur?" she asked. She reached for a piece of fruit, and her hand grazed his thigh.

"No, thanks," he said, rising.

She rose, too, but very slowly. "You know," she said, "you remind me of a model all the menswear companies have been using lately. He's hot these days. Very hot."

"Too much heat down here if you ask me," said Bermudez, moving toward the door. "Me, I like winter."

Back at the hotel, Bermudez checked the time of his flight to Mexico City, took a shower, found out that the thing in the bathroom he'd taken for a telephone was really a wall-mounted hair dryer, and set the clock radio for six—the flight left early, and he wasn't sure how long it took to return a rental car at the airport. He tuned in the radio to a country-music station he'd stumbled over using the nifty scan function in the car.

Country music was the most Texan thing about Texas so far. Tad Gill had an accent, but a lot of people here didn't. Bermudez had expected something different, but he wasn't sure what. Cowboys, maybe. Sheriffs going after the bad guys.

Which is about what he'd expected when he joined the New York police force. Which had turned out to be a joke.

He popped open the can of beer he'd brought up with him and lay down on top of the bedspread. They'd turned his covers down while he was gone. He felt something hard under his back. Mints.

The copy of *People* with Connie's picture on it was on the night table. Bermudez didn't have time to send it to New York and get it autographed for the Trans Rio secretary. He had decided he didn't like the inside pictures of Connie after all. They were supposed to be candids, but he knew from what she'd told him they were posed.

The way she could fake it so well scared him.

He wondered how he was doing at his end, if he was carrying it off at all. She said she could detect his ambition in the way he stood. How about the way he made love to her?

He told himself there was nothing in it but ambition.

Down here, he was the one who was posing. Fowler's wife said he looked like a male model.

He was turning into one of those fake cops in those fake cop movies he patrolled, the ones that need technical advice.

Bermudez reached behind him for one of the foil-wrapped mints and lobbed it toward an ashtray across the room. It landed dead center.

It was time to walk away from the rain sprinklers and the sidewalk lights. This was Bermudez's chance to make it real again. He was going to get the guy in those vacation snapshots. Live and in person.

# 11

To CERTAIN RESIDENTS of Mexico City, the earthquake was a special kind of disaster. It meant you could no longer find hypoallergenic contact-lens solution because your *favorite* optician's office had been shattered into *smithereens*. It turned your lunch date with a Very Important Someone into *total confusion* because that little French bistro on Humboldt where you'd arranged to meet was absolutely GONE. And it had you looking like a *fright* because that GENIUS hairdresser you depended on *perished in the disaster*, and no one else in this city *understands* baby-fine hair.

These and other tragedies of similar magnitude were detailed in a recent Doris Pike column, which had been transferred from a page of the *Mexico City News* into Brian Fowler's hip pocket. Both it and he were now on their way to 6-A Mata Street, which, according to this same column, was now the liveliest social spot in the entire Federal District—a Little Ray of Sunshine in our *poor, blighted* midst, as Doris Pike put it.

Fowler walked the seven blocks to Mata from Santo Domingo Plaza, where he'd been unlucky enough to spend the last few nights. He could always depend on an early wake-up call over there. The public typists and letter writers set up shop on the benches near the church every morning, just as they'd done for years. It made no difference to them that fifty-odd families driven from their homes by the quake had set up a tent city on the plaza. Business was good, one of the scribes told Fowler. Everyone was writing to someone for money.

That included Fowler, who thought about making a quick detour to the post office on his way to Mata Street, but decided against it. It was about noon, too early for today's mail to have been sorted for the *lista de correos*. The clerk at the *lista* window took his time, especially when it came to giving a good, hard, mocking stare at Fowler, forced to spend five minutes daily on a task that should have taken ten seconds. The roster of mail recipients was brief—and getting briefer each day as the pipeline of tourists dried—but the distortion and reversal of foreign names turned it into a rebus. There was always the chance he'd missed a tortured approximation of "Plano Associates."

But nothing ever came close. Fowler was nervous: The letter should have arrived by now. Had his own letter gotten lost in the afterquake chaos? Writing again would be risky. He could predate the letter—given the usual state of the Mexican mail and the dimensions of the disaster, even a two-week lapse between mailing and arrival would probably seem plausible. But this time there'd be a huge postmark lag. Dead men don't flip letters into mailboxes.

That's why Fowler was going to 6-A Mata Street, one of Doris Pike's favorite hangouts these days, and the place from which she claimed to have phoned Cincinnati to order that elusive contact-lens solution. If Doris Pike had phoned Cincinnati from 6-A Mata, then 6-A Mata was truly something fantastic. In all the rest of Mexico City, long-distance service was still kaput. A few calls had been crackled in from outside, but transmission remained impossible. Fowler had an urgent need to transmit.

The building turned out to be an elegant terra-cotta town house with a discreet brass nameplate identifying it as the headquarters of the Mexican Press Club. At least Pike had gotten the address right. He gave the knob a tentative twist, and the door swung open.

Once inside and standing on a carpeted foyer, he was

seized by something like stage fright. Beyond him was a clutch of young people—North Americans or Europeans—chatting together as they faced a wall. Fowler could smell the stink of his armpits under the cheap, new shirt he'd bought that morning with some of his last 1,000-peso notes. A few hundred pesos more had bought him a shave at a Centro barbershop, but showers weren't so easy to come by. The public baths near the railroad station were still without water.

He wondered if he'd manage to get through this. It would be one thing if reporters were still those crumpled-fedora guys of thirties movies. Nowadays, they tended to emulate the people they interviewed. The group in the room beyond him looked casual but well groomed, the men in crisp shirts and slacks, the women in blouses and skirts—probably writers for general-interest newspapers. Fowler's wife had to do better than that; she covered the fashion business. Her wardrobe ate most of her salary, but she insisted she needed it to win access to important sources.

"Access" and "sources." He'd heard those words often enough to absorb them. A handful of other terms had burst through the dense barrier he erected to shield himself from wifely career babble. Now he wished he had listened more closely. Last night, on the cold stone floor of Santo Domingo Plaza, he'd tried to reconstruct her gossip and anecdotes, but all he could come up with was phrase-book-level vocabulary.

That would have to do because a couple of the young people in the cluster were glancing his way now. Time for his entrance. Fowler was about to impersonate his own detested wife.

He stepped forward and saw that they'd been reading news clippings and notices off a bulletin board and discussing them among themselves.

"Hello," said one of the young men, breaking off from the general conversation. The "hello" had an accent. English, or maybe just Canadian. Fowler mumbled something in response, not quite as newsmanlike as he planned.

"Just arrived?" asked the greeter. He was English, that was obvious now. Fowler, who didn't think much of the English, hoped he wasn't a club official.

"Just arrived here." If the next question asked who he was working for, Fowler had several names of apparel trade magazines on tap, including those his wife worked for and ones that had inspired tantrums by turning her down. He wasn't afraid of that. "Is there some kind of fee to use the club?" That's what he was afraid of.

"Just wire fees if you file from here. They've got three kinds of machines, but I can't get the hang of any of them. If you need to use them, better ask somebody else."

A young woman turned around to face Fowler. "I can—"

"Thanks. I won't need them."

"You must be one of the lucky ones," she said. "Your newsroom's still in one piece?"

Fowler didn't want to answer that one. He was thankful that the question came from a woman, and a very small one at that. It seemed perfectly natural to ignore her and address the man.

"Phone around here?" He tried not to salivate.

"Up in the bar," said the Englishman, indicating an iron-railed staircase. "Carlos clocks the time on it. Better keep an eye on him. He's not all that accurate."

The Englishman gave Fowler a you-know-these-Mexicans look. Fowler returned the look, feeling his facial muscles assume a familiar, nearly forgotten, position. He walked up the stairs with a spring in his step. He was in.

There was a bar all right, the type a middle-class Mexican might have at his beach house in Puerto Vallarta. Fairly well stocked, but don't ask for Pimm's Cup 5. No one was tending it at the moment, and none of the twosomes scattered over the couches and armchairs of the big room seemed to be drinking.

A small balcony beyond a set of ornate French doors seemed to be the main attraction. About half the bar's occupants, five or so people, were concentrated there. But Fowler knew where he wanted to sit. Right here in the bar area. Near a woman who was talking into a black plastic mouthpiece, speaking English loud and clear.

Since she made no effort to keep her conversation private, Fowler gathered within moments that her kids were fine but freaked out, that for the first time since moving to Mexico she had more assignments than she could handle, and that, terrible as she knew it sounded, she found the earthquake had been great for her career.

More importantly—and this is the part that made Fowler's heart pound—he picked up the fact that she was talking to her mother, and that her mother was in Denver. Denver, Colorado. U.S.A.

"You want take a drink?" A Mexican had crept next to Fowler, who began responding in Spanish but checked himself. His wife didn't speak Spanish. Should he? Confusion made him order a beer in English. The pesos were disappearing.

The woman hung up, glowing from her talk with Mom. Her eyes fell on Fowler. Oh, no. Chit-chat.

"Are you the guy from Amsterdam?" she asked. So he looked that bad. "Hans was looking for you."

"American," said Fowler. The beer arrived, and now the Mexican was taking the woman's order, blocking the coffee table in front of her and the black, delicious rotary-dial telephone sitting on it.

The waiter moved away, and the woman asked Fowler what publication he was working for. He named an obscure California apparel trade magazine, hoping she wasn't familiar with it.

She'd seen it. "Stringer or staffer?"

"I do some free-lance for them," said Fowler, slightly off balance. His wife "did" free-lance.

"Based here or up there?"

"Up there." No use getting into addresses.

Wrong answer. A buzzer went off, he could tell that by the lift of the woman's eyebrows. "They sent you down here *now* to do some free-lance?"

Thank God for the beer. Fowler lifted the bottle to his lips and tried to figure the way out. This woman wasn't going to be as easy to ignore as the one downstairs. She was older, for one thing, about his age. She had an intelligent look in her eyes, she sat leaning forward with her palms on her knees, and she had ordered her vodka and tonic in competent, if flawed, Spanish. This type was trouble.

But by the time he lowered the beer, he could see he was off the hook. She wasn't sizing him up, she was mulling something over.

"Big story, what's going on in the garment district," she said. "*Woman's Wear* contacted me, asked me to do a couple of stories. Fairly good money, but I'm swamped as it is. Oh, sorry. I haven't even introduced myself." She gave her name—same last name as one of the members of the U.S. Cabinet—and met Tom Dixon.

"Mostly," she said, "I string for *Newsweek*." Maybe she was actually related to a government official—Fowler's wife always claimed you had to have connections to get into the big-league magazines. "Gotta get back to work. They want six files this week. For once, they're actually using most of the stuff. This your first disaster?"

Fowler nodded. His wife would have nodded. "Does this phone call anywhere in the States?"

"Yeah, but it costs a fortune. It's cheaper to use the teletype machines downstairs."

"I have to do something by phone."

"Be my guest." She rose, and pulses tingled in Fowler's fingertips. He looked around furtively to see if anyone else was approaching, an animal protecting his kill. "Just signal to the bartender when you make your connection. *Newsweek* is going to freak when they see my tab, though it's a little cheaper than the usual rates. They did a special hookup through Monterrey."

Fowler's untrimmed fingernails scraped against plastic as he dialed the long string of numbers. The dear, welcome drawl of the operator came through clear as a bell, clear as

Southwestern Bell Telephone. He was home safe, talking to directory assistance in Dallas.

He had no paper or pencil to note down the number of Citizens National Bank, so he chanted the numerals like a mantra as he dialed again. The Mexican bartender approached him as he did so. Fowler waved him away with the customary gesture he used in Mexico to dismiss members of the servant class. There was nothing unusual about the gesture; perhaps it was slightly more deprecatory than the gesture Fowler might have used north of the border, but that was part of his bilingualism. Still, he saw the bartender's face harden in anger.

After several light years, he was connected to the bank's customer-service department. Eons later, Plano Associates' account number was unearthed. The pace picked up with the checking of the address and the tax identification number. It was all very impersonal and mechanical, just the way Fowler wanted it. A routine call that would leave no record.

"There's a balance of forty-three dollars and fifty-seven cents in this account," droned the customer-service voice. "Is there anything else I can help you with?"

But Fowler had been helped all he wanted, helped enormously. Fifteen thousand dollars had been withdrawn. The money was on its way. He only wished he had made a closer guess at the balance. An extra forty bucks would have been welcome.

"Where you made calls to?" The bartender was hulking over him. Tall for a Mexican, this one, and Fowler would have preferred "Where you made calls to, *señor*?"

"Dallas, Texas." Fowler remembered now that he'd neglected to signal the starting times. He waited for revenge in the form of an overcharge, but the amount seemed reasonable enough for a daytime Monterrey-to-Dallas connection. As anticipated, the tab neatly wiped out the remainder of Rigg's loan.

But worth every peso. Fowler drained the beer bottle. He was ready to go out and face the post office.

Halfway down the stairs, he heard a voice behind him.

"Next time, please use the operator. Do the favor of ask the operator that she calls us with charges." The bartender looked larger than ever from this perspective.

Fowler cursed him out in Spanish so rapid and colloquial that he doubted it could be understood by any of the foreign reporters milling around on the ground floor. He no longer needed the Mexican Press Club and its telephone. He was a free man. Greenbacks were coming.

As it happened, they had arrived already. That afternoon, Fowler traced the words ASOCIEDED PLENO on the *lista de correos*, alphabetized between "Mary ANN O-Connur" and "Rosario BASQUEZ de Rivera." He'd run up a phone bill for nothing. Not that those few thousand pesos mattered now.

The clerk made a sadistic show of sorting through his tiny pile for the envelope.

"Identification?" he asked, after a five-minute perusal of the address.

"It's addressed to my business. You shouldn't need personal ID for that."

"I need something." The clerk smoothed the envelope in front of him, leaving the Citizens National logo tantalizingly visible. If it had been within snatching distance, Fowler might have made a move, but the clerk was careful to keep it away from the hole in the window.

"I lost my tourist card in the earthquake. I lost everything. I was buried alive." Fowler saw in the dull eyes before him that this was the wrong approach. No use appealing to the milder side of someone who had none. Fowler had seen the clerk's face and body a thousand times, on the Metro and on the streets. Square and neckless with unanimated features: a chess rook of a man.

"Oh, you are a tourist?" So, the jerk had taken him for a local. Now he seemed more interested. "You are expecting dollars?" He held the envelope up and rattled it.

"It's a check," said Fowler, seeing what was coming next and automatically lowering his voice. "I'll give you a cut as soon as I cash it. I've got nothing on me now."

The man named an exorbitant amount. Impatient, Fowler carried out the pretense of bargaining. What did the amount matter when he'd never be back here? He settled on 15,000 pesos, more than thirty dollars. The clerk looked surprised.

"I'll bring it tomorrow."

"You bring it, or you don't get any more letters."

Fine.

He carried the letter in shaking fingers to a dim corner where the *lista* troll couldn't see him.

Soon after, however, he had moved to a lamp, to check what he couldn't quite believe. A check for $500 was in the envelope. Just that one check. He'd already turned the envelope inside out.

The letter said "the others" would follow, each in a separate envelope. Per his instructions.

His instructions. He remembered standing here in this same post office, writing and rewriting the letter. He'd asked not to have the whole amount in one lump sum because of the difficulty of cashing large checks. No, the phrase "one lump sum" had eluded him.

He'd said not to send it *all at once.* That's what he had written, pidgin English. He was losing his mind.

It wasn't that bad, he told himself when the grunts in his breathing had stopped. He had a check for $500, more than he'd seen in a long while. Tom Dixon would stay in a hotel tonight and take a shower. He would rub cream on his sun-scorched face and powder the itching places between his toes.

And the other checks were sure to follow soon. "I'm not sure what you meant, so I'm spacing them out every three days or so," wrote the banker, who also hoped Fowler had "gotten through the earthquake okay." Beautiful. The premortem date on the letter had been noticed.

The troll of the *lista de correos* would get his 15,000 pesos after all, and, inevitably, more after that. As for the gentlemen who operated the scabrous money-changing house where Fowler was now headed, more checks to be cashed without identification would probably heighten their usurious demands.

But it didn't really matter. The plan would go forward, just a little more slowly now. Right-handed, he'd endorse the check with a fine flourish of his left so that if anyone should discover the account at some faraway future date, they'd see that the late Brian Fowler's signature had been forged. Meanwhile, the money changers would have no trouble with collection because no one was going to stop payment.

Once the entire $15,000 was in his hands, Fowler would leave this stinking, ruined city and start a new life elsewhere. With $15,000 he could buy a house somewhere else in Mexico, a business, maybe take a new wife. Monterrey, perhaps—no, that was out. He could bump into Rigg there. But the country was large. Or he could buy himself a counterfeit passport and slip into Argentina or Chile, where his European looks would draw less attention.

He would be his own boss, not a whipping boy for some corporation. What that woman reporter said on the phone was absolutely right. The earthquake could do a lot for your career.

$\triangledown$

# 12

Bᴇʀᴍᴜᴅᴇᴢ ʟᴀɴᴅᴇᴅ ᴀᴛ Benito Juárez Airport with plenty of daylight to spare, grabbed a good street map at one of the gleaming airport kiosks, rented a Chevrolet, and drove out into a city that somebody had stubbed out.

The damage wasn't too bad as he swung south on Aeropuerto, but a little way west on Eje 2 and he was in the thick of it.

Still, the Hotel Toronto came as a surprise. This was Fowler's last known address, the place Bermudez was going to canvass, asking the hotel workers if they remembered the guy and if they had any idea where he was headed next.

It just wasn't there anymore.

Some people apparently thought it was. Whole families were buzzing like bees with nonstop prayer around a big steaming heap of pulverized concrete. You could hear them between the killer blows of a wrecking ball that had chewed up most of the mess and was now making moves toward the one wing still standing. Standing, but not very tall. It was all squished together like a New York deli seven-layer cake.

Bermudez couldn't quite take it in. This place hadn't been on the list of blitzed hotels he'd been given by the Mexican Consulate in New York. They'd babbled on about some Hotel del Prado and how they had to rescue a Diego Rivera mural before the explosives moved in.

The Toronto must have slipped their minds. Maybe for lack of murals.

"You lose somebody in there?"

Bermudez turned to see who'd tapped him. It was a man with tear streaks down his face. The dust on his knees indicated his affiliation with one of the kneeling families.

"I was looking for a man," said Bermudez.

"Someone who was in the hotel on Black Thursday?"

"Maybe. Or maybe he stayed somewhere else."

But Fowler had been there all right. Trans Rio's annotated schedule showed him sticking close to schedule.

"If only you'd come a few days ago," said the man. "The bodies that weren't identified were taken to the *fosa común.*"

The common grave. No niceties with morgues here.

"This bunch doesn't care about the bodies. Look how careless they are with their equipment." The man gestured toward the soldiers ringing the site. "We'll be lucky to salvage a few bones. It was different when the rescuers were here."

"Rescuers? Army rescuers?"

The man looked at him curiously. The question, Bermudez realized, marked him as a foreigner. The man explained that volunteer rescuers had been pulling corpses out so that the families could bury them properly.

"Maybe there aren't any more."

"There are," the man said softly. "My son was there."

Jet lag, airplane food, Mexico City driving, and general confusion left Bermudez with nothing to say.

The man mistook the look on his face for bereavement. "May your friend rest in peace," he said before shuffling away.

Bermudez stared at the pile of masonry where Fowler had probably died, and he felt rage and frustration because he might as well fly back to New York tonight and tell Connie he'd failed. He hated himself for caring about it at all with everything else that was going on around him. And he loathed this city and the praying families for blowing tragedy up to such huge dimensions that you felt like staying in a tiny corner of the picture where you couldn't see the rest of it.

The only way to get through it was to put blinders on. The

bereaved man had mentioned rescuers. Bermudez had to find out whether they'd taken any people out alive before they started digging for the stiffs.

The vendors selling flavored water on the sidewalk had the air of being a neighborhood fixture. Doing good business, too, even though the newspaper Bermudez had picked up at the airport warned people not to buy from those guys.

The guy smiled with anticipation as he approached.

*"Horchata? Limón?* It's all made from rainwater I collected myself."

Right.

Bermudez gave him a small coin and accepted a glass. He asked the vendor about the rescuers while he surreptitiously watered the curb with almond-flavored drink.

The vendor said this was his regular commercial venue, but he'd still been in bed when the earthquake hit.

"My family was all right, thank God, but there were relatives to check on, friends. I didn't come out here until Saturday. I thought no one would want *agua fresca,* but I was wrong. The *sismo* brought new customers."

Bermudez followed his index finger over to the familial clusters.

"You wouldn't happen to remember which of those people were here on Saturday," prompted Bermudez as he laid another coin on the pushcart.

"Sure. Those three ladies over there. They're the only ones." Bermudez followed his glance to a group that looked more patient than pious, sitting quietly on cardboard boxes while everybody else bowed heads together. Their reverence must have been all tapped out by now. "The grandma likes orangeade. The granddaughter, too. The daughter buys Coca-Cola from the *tienda* on the corner. Such extravagance in these times!"

Identification by soft-drink habits. All right, whatever worked.

"The others from Saturday have gone. They took their dead already, hotel employees mostly. The guests were from out of town. It took time for their families to notice they were missing."

Bermudez advanced toward the three women, but the vendor drew him up short.

"Excuse me, sir? The glass."

Bermudez backed up and returned the streaked tumbler to the man's pushcart so that it could be dusted off and used for the next customer. He remembered this custom from his early childhood in Puerto Rico. Third World recycling.

The female trio represented three generations. Bermudez played it down the middle, addressing the middle-aged one. He figured she was the smartest, sticking to Coke.

The best thing would have been if they'd arrived before Saturday and seen what was going on. The woman said they hadn't. However, someone had told her that survivors had walked away from the wreckage on Thursday.

"A man with his arm in a sling," she said. "He was here with the rescue brigade. He couldn't work because of his arm, but he was helping the others with communications. The arm had been broken in a rescue, he told me."

She had a first name for him, Abel, and a strange description.

"Short and skinny. He must have been a *topo*."

A mole?

She saw his confusion. "The little people who dig tunnels and bring people out. 'Dig, dig!' he kept telling the others. He had more hope than they did, because he knew some people had survived here."

The woman cast down her eyes. "Maybe if he had stayed. But his arm swelled up outside the . . . the thing doctors put on for healing."

"The cast," prompted William.

The woman nodded. "He stayed as long as he could, but then the cast started cutting into the skin. He said he had to go back to the clinic and get it loosened. It's probably best not to wear those things. Isn't that true?"

That's the attitude you developed when you couldn't

afford things. Mexicans didn't have Medicaid. If this woman broke her arm, she'd probably just put it in a sling and hope for the best. The beggars with shriveled limbs who'd approached Bermudez outside the airport proved how well the home remedy worked.

She had no idea where the injured man lived or worked, and she hadn't seen his companions since the army ordered them off the site.

Okay. Off to find a man with a broken arm in a city that must be full of them.

Here came the tedious scut work that Bermudez knew he could have looked forward to had he been interested in making detective. The map in his pocket had a list of hospitals and medical centers. "Clinic" was the word the woman had used, and there could be thousands of private ones. You had to start somewhere, so Bermudez nosed the rental car to the big medical center–general hospital complex off Cuauhtémoc Avenue.

The detours he was forced to take around busted streets kept him so busy that he was almost there before he remembered all the news reports about the biggest cruel joke of the earthquake: The principal hospital had come tumbling down at the time it was most needed. Already he could see the devastation, big enough to make the Hotel Toronto seem like an anthill.

He did a U-turn to get out of there and go to Plan B, but the detours took him in a circle, and he was smack-dab in front of another part of the structure when he noticed all the commotion going on at one end of it. Some army trucks were pulled up in front of the site, and there were a lot of olive-drab loiterers around. The real action, though, was strictly civilian. Maybe a half-dozen men were scrambling over slanted slabs and exposed rods, playing a dead serious game of king of the mountain.

After he'd parked and come closer, Bermudez saw what the problem was. This part of the building had come down at a sharp angle. The men were trying to shimmy up to what used to be the tenth or eleventh floor—it wasn't easy to count when all you had to go by were some remnants of ceiling and floor with not too much room between them.

The slabs had fallen in such a way that it must have been hard for a foot to get a purchase on them. So the fellows on top kept sliding back.

"What's going on?" Bermudez called to them. "You need help?"

"There's a woman in there," somebody shouted down. "We're trying to reach her."

"I'm coming up," said Bermudez.

After what he'd heard at the Toronto, he wouldn't have been surprised if one of the soldiers had rushed him with a bayonet. Bermudez was feeling naked without his off-duty six-inch-barrel .38 Ruger. He'd had to ditch it in Texas when he found out that you couldn't bring arms into Mexico except for shotguns during hunting season.

But the soldiers seemed content to wait around and gawk, and a gun wouldn't have helped much with this job. Climbing to the plateau where the rescuers were stalled took some real concentration. Much of the concrete had cracked and crazed, and many of the reinforcing rods had popped out beyond the masonry, producing a barbed-wire effect. There was only one narrow route up, and Bermudez discovered that he had to check each foothold carefully before shifting his weight onto it. Edges of concrete kept loosening and crumbling away. This must have been a real spit-and-Scotch-tape building.

Five sweaty men wearing backpacks were standing on part of a slab that had managed to stay parallel with the ground. One end of it was cantilevered over thin air, and that's where they were. Now that Bermudez was closer he could see that all of them were little guys. As for himself, he preferred to keep clinging to the side of the pile, where a little groping around had found him some nice rods to grasp with his hands. There was no telling when that ledge was going to reach maximum capacity.

Looking above, he could see why they couldn't make it any farther. For about six feet over his head the concrete was all powder and pebbles. There was no way a foot could stay firm on that. Bermudez noticed a thin piece of insulated wire traveling the length of the inaccessible expanse. Speaker wire, it looked like. It disappeared into a gap above the debris.

"One of us made it up and tunneled in, but as he climbed, the concrete disintegrated," a member of the rescue team explained. "Rodrigo's got a microphone with him. He's in contact with a woman who's trapped in there, but he needs us to help him."

"No other way to get there? From the other side maybe?" Bermudez felt his fingers and toes beginning to cramp.

The man shook his head. "It's worse there. The rods are sticking straight out. It's like an iron maiden."

"Looks to me like if you stand on my shoulders you can make it," said Bermudez.

The men on the ledge smiled. Mexican courage and solidarity had taken them this far; they needed the Puerto Rican's height to finish up. Hispanic children grew taller in the United States. These guys were going to get a boost, thanks to food stamps, a diet heavy with milk, and free New York public-school lunches.

Static crackled out of a small speaker that one of the men on the ledge held cradled under his arm. Bermudez saw now that he had guessed right about the wire.

"Tell Rodrigo you're coming up," said the American.

"We can't talk to him, we can only hear him." The man in charge of the speaker fiddled with a connection. "He hasn't said anything for a while. I think maybe the mike filled with dirt, or the system broke down."

As if insulted by this accusation, the speaker—probably grabbed hurriedly from somebody's cheap stereo system— screeched out a message.

"What'd he say?" Bermudez asked.

"He needs a saw." Everyone looked very glum.

"I'll get you up there," Bermudez promised. "Some of you,

anyway. Enough of you to saw through some concrete if
you've got the right tools. I would go in with you, but I doubt
I'd fit through the passageway. You're all *topos*, I take it."

"The kind of saw he needs is for bones, not concrete," the
man said quietly. "The woman is trapped by her leg. And,
yes, we have the tools." He tapped his backpack. "We're
*topos*, but we're also medical residents and students. The
woman is our *compañera*, a student of medicine. She was
at the hospital doing rounds when the quake hit. It's been
a long time. She's very weak, very dehydrated."

Bermudez was worried about moving onto the ledge.
There was no handy placard about maximum weight capacity like the ones on elevators, and no way to test the limits.
A failed experiment might have resulted in a dead cop. And
all the available medical personnel would be lying in a heap
with him.

The group selected two members to complete the rescue,
and it was agreed that the man with the speaker—Bermudez
had started to think of him as Sparks—would stay on deck
to run communications in case they needed something.
The remaining two guys were to return to terra firma. Before
they did, there was the grim business of pooling the medical
equipment in the backpacks and selecting the proper hypo-
dermics and sedatives; Bermudez tried not to look at the
saw. Then the two superfluous men inched over to the end
of the ledge.

"No rope, huh?"

"We had some, but we gave it to Rodrigo for bringing her
down," somebody answered. "Maybe that was a bad idea,
but it's too late to fix it. He has to stay by her side now."

With just one path of descent viable, the only way to
change places was for Bermudez to let them use his body as
a chute to the footholds below.

The trick was to have them ride piggyback for only a few
seconds, allowing them to grip him by the waist and slide
down his legs until they could find places for their feet. The
hands, they decided, wouldn't be too much of a problem

because there was so much rod jutting out. Bermudez's feet seemed secure, and the metal he'd grabbed was holding fast, even if his fingers had grown pretty stiff, so he figured he could hang on if they did it right.

The army must have had some ropes, and probably some better communication equipment, but he imagined the Mexican rescuers had their reasons for not even trying to ask.

The first descender was a bit stocky, but he handled himself gracefully, and it all went smoothly.

He expected no problems with the bantamweight remaining, but the guy panicked as he hung from Bermudez's belt, yelling that he was afraid of falling. Bermudez felt gravel forming beneath his shoes as the man pulled heavily on his waist. Soon his feet had popped away from the wall, and he had to depend on hands that had forgotten how to make a fist tighter.

The monkey on his back slid off, miraculously finding contact points now that he had to. Bermudez wasn't so lucky. Dangling by his arms, he treadmilled the wall. Chips flew, but his feet found no place to stay.

It was time to go for the Olympic gold. His high school hadn't had enough cash for decent baseball bats, never mind rings for gymnastics. Nonetheless, he'd have to score at least an 8.8 now, on his first try.

"Clear a spot for me," he told the three on the ledge. "I'm heaving myself over."

It was risky doing this with numb hands, but he was going to have to swing his legs far to the left and bring them up and over to the plateau on the right.

Maybe a Romanian judge would have deducted a few points for bad interpretation, but he landed close enough for the ledgemen to haul him to safety. From there on, the event changed to acrobatics. The two rescuers took turns getting on his shoulders and scrambling into the tunnel at the top of the slippery slope. This was not a problem. Probably their backpacks weighed more than they did.

"It all went like clockwork except for that panic attack

your friend had on the second trip down," Bermudez commented to Sparks.

"Yeah. Well, that guy's a proctologist."

They pretended to clown around for a while, but both of them had their minds on the scraping sounds coming through the speaker.

"They're probably helping Rodrigo get her into position," sparks said.

Nervous, Bermudez cracked his knuckles and was sorry he had. He wondered what kind of noises would come out of that speaker next.

Soon everything ceased except human voices. Bermudez couldn't make all of it out, but he gathered that the men were asking the trapped woman if she really wanted to go through with this.

"A formality," said Sparks with a catch in his throat. "There's no other way."

Then a clear female voice cut through the static.

"Doctors," it said, "you know your duty."

▽

# 13

THE INTERNS WHO'D climbed down managed to scare up a Red Cross van, so there were extra ropes and a stretcher waiting for the woman when she was finally extricated. One of the mole-docs accompanied her as the van squealed off, bound for a hospital in another part of the city. It was getting dark as Bermudez and the others finally clambered down.

They shook the New York cop's hand, but he didn't want thanks. He wanted to know where they thought a man might have had a cast put on his arm one or two days after the earthquake.

"How about that hospital your friend was taken to?" Bermudez suggested.

Sparks shook his head. "With this medical center gone"—he motioned to the fallen behemoth behind him—"all the other hospitals are completely overloaded. They take only the most serious cases."

"A private doctor then?"

"Possibly. But nobody's been all that private since the earthquake."

"Come again?"

"We're all in the streets, *cuate*. Doctors, nurses, architects, engineers. What you want to look for is a street clinic. They're all over the place. Start at the big one in the churchyard in Tepito. Lots of bones set over there. Somebody dug up an X-ray machine, and, boom, they were in business. The government's not doing anything. We're doing it all ourselves."

Bermudez got the address and poked his way through the detours to the address Sparks had given him.

In Tepito everyone really was in the streets, and so were their furniture, their plants, and their dishes. Bermudez finally found parking about two dozen blocks from the self-help clinic, locked up the car, and ran right into a clothesline that somebody had erected on the curb. Family after family seemed to have gone camping permanently under tents jury-rigged out of metal tubing and sheets of plastic. Guys in their undershirts had settled into easy chairs on the esplanade, guzzling beer and enjoying a show on television, courtesy of the electricity they'd cadged from a hookup to the utility poles. Women changed diapers and puttered around under the traffic lights. Soup was on, spluttering in pots, alfresco style.

The odd thing was that the buildings around here looked intact.

Bermudez couldn't figure any of this out, but the people who'd set up a mini–merchandise row alongside the campers seemed familiar enough. This might have been Anyblock, Manhattan, on a Saturday night, with people selling pirated cassette tapes, hubcaps, and assorted bric-a-brac off blankets.

"A toy for your children, *señor?*" somebody urged.

Bermudez took a look. The vendor was pulling strings at the base of a fake chicken foot, making the claws flex and extend. Pretty macabre, but not so different from the battery-operated plastic hands that always drew an audience around the illegal peddlers on Times Square.

Bermudez asked the price. Less than a dollar, and a helluva lot less than they were getting for those hands in Manhattan. He bought a couple for his nephews and tried them out. They clawed up nicely enough and sure looked realistic, though the pieces of aluminum foil around the base of each foot spoiled the effect a bit. He tossed them into a shirt pocket.

The next retail display that caught his eye was a rack of ballpoint pens sheathed in woven covers that spelled out various first names. Bermudez scanned them. Luz, Eugenia,

Marta, Xiomara, Patricia, Javier, Daniel, Rafael, Beto, Abel. Abel. It was that common. He wondered why he was wasting his time.

The self-help clinic, located in the courtyard of a converted church, had the official name of Tepito Cultural Center. Now its cultural offerings consisted of two enormous hand-lettered signs hung on the gate around it. One read, DON'T URINATE OR DEFECATE IN THE STREET. Said the other, IF YOU HAVE DIARRHEA, GO TO THE RED CROSS.

Bermudez shoved through the mass of humanity giving and receiving services and asked for the head honcho. The head *medical* honcho, he had to specify, because the place apparently ministered to housing, employment, and sundry other needs as well. After a fifteen-minute wait next to a communal bean pile from which women were gathering raw materials for the night's supper, he was shown to a damp-haired young woman named Dr. Gavela.

"A man named Abel who broke his arm in a rescue?" she repeated.

"Right." Bermudez felt foolish. Embarrassed enough, in fact, to feel like hiding behind the bean pile.

"That'd be Abel Castellanos. An accountant. He lives near here." She pointed to the doorway. "Go left three blocks and turn right. He's in the big apartment building, the only one on the block. Or," she added helpfully, "on the street outside it."

She saw the shock on his face. "We know all the rescuers around here," she said, "and it's not that common a first name."

Because relief had turned him into a babbling idiot, Bermudez told her about the ballpoint pens.

"No kidding. And they never have my name, Dimpna. What's yours?"

"William."

"Now that's a strange one."

He exited through the gate, passing one final sign posted so that people would be sure to see it as they left. It said, HELP

THE NEIGHBOR WHO IS MORE FUCKED UP THAN YOU ARE.
Two turns and three inquiries took him to Abel Castellanos, a small man lounging on a couch along with several small children. It was a typical domestic scene except that the couch and the rug in front of it were surrounded by asphalt.

He swatted the little kids off the couch, brushed a young adolescent boy off an easy chair, and urged Bermudez to take a seat. Nearby, a woman was nursing an infant. Abel's wife, presumably, unless the stouter female busy with some needlework was his wife. The tent arrangements flowed together, making it hard to see where one family ended and another began.

Yes, Abel said, he was the rescuer who'd been at the Hotel Toronto on Saturday the 21st, two days after the quake, and he knew for certain that some people had survived there.

"Another rescuer told me, a fellow who was at my side all day on the twentieth. The Toronto, I'm sure of it. He said he pulled one live person out after the quake, but he had to leave after that and check on his relatives. You remember what the first day was like."

Bermudez shook his head. "I just came from the States."

Abel raised an eyebrow. "Looking for a relative, eh? We're trying to get the news back to the States about the people who are safe, but the damn telephone lines are still down."

Bermudez produced a noncommittal grunt. "Where's this fellow rescuer of yours? I'd like to talk to him."

Abel studied his shoelaces. "We were working at Calzada de Tlalpan and Calle Cuatro on Friday at seven-thirty P.M."

"And?"

"I forgot. You're from the north. That was when the second earthquake hit, *hombre.* Our building came down. I got this"—he lifted his arm in its sling—"and the man you're asking about got buried."

It was absurd to sit in this scene of mass displacement listening to a story about death and feel unlucky. Still and all, Bermudez managed.

"You wouldn't happen to know if the person he rescued at the Toronto was male or female."

Abel threw his head back and screwed up his eyes. The guy was really trying to be helpful.

After a long pause, "No."

"And you wouldn't know the rescuer's name or where he lived so I could ask his friends or family if he talked about it?"

"Sorry. Who did you lose?"

"Actually I'm doing an investigation for a friend. I'm a cop."

I was like those Transformer toys that the kids played with in the States: With a few minor movements—a stiffening of the body, a pursing of the lips—Abel converted from helpful, sympathetic neighbor into cold, wary android.

Bermudez, of course, had turned into a pig. This was a condition in which he always found it hard to continue talking, despite many years of practicing porcine conversation with black and Latino youth and people of Ernesto's political stripe. One of the perks of working for the Movie and TV Unit was that no one bothered to oink at him anymore; now, he was just a joke.

It wasn't that he didn't understand the thinking. Before joining the force, he'd been stopped more than once for DWL, as the joke in his neighborhood went: Driving While Latino. He'd be the first to admit that there were racist cops and brutal cops—and, God knew, after the incident with Griswold—crooked cops. But there were also drug dealers and skels and murderers and rapists, and it was the cops who put their bodies out there to protect the taxpayers.

He knew there was no use talking about it with a cop hater, so he mumbled the usual things and got up to leave.

"Why are your clothes torn?" Abel was looking at him through narrowed eyes.

Were they? Bermudez looked down and saw that the nice outfit he'd picked up at a Dallas shopping mall, specially to avoid problems with immigration people at the airport, was now suitable only for landfill. His hands looked like they needed to be washed in industrial solvent.

None of this guy's business, but he tossed off a brief description of what had happened at the medical center.

Abel was on his feet, extending his good hand for a shake. "You participated in that rescue? We heard about it on the radio. It must be true what they say, that the North American police aren't like what we have here. Lupe!"

The woman working with needle and thread turned around.

"I'm taking our American visitor for a drink."

Hell, why not. The pseudosirloin and dessert square consumed by Bermudez on the plane had been digested many hours ago, and he realized he was weak from hunger.

Abel assured him that the area restaurants were operating normally. On the way over Bermudez had a chance to ask what gave with the families on the street.

"That's my building over there." Abel pointed out a low-rise across from where they'd been sitting. Only about six floors high, but it hulked over the rest of the neighborhood. "If you went inside, you'd see cracks all over the place, walls out of joint. We felt the quake all right, even if no one got hurt. We're not sure it's safe. Another temblor could topple it. In the daytime, it's okay, you can go inside if you're ready to run out at any moment. But at night, when we're sleeping . . ." He shrugged his shoulders.

"These one-story structures must be safe, though," Bermudez remarked, and it seemed to him that the low-slung buildings made up 90 percent of the area.

"Not at all safe," said Abel. "They were put up cheaply years ago. At first the rents went up like crazy all the time. Then the tenants marched and protested, and the rents were frozen. The landlords retaliated by refusing to fix anything. It's lousy housing, families of eleven or twelve people shoved into a little room with a sleeping loft, communal toilets and sinks in the courtyard. Some of them were ready to come down even before the earthquake. We're waiting to get them checked."

Most had been chained up. To protect the possessions from thieves, Abel explained. He and Bermudez passed one with an official notice on the door reading: UNINHABITABLE.

"Well, these people have their answer," said Bermudez.

"Not at all. The landlords came around with their own so-called experts and condemned everything. This is prime real estate location, the middle of the city. They've been wanting to kick us all out for years and raise the rents. We're going to hire our own experts."

They had to maneuver around a long table from which women were dispensing food to a long line of supplicants.

Abel stopped short, as curious as William. "Every day, there's something new here," he said. "I know only about the Tepito Cultural Center, where the young kids have set up a shelter. We'll pass that, too. This is good. Another collection center."

"This must be from the money the U.S. sent—"

"Donations, all collected here. From the neighborhood. The official shelters are terrible. You get robbed, beaten, if you sleep there. The army steals the blankets and food and sells them."

The restaurant reminded Bermudez of the places Puerto Ricans used to run in New York when he was a kid. Just a bunch of tables in front of a stove with some cats sniffing around them. And Abel's nonstop antiestablishment rap reminded him of Ernesto.

He was negative about everything. He asked where Bermudez was staying and waited for him to find the hotel name on a scrawled note in his pocket. Bermudez had yet to see the place; his bags were still in the car trunk.

"The Marquesa," Abel repeated knowingly. "Near the U.S. Embassy. Nice neighborhood. But keep one eye open all night in that hotel. The aftershocks are still coming."

"The Secretariat of Tourism said it was safe. I got the referral at their airport kiosk."

"Good old SecTur. The owner of the Marquesa is very friendly with SecTur. They'll tell you the experts have been through to inspect. They probably have. With their palms open."

On one important point, though, Abel was positive. He thought there was a good chance that Fowler was alive.

"When I was out at the Toronto on Saturday, I saw that the low floors on the west side were pretty bad, but maybe survivable."

The west wing. That was where the army wreckers were working.

"*Hijos*," spat Abel, when he told him. "They're killing people." One of the restaurant's cats had been trying to climb on their table but skittered off at this display of rage.

"There must be a list somewhere of the casualties," Bermudez prompted. "Maybe I'll try the police tomorrow. Bureau of Missing Persons. It couldn't hurt to try."

Abel snickered. "About a thousand people are missing, and the last people to care about them would be the police. Unless you have some cash to offer them to investigate."

Bermudez wiped his mouth with a single-ply paper napkin. Abel's information about the west wing was encouraging, but not much else was, and he wanted to go. He didn't have to hear any more. He'd spent enough time with Ernesto to know all about this political posturing.

While they waited for the check, the cat finally managed to achieve the tabletop and sniffed earnestly at Bermudez's shirt pocket.

"A calico," Abel observed. "Calicos are always female. That's why she's so nosy."

Bermudez knew several U.S. Latinas who would've wanted to kick him in the groin for that.

"What do you want?" Bermudez asked the cat. He reached into his shirt and pulled out the toys he'd gotten for his nephews. "Plastic chicken feet?"

Abel's laugh gave him the answer. Bermudez unwrapped the aluminum foil he'd been wondering about and found unmistakably real bones. He tugged on the strings again. The claws contracted because they were attached to the bird's tendons.

Disgusted, he let the "toys" fall to the ground. The cat

plunged after them. No wonder they'd been so cheap.

It wasn't like the Upper West Side here, after all.

As he counted out money for the waitress, three loud blasts rang out. Reflexively, Bermudez reached for his non-existent gun, then noticed bands of yellow slicing through the night sky. Everybody else was either scrambling to their feet or on them.

"Rockets," Abel explained, overturning his chair. "That's our code. A family's getting evicted. Damned bloodsucker landlords. We're going to go over and stop it."

More fireworks streaked overhead.

"They're from over there," someone yelled. "Near the Palacio Negro."

Bermudez watched Abel rush off. Hundreds of people, it seemed, were running in the same direction.

Something was happening here that was different from Ernesto's hip, intellectual, foundation-funded posturing. Or maybe it was the same, but the stakes were so much higher and so many more people were playing.

He thought about all of it later as he lay in bed at the Hotel Marquesa, where each noise in the hallway sent plaster drizzling down from the damaged ceiling.

He wasn't going to close the case. Abel thought there was a good chance he was looking for a live man.

He would check to see if the casualties were recorded anyplace, but he would also check the hotels. For all he knew, Fowler was here at the Marquesa, paying, like he was, for a room with a blown-out window, ripped wallpaper, and walls meeting at odd angles.

Paying how? Trans Rio said they'd given Fowler a modest advance on his expense account to stay at the modest hotels on their list of potential acquisitions. It was surprising he'd never phoned for money toward the end, they said. Then again, he'd seemed "somewhat riled" with them.

Maybe there had been some action in his personal bank account or on his credit cards. Bermudez would wire Dallas tomorrow and check on that. Or someone here could be supplying him with money. No, the wife said he had no friends here.

But he must have some friends in the States. They might have been sending him money. Through Western Union, or whatever they had down here. Maybe directly through a bank. Maybe via the U.S. Embassy.

There would have to be a money trail. If Fowler had been pulled out of that mess at the Toronto, he must have needed funds to keep himself afloat. Veins were feeding Fowler. Veins that could be traced.

After all, thought Bermudez, tossing with restlessness so that the headboard knocked against the wall and sent plaster flakes down on his head, being rescued wasn't the end. Once saved, people needed food and shelter. And it wasn't as if a big executive like Fowler was going to get those things at a place like the Tepito Cultural Center.

Not long after Bermudez drifted off to sleep, he was wakened by a commotion on the street below. He stumbled to the window and pulled away the plywood. A Federal District police patrol car was parked in front of one of the fancy stores across the street. The light on its roof illuminated a cop talking to a man who carried a large bundle. A burglar alarm rang faintly from somewhere. Bermudez assumed there was a store with broken glass nearby. So, the cops were on the job, after all. The situation seemed to be in hand. Bermudez would contact the PD tomorrow, sort out the people in charge.

The argument on the street escalated for a while, drawing onlookers. Then the cop started digging around in the other man's bundle. After he found something he liked, he got into the patrol car and drove off. The onlookers dispersed, and the man with the bundle went on his way.

Bermudez replaced the plywood on the window. He owed Abel an apology.

⬇

# 14

"I'VE GOT A new one for you, Mr. Dixon."

Fowler cracked his knuckles and pushed the remains of his *huevos rancheros* aside. Breakfast hadn't been bad today, better than the pancakes yesterday, and even they weren't too shabby. Except for the erratic water supply, this hotel had turned out better than expected.

It was one of those dank places near the Monument to the Revolution, a spot on the ten-dollar-a-day tourist map and pretty empty these days. The newspapers were full of talk about the "normalization" process, but the tourists hadn't heard. They were taking their ten dollars elsewhere.

Which gave the green-eyed waiter more time to try out some jokes on Fowler. As good a pastime as Fowler could imagine, and he did need pastimes. Today made three days since the first check had come. It was time to go back to the post office. Fowler had forced himself to stay away till now. No use facing the troll until he had to. The troll would want another *mordida*, a bite, and Fowler's first $500 was already well-bitten by the money changers and the reservations clerk here, who complained daily and bitterly about his lack of a tourist card.

Mario the waiter, on the other hand, never had a glimmer of complaint in his green eyes. Fowler kicked a chair out for him. Mario dumped his laminated menus on the table and settled in. He lit a cigarette, flashing a silver cigarette lighter the size of a paperweight. A new gift from his woman friend, he said. Fowler made all the right admiration noises, and the lighter went back into the pocket of the synthetic, white waiter's jacket. On someone else, that might have seemed comical. Not on Mario. Synthetic clothes hung on Mario like they'd been synthesized just for him.

A few days in the company of washbasin and bed had returned Fowler to his normal robust state. Fifteen years ago, he would have been classed close to Mario in the appearance tournaments. Even now, he believed many women would prefer him to the younger man, and not only because he was an American executive while Mario was an ignorant nineteen-year-old from some groaning city slum. Where Mario lost points was in the self-conscious way he wore his good looks, making it painfully obvious it was all he owned.

Still, the looks match would be a close contest, and Fowler liked close contests. His after-breakfast sessions with Mario reminded him of his normal life in Texas. He missed the business breakfasts, the racquetball after work—buddy-buddy stuff with an edge that kept you on your toes. He could imagine Mario doing well in the United States on looks alone.

That is, if the kid could learn English, which was doubtful. He was dumb as a stone.

Mario had some earthquake jokes today, but Fowler had heard them all.

Q.: What did Paloma De La Madrid say to Nancy Reagan when she came down with the $1 million check?
A.: Hi, Nancy. Excuse the mess.

A subspecies of earthquake joke harked back to last year's disaster, when a gas-tank explosion in the San Juanico section of the city had left hundreds of people dead and burned:

Things were really shaking at the blast in the Centro, but the blowout in San Juanico had better sounds.

Last year the Mexicans were playing with matches, now they're playing hide-and-seek.

*"Pssst."* Another waiter was standing in the opening between the swinging doors that led to the kitchen. This was Mario's relative, a skinny, middle-aged man with a perpetually worried look on his face. Often the look stemmed from his concern that the manager would catch Mario goofing off.

Mario motioned for him to get back in the kitchen.

From jokes he progressed to tongue twisters, laughing and thumping his fist on the menus when Fowler got tripped up. Some kind of free-association process connected tongue twisting with tonguing, and Fowler was treated to explicit descriptions of Mario's latest tryst with the married woman who'd given him the cigarette lighter. Her husband, who ordinarily came home for lunch, would not do so today. Today Mario hoped to have her the ultimate way.

Fowler, who didn't share the Mexican passion for the anus, said something paternal about sexually transmitted diseases. But Mario thought of this as a purely North American problem, like drugs and sunburn. For some reason he had fixed on today as the deadline for overcoming the married woman's resistance on this point. He had a battle plan: He would return to the kitchen now to help finish up the dishwashing, slip out the alleyway door at eleven, and return in time to serve lunch with mission accomplished. Several bets were riding on it. Fowler was invited to place his own.

*"Oye,* Mario." The relative had popped out of the swinging doors again.

"Coming." Mario snubbed out his cigarette. He began gathering up the menus, then put them down again.

"I've got to show you something." He thumbed through the laminated placards, found what he wanted, and removed the top half of the pile as if cutting a deck of huge playing cards.

Atop the remaining pile of menus was a stack of papers. Fowler was looking at a badly reproduced copy of a photo that had never been good in the first place.

It was the typical kind of photo taken by a Polaroid identification-card machine. No one came out well, but the machine was cost-effective. Any employee could be trained in an hour to use it. Fowler's secretary had learned within minutes. She had photographed the entire staff, starting with this photo of him.

It looked a lot different with "Wanted" printed over it in English and Spanish.

By the time Fowler had adjusted his features into mild curiosity, it was too late.

"It really is you," said Mario. "I thought it was just some other gringo who looked like you."

"Where did you get these?"

"I was out at registration this morning looking for the Whale." The Whale was the staff's name for the corpulent submanager who patrolled the registration desk. He was the one who'd made the decision to admit Fowler to the hotel despite his lack of a tourist card. He was also the one who'd demanded something extra as the price of admission. "A guy came by and dropped these off. Said to distribute them among the staff."

"What did the guy look like?"

"A *prieto*." That was Mario's deprecatory word for anyone with skin a shade darker than his.

"Not American?"

"Nah. An Indian." His usual description of his compatriots.

Fowler flipped through the stack. Two dozen or so. He peeled the top one off.

"Did the Whale see them?"

"No. I took them. I thought they were a joke. I thought you sent them."

Fowler wanted to think of an explanation. It wouldn't even have to be too plausible; Mario wanted to believe it even before it was uttered. But he could only sit there, reading.

"Hey, look, take them all. I've got to run." The chair scraped back, and Fowler heard the sounds of someone scrambling out of it, hastily and clumsily. These were not sounds his charming pal Mario would make.

The leaflets said that law enforcement authorities in

Texas, United States of America, had a warrant out for the arrest of Brian Fowler (pictured above), an American businessman last seen in Mexico City before September 19.

Persons with information were advised to call a telephone number with an extension. The extension struck Fowler as odd. Even odder were the incorrectly spelled words and grammatical errors in the English translation that followed the Spanish.

The Spanish, too, was peculiar. It would have surprised him less had it contained the type of errors foreigners were prone to make. Instead, it contained a number of words that seemed almost archaic, and the Spanish misspellings were the kind that uneducated natives made, *b* for *v* and so forth.

But it was good enough Spanish for even an ignorant young hotel waiter to understand.

The reward offer was a serious misstep, Fowler thought. There was no need to offer such a large amount to Mexicans. Half would have been more than sufficient.

Fowler went upstairs to his room and packed his two extra shirts and one pair of pants in the plastic bag from the drugstore where he'd bought some rudimentary toiletries. He packed the toiletries, too, first extracting one item and putting it in his pocket.

Matches had been supplied with his room—an extravagant touch for a budget hotel in a country where matches weren't free, Fowler thought. He used them to make a small bonfire in the bathroom sink. The leaflets curled up like snakes. He ran the faucet to rinse them away. They left a forbidding black stain in the sink.

The hotel operator gave him an outside line, and he called the number on the leaflets.

"Hotel Marquesa," said the voice that answered. Maybe Trans Rio was paying for this and not Connie Oland after all. Or maybe Connie Oland was as tightfisted as Trans Rio. The Marquesa was nothing to write home about.

Nobody answered the extension, which Fowler now recognized as a room number. He made another call to the desk downstairs and told them to have his bill ready.

"Leaving us so soon?" The Whale, who'd been looking forward to more "stuffing"—the apt name he preferred for his bribes—looked genuinely disappointed. Disappointment was the only emotion Fowler saw in the triple-chinned face. Mario hadn't shown the leaflets to the desk staff. Yet.

Fowler walked out the front door and checked his watch. Twenty minutes to eleven. People were walking down the busy street outside, and he joined them, turning after a few blocks to backtrack. For fifteen minutes he repeated these motions. He would have liked to quench his dry mouth with a mineral water or soda, but shopkeepers might remember him later. He stayed dry.

As he walked, he decided that he had to jettison the plastic bag. For this purpose, he selected an untrafficked side street with a refuse basket. It pained him to discard the shaving cream and toothpaste he had just bought, but more checks would be coming soon, and he could easily replace them. The bag would only slow him down.

A second later, he was pulling it back out of the basket and searching for his sleeping pills. While the earth still trembled daily, he needed them. And he had an inkling that soon he would need them more than ever. He placed them in his left pocket, next to the wallet he'd shifted when packing his toiletries.

At five minutes to eleven he was back at the hotel, having circled the block so that he wouldn't pass the main entrance again. The garbage cans by the alley door to the kitchen were already bulging, but he feared that someone would come out and fill them further. Flies lit on his arm as he reached into his right pocket.

Mario came out of the door, ten minutes late. It was essential to approach him from behind. He was only medium height but well muscled; Fowler needed the element of surprise. He banged the garbage cans as he straightened from his crouch, but the boy didn't look back. Still, the awkward scrambling cost Fowler time. Mario was almost out of the alley and onto the street by the time Fowler caught his arms and pinned them behind his back.

Fowler's plan had gone awry. Someone might pass by the entrance to the alleyway and see a taller, older man throwing a boy to the ground. But no one passed, and no one came running in answer to a scream, because Mario—perhaps sensing that his self-conscious beauty already made him somewhat feminine—did not cry out. He fought bravely with his legs, but Fowler managed to keep them pinned under his heavier American body, even when he shifted the boy around so that he could see his face. It was essential to let Mario see his attacker.

Because Mario kept quiet, he probably heard Fowler's warnings and his threat to return with worse if the number on the leaflet were called.

The scream finally came, later, when Fowler had already done his work with the razor blade. By that time, Mario's beauty was something of the past, separated from the present by a thin red line. Fowler had meant to draw it delicately down the outer edge of the face, stretching down the forehead over the cheek, and stopping at the jawline. After all, it was only a warning. But the boy had struggled too hard, and Fowler had not been able to lift the blade when he was finished.

There was blood, more blood than Fowler had expected, and the worst of it seemed to be coming from the neck. The boy had stopped crying out. Fowler left him facedown in the alley and merged into the street. He remembered to walk naturally. Later, he was proud of that.

Blood was crashing in waves through his brain. His thirst was enormous, yet it seemed repellent, almost unimaginable, to stop and drink. By the time he arrived at the post office, his pulse was returning to normal. It was better this way. Aside from Rigg, no one but Mario knew who he was. Juan Antonio had known, but the earthquake had killed him while Fowler had survived. Fate, an accident. People got into accidents. Connie Oland's grandfather, for instance. It had been an accident, and partly his own fault. He should have been in a nursing home, in his condition. Mario shouldn't have struggled at that moment.

No one would be after Fowler for it. The police were tied up, and Mario was just a waiter from a slum where life was cheap.

In fact, he came from a district not far from San Juanico, where the people killed in the gas-tank explosion had never been definitively counted.

As for the leafleters, they would give up looking for Fowler, too. By now, they would have seen the remains of the Hotel Toronto. They were probably looking halfheartedly, making a show of it so they'd have something to report to their employer (Connie Oland? Trans Rio? The Texas DA?). They would conclude that Fowler was dead. Chances were they hadn't leafletted the children's brigades in Condesa or the tent people in Santo Domingo Plaza. They would think Fowler was dead because there was no one to tell them anything different.

The *lista* wasn't up yet. Fowler stood away from the window so that the troll wouldn't see him. But he felt other eyes on him, stares boring into him from the stamp windows and from the postal patrons furiously licking and addressing envelopes at the counters, making Fowler's idleness all the more obvious.

A dark-suited man, obviously foreign, was gliding the length of the post office with head upturned and a hand busy jotting something in a notebook. Fowler picked up his cue and pretended to be admiring the building's interior. There was often art-lover spillover here. The big museum, the Bellas Artes, was right across the street.

The Bellas Artes had weathered the earthquake well, Fowler reflected a little later, when, tired of feigning interest in chandeliers and walls, he settled for staring out the window. It looked like rain. He imagined the rain washing away the blood in the alleyway. He started and swung his head around, but there was nobody behind him.

There was, however, movement at the *lista* window. He turned to see the troll opening the little glass case to tack up the list. The troll looked back, and even from this distance Fowler could see eagerness in those little eyes. More money was in.

It said SOCIADO PLANO this time. Alphabetized below Herbert Lewis SENIOR.

He was still stooping before the glass when the dark-suited foreigner hurtled out of a corner to beat him to the *lista* window. So he'd been combining a little study of the plateresque style with his mail pickup.

It was just as well that the man—probably Herbert Lewis, Sr., himself—had hotfooted it to the window. Fowler didn't want anyone behind him when he said what he had to say to the troll. He had no intention of paying the agreed-upon bribe. The second check would be one of the small-change ones he'd asked for, another $500. Nights spent in self-loathing had recalled to him every word of his disastrous letter: "four checks for $500, three for $1,000, one for $10,000." He had to start the troll off small, because the troll was certain to escalate his demands. Later, when the big money got here, that wouldn't be as much of a problem.

The problem would be getting to the post office. He wondered if they were watching the intercity bus stations and the train stations. The airport was out; no tickets even on domestic flights without a tourist card. If he didn't go too far, he could have a car take him into the city. It was only a short ride from Cuernavaca. No, that was too obvious. Maybe Querétaro or Celaya. They'd never think of Celaya.

The troll undoubtedly had misfiled the mail for Herbert Lewis, Sr., because the broad dark-jacketed back was still leaning forward into the window. Finally something was withdrawn from his pants pocket—a tourist card, Fowler assumed enviously.

At last Herbert Lewis was gone, and Fowler stood across from a very unhappy troll face.

"You didn't keep your part of the bargain. I gave you the

letter. You were supposed to bring me my money the next day."

"Check-cashing problems," said Fowler. "You think it's easy to cash a check with no tourist card?"

"The consulate can replace tourist cards."

Fowler was taken aback by this. He didn't expect the troll to have a worldview that included consulates.

"They're too busy counting injured Americans," he said. "Where's my mail? I've got money for you now."

He counted it out, half the agreed-upon amount. The troll swept it off the window ledge as if it were dust.

"That isn't what we settled on for even one letter, and now you want two letters. You know that I'm not supposed to dispense without identification. What if I'm giving mail to the wrong person? I could lose my job."

If it was easy to draw a line down a handsome face, how much easier to destroy this hated one. Fowler's forehead throbbed as he thrust it against the bars. "Give me my mail, or I'll watch you when you leave work," he said in a cracked whisper. "I'll make you sorry for this."

"Criminal!" cried the troll. "The consulate won't give you a card because you're a criminal."

Fowler took a step back. He swiveled his head around quickly to see who had heard. The man in the dark suit was still in the post office, ostensibly reading a letter, but peering over it in Fowler's direction.

It was like the moments after the earthquake, the bed pinning him in, the springs pushing at his chest. Fowler remembered now that the man had approached the window without first consulting the list. No one asked for mail without looking at the list.

The dark-suited man was approaching him now, walking slowly and deliberately toward him.

"How much did they pay you to finger me?" Fowler demanded of the troll. "I will give you double."

"One hundred dollars," the troll said promptly.

There wasn't enough time to figure it in pesos. Fowler shoved most of the contents of his wallet at the troll.

"More later," he panted. "Tell him it wasn't me."

It had to be the honor system now. He hoped the troll's honor would last for as long as it took to get from the *lista* window to the door.

Outside in the wet slop he broke into a gallop, dodging the people who hurried by, newspapers held over their head. "*Granizos!*" shouted a group of children who rushed by under a single sheet of plastic. They always yelled that when it hailed, but Fowler flinched; it seemed to be meant for him.

He looked behind him for his pursuer, but it could have been anyone. Everyone seemed to be running. His parched mouth hung open as he pounded down the street. Hailstones as big as marbles pelted his arms and back, punishing him.

A bus was jerking away from a corner. Fowler flung himself into it, searching his pockets for the fare. Eighty centavos. He still had eighty centavos.

Inside the post office, the man in the dark suit finally spotted a second chap who seemed likely to speak English. He asked him for a pen. The chap didn't have one, but at least he acted perfectly normal about it.

# 15

WILLIAM BERMUDEZ NEVER would have believed people were capable of treating a police officer with such awe and respect. Sure, that happened for a while after the award ceremonies and the supercop coverage, but everything snapped back to normal pretty quick.

This time, though, it wasn't happening to him. It was happening to that French cop in the lobby, and Bermudez was surprised at how jealous he felt.

The door of the Hotel Lara's elevator slid open, depositing three small children and their mother to Bermudez's left.

"Aurore!" cried the largest child, and soon six little feet were running across the lobby toward the German shepherd. The dog stood near its uniformed master, patiently enduring the pats of four or five other children. The new arrivals knelt next to the animal and waited for a petting vacancy.

"Don't bother that dog," called out the mother, still nearer the elevator. "It needs its strength to work."

Bermudez seized this opportunity to hand the woman one of his leaflets. She took it without examining it, letting it drop to her side as she clacked across the stone floor. There weren't many seats left for the dog-and-cop show, but someone squeezed over on a couch to make room for her. She looked at the French cop like she would've liked to have given him some of what the dog was getting.

Bermudez envied the Frenchman's high-laced black boots, navy fatigue pants, and waist-length zipper jacket. The hat was all right, though it reminded him of the Pittsburgh

Pirates. A military look, though he gathered the guy was in a civilian police force. The uniform was a hundred times better than the clunky NYPD outfits. Those got periodically updated by big Seventh Avenue designers, but despite the press hype, they always turned out about the same—nothing to balance all the junk around the hips. Between the belt, the holster, the citation book, and the keys, you got a pear-shaped effect no matter how much time you spent at the gym. The French had the right idea. Bermudez wondered if Pierre Cardin or someone had had a hand in it.

He thought of asking the cop about it. The cop had already answered every other conceivable question: Yes, the dog could smell dead bodies as well as live ones. No, the dog didn't fight with the German and Swiss rescue dogs; only the humans fought. No, the dog didn't drag people out, but she did indicate the best route to take to get at them. Yes, the dog understood French, she was very smart.

The cop understood and spoke Spanish, but not tremendously well. He seemed relieved when one of the men got up off his couch and told everyone to let the "heroes" relax on their day off.

"The dog doesn't *want* your Chiclets," Bermudez heard one of the fathers advise as the crowd hustled past him into the elevator. The dog did, however, want the big ashtray filled with water that someone had set beside him. The Frenchman sank heavily into an armchair, waiting for the lapping to stop. With embarrassment, Bermudez saw that several of his leaflets had been left on the seats and coffee table. Well, he had no other choice but to walk over and collect them.

He'd brought just an armload or two with him, figuring he could swing back to the Marquesa when he needed a refill. But this Hotel Lara turned out to be farther than he thought. It was in a funny part of the city for someone like Fowler to have stayed, though of course that had been for business reasons. After this, Bermudez would continue bombarding hotels where Fowler might be staying now. He'd already covered the lists in the Fodor and Arthur Frommer books, but American Express had given him the names of some new ones. Leaflets could not be wasted.

The method was crude, a last resort he'd had to resort to. His field investigations around the Toronto had turned up nothing.

He still didn't know if he was looking for a stiff. The people in charge of the common graves laughed when he asked if they'd kept records of physical descriptions. They suggested he might want to come back after a good, hard rain.

"Is this yours?"

Bermudez drew his head out from under a couch and saw the Frenchman examining one of the wayward leaflets. Bermudez nodded.

"Texas?" asked the Frenchman, reading. "Police?"

"Police," said Bermudez. It was easier than describing the private detective bit.

"New York! Fantastic place!" The Frenchman had switched from Spanish to English, looking like he'd loosened a tie in the process. "Detective work, eh?" He flicked a finger against the leaflet. "Tell me about your case."

It soon became apparent that Officer Etienne Gauthier of the Compagnies Républicaines de Sécurité liked being the one to ask the questions. The dog finished the water and lay with eyes closed next to its master's knees as Bermudez outlined the basics.

Gauthier was interested. He said he liked detection and had studied its techniques, though opportunities to apply his knowledge were scarce. Like Bermudez, he'd done routine police work before joining a specialized force.

He was surprised that the New Yorker liked his uniform.

"This uniform is despised in France," he said. "The CRS are basically riot police." It happened that his company was a special one that did mountain rescues and lifesaving. They were civil police, all right, but they lived in a barracks under military-type discipline. Most of the other men were tenting near a big rescue site here, the Multifamiliar Juárez. They'd put him in a hotel because his dog was nervous.

"She's the best," he said, giving the dog a pat. "But she's a woman of expensive tastes."

He wanted to know more about the leaflets. "Why are you giving these things to the guests here?" he asked. "Most of them stay only two, three days. They are business travelers and their families, most of them. They were not here before the earthquake."

Bermudez explained that he was working the Lara hard because this is where Fowler had stayed until he went somewhere else to tuck himself in for Black Thursday. At other hotels, he dumped the leaflets at the desk. Here, he'd already interviewed some members of the staff. A clerk had shown him Fowler's name in the registration log, but no one knew if he had actually proceeded from here to the Toronto.

He mentioned to Gauthier that the other hotels on Fowler's itinerary had been checked, revealing that Fowler had followed his plans to the letter.

"In that case, it seems that he went to the Toronto," mused Gauthier. "A big mess, that place. And they demolished the remains before we got there. You are working, of course, on the assumption that he survived?"

Bermudez nodded.

"How is he subsisting?"

"His employer and estranged wife are keeping an eye on his bank balances in the U.S."

"And?"

"They wired me back already. No withdrawals. No credit-card activity." Bermudez also described how he'd checked the possible entrance points for money, operating on the assumption that Fowler had no fixed address. He'd been to the telegraph office, the U.S. Consulate, and American Express. Nothing.

"So, he survived with his wallet."

"I'm leafletting hotels, checking guest registers at the most likely ones."

"You have police authorization to check guest registers?"

"I have money. That opens things up here."

"You say you know the most likely hotels." One of the Frenchman's eyebrows was raised. "Are you sure you know which ones are most likely for your man? Do you understand your man? That is the critical thing."

Bermudez crossed his arms, then uncrossed them. No use trying to appear coplike in the presence of another cop. "He's an American businessman. Made lots of money. I met his wife, saw the house he used to live in and where he worked. I know the type."

"He is American born?"

"Of course."

"And you?"

Bermudez's face felt hot. "I'm Puerto Rican. What the hell does that have to do with it?"

"Take it easy. I'm just trying to make you realize maybe you don't know what's happening in the mind of our"— Gauthier consulted the leaflet—"Mr. Brian Fowler."

Bermudez tried to compose himself. The European was only being helpful. Restless, he rubbed his hands on the arms of his chair. The upholstery felt cheap, made out of the same kind of material his mother protected with plastic covers.

"You know, maybe you've got something there, about trying to get into the guy's mind. I wouldn't have thought a corporate exec would stay in this dump, though at least it's in a solid condition. My hotel's fancier, but it's got earthquake cracks."

"Oh yes?" said Gauthier absently. "Perhaps you should change. We have done several rescues at buildings that fell from the aftershocks." He was thinking. "Maybe your man is still here in the Lara," he said slowly. "Hidden by the staff, so that no name appears in the register."

"He could do that anywhere if he had sufficient bribe money."

"But here he already knows the employees. He stayed here before. It would be less awkward to ask for help. Maybe he has no money, but they are giving him credit."

Bermudez tapped the leaflet that Gauthier still held. "You ever see this man?"

"No, but I am out day and night. This is my first free time since we arrived."

"If he's here," said Bermudez, "my troubles are over. Someone will recognize him and call me for the reward."

"Nonsense! The ones who hid him will not betray him, because he'll promise them even more money. And the others will not identify him, because they cannot tell foreigners apart. They mistake me for a member of the German rescue team. They mistake my dog for the first one I brought here."

"You changed dogs?"

"Certainly. There are too many children staying here for Aurore. This one doesn't bite children."

Several moments passed before Bermudez noticed the trembling on the Frenchman's very serious face. Then Bermudez himself burst out laughing, the first laugh he'd had since arriving in this grim, ruined place to search for a ghost.

"Come," said Gauthier, wiping the tears from his eyes, "we'll discuss this over coffee." He rose, and the dog bounded up. Bermudez was already behind schedule, but Gauthier's advice could come in handy. And, damn it, he could use a cup of coffee and a friendly talk.

They had planned to have their coffee in the Lara's restaurant, but they found the door closed with a chair set in front of it. A custodian passed by and explained that most of the staff was gone for an hour or so, attending a memorial for a coworker who had died in the second earthquake.

"A rescuer like you, *señor*," said the custodian, with a deferential nod that included both the Frenchman and the dog. "The bar is still open," he suggested.

But neither Bermudez nor his new friend were big daytime drinkers, so they adjourned to a taco stand on Guerrero, thereby missing Rigg, who at that moment was in the bar, pickling himself in hops.

\*   \*   \*

The woman narrowed her intelligent eyes at Fowler and said, "You know I never would have figured you for a fashion reporter."

Fowler was back at 6-A Mata Street, the Mexican Press Club. He'd gotten past the glass doors on the second floor this time and was out on the patio, sitting at a white wrought-iron table with the *Newsweek* reporter.

Ellen was her first name. Her last name, Weinburger, was actually one letter shy of a match with Casper Weinberger, U.S. secretary of state. It was a common mistake, Ellen said, and she didn't mind at all. *Newsweek* had hired her because they thought she was related to someone important, and they could go on thinking it as far as she was concerned. Ellen was an operator. Fowler was back here to operate.

The bartender came out on the patio with an apple-cider soda for Ellen and a black look for Fowler.

"How come you insulted Carlos the last time you were here?" she asked when the French doors were closed again.

"He complained about it to you? Does he want you to write it up for *Newsweek*?"

She wiped the top of the soda bottle with her sleeve and started drinking, ignoring the glass that had been brought. She could be halfway attractive, Fowler thought, if she acted more feminine. "Everyone likes Carlos," she said. "He's one of the guys here."

Fowler shrugged. Carlos gave him the creeps, more than ever now that the deed had been done in the alleyway. Ellen sipped, neglecting to offer some of her drink to Fowler, who had ordered nothing because even a soda cost a few hundred pesos.

He doodled "Tom Dixon" on the cover of the notebook he'd bought in a stationery store. It was the wrong kind of a notebook for a reporter, he knew—short and wide with the spiral coil on the side instead of the top—and he wished he could have doodled some other fictitious name on it. "Tom Dixon" is how Ellen had greeted him this morning, much to his annoyance. She seemed surprised when he remarked on her memory.

Remembering names is part of my job, she said—"*my* job," not "*our* job." Tom Dixon wasn't in the *Newsweek* league. It was something Ellen couldn't let Fowler forget. His slovenliness, on the other hand, didn't seem to faze her.

And there was quite a lot of it to overlook. He had spent the night in Garibaldi Plaza, another tent city like the one in Santo Domingo Plaza, but one where the tents didn't go up till the tourists left. Garibaldi lived on tourism. The domestic travelers were back, almost in full numbers, either lured by the government's announcements of "normalization," or because they were in the capital to bury a loved one or two. Once again, the revelers were doing it up in Garibaldi Square, hiring bad mariachi bands, buying cheap moonshine from men who sold it out of coat linings, celebrating till all hours with noise and vomit.

Slept-in clothes didn't bother Ellen at all. But with a word here, a look there, she ranked Tom Dixon with the kind of journalists who worked for *National Home Centers News* or *Chain Store Age Executive*—the kind of publications Fowler's wife sneered at after she'd been sneered at herself.

Ellen's sneers told Fowler he was playing his part well. Tom Dixon was just a two-bit free-lancer for the trade magazines covering an earthquake sideshow. But he was a free-lancer with some spare time on his hands. That's why he'd come back to ask Ellen about those *Women's Wear Daily* assignments she'd mentioned.

Ellen was delighted to pawn them off.

"The editor's going to be thrilled I got somebody to take this," said Ellen. "And I want *Women's Wear* to be thrilled with me."

"What for?" Fowler asked.

"Future assignments."

"You do *Women's Wear* often?"

"Hey, the earthquake's going to get old soon. Everyone's revving up for the World Cup, including yours truly." Next year's international soccer championship was going to be hosted in Mexico. President De La Madrid had made noises about canceling it out of reverence for the earthquake victims, but *fútbol* won out over reverence.

"You'll do a soccer piece for *Women's Wear?*" He was becoming bold now, talking shop like an old pro.

"Sure. What Everybody's Wearing at the World Cup. I don't know sports, I've got to do something. Keep that editor smiling."

Ellen was so pleased that she agreed to Fowler's curious request that she pay him the $100 fee out of her own pocket. Seems he was off to Europe tomorrow to try developing a speculative story, and he needed instant cash. Ellen was very understanding. She agreed to pay up—just as soon as the story was in her hands. Despite all her contempt for the business press, she was quite a sharp businesswoman.

It was a little before 10:00 A.M. Deadline for turning into a professional journalist was 5:00 sharp. How hard could it be if his wife did it?

Fowler rose to leave, and Ellen wished him luck. "Don't do the corruption angle," she added cryptically. "*Women's Wear* couldn't care less."

▽

# 16

Bᴜᴛ ᴛʜᴇʀᴇ ᴡᴇʀᴇ others for whom "the corruption angle" was the real story. That was the first thing Fowler learned when he got to San Antonio Abad. The Metro spat him out at the elevated station and roared past, partially blocking his view of the sewing factories across the wide boulevard. Finally the last orange train car pulled away, and he saw the long bench that had been placed in front of the Omaha garment plant, presumably by the people who were jammed together on it. Nylon shopping bags bulging with food were packed around them, provisions for a lengthy vigil. A banner running the length of the bench identified the bench sitters as relatives of seamstresses seeking justice from the factory owners. "Corrupt" factory owners, it said.

Fowler wasn't particularly interested in finding out what their beef was. There were banners like this all over Santo Domingo and Garibaldi. Landlords and government agencies were accused of poor building construction and inspector payoffs, as if any of this was news. A fresh coat of political graffiti was coating the city. Even the blue-and-white-tiled side of Sanborn's dripped with a question: "Where is the international aid?" It was the old battle between the leftists and the PRI, the one party in a one-party system. Fowler was familiar with this kind of protesting, more familiar than most U.S. businessmen were, he thought. When he was in high school here, some of his Mexican classmates had wanted to do a Gorky thing as the class play.

On the whole, Fowler didn't regret the experience. There

had been a time when a union had tried to organize employees at Trans Rio. Knowing the rhetoric had helped Fowler put a lid on it.

He opened his notebook and started jotting down notes about the physical condition of the factories. The sides of the Omaha plant had peeled down from the top, exposing floors and ceilings separated by mere inches of space. Clenched between them were rags and corkscrews of metal. A crane buzzed around the ruin, presumably for demolition purposes, though it seemed to be making slow progress.

The Annabel factory next door may once have been the Omaha's twin, but now it was twice as tall. Oddly selective, the earthquake had left the Annabel alone after slamming down a few top floors. Fowler noted a group of women leaving it. Could it still be in operation?

"Journalist?" As if caught in a lie, Fowler slammed his notebook shut. The question came from a middle-aged woman wrapped in a black rebozo. All her clothes were black except the gray T-shirt with the word "Gucci" splashed across it. He had seen her before, picking her way across the street.

"Tourist," answered Fowler, who wished her back on the bench she had come from.

"This is no place for tourism, young man," she said. "There's tragedy here." She shoveled some crumpled pages of newspaper at him. "Tell your countrymen about this."

The top was torn from *La Jornada*, one of the leftist tabloids Fowler had stooped to reading in the days when he was searching for word of Connie Oland. An article had been circled in pencil.

JEWS RESCUE MACHINES, ALLOW WORKERS TO DIE
On San Antonio Abad, equipment continues to be brought out of factories owned by the Jews Sergio Goldemberg, Nathan Levi, Lazaro Bass, and Jose Silver while rescuers are denied access to the site.

The article went on to accuse "the Jews" of thwarting rescue efforts in order to conceal illegal child-labor practices and the exclusion of some workers from benefit plans.

The second newspaper clipping was from *Unomásuno*. A column by Marcos Tonatiuh Águila M. denounced "the Abrahams, Jacobses, and Moseses without tablets" for removing, along with their strongboxes and precious fabrics, "the dignity of the uniformed personnel who have become their allies."

"Nobody's alive in there anymore, *señora*," said Fowler. "It's too late." He took another look at the crane on the Omaha site, wondering how it retrieved equipment out of that mess. Industrial sewing equipment was quite expensive down here, he imagined.

"What about the miracle babies?" The television news was bubbling with reports about the newborns just rescued from the crushed maternity ward of Juárez Hospital. Mysteriously, the babies had survived while the mothers and nurses perished.

Fowler shrugged. He didn't like to be reminded of the babies. Mario had often spoken about them.

"We want the dogs and the *topos* here to search for our relatives. If they are alive, we want them saved. If they are dead, we want the bodies so that we can give them a decent Christian burial."

If lack of interest couldn't drive her away, maybe a bad joke would. "I'm just a vacationer," protested Fowler. "I thought maybe I'd see Plácido Domingo here." It is well known that the opera singer had been standing in front of a Mexican apartment building since the day after it crumbled, waiting for the bodies of his uncle and aunt to be brought out.

Which just went to prove Fowler's point: You never knew what rich celebrity you might be pissing off. Who would have imagined that a world-renowned tenor would let his uncle live in a cheesy government-owned complex?

"Not here," said the woman. "He's over that way," she said as she jerked her finger north. "With our comrades in

Tlatelolco." So they were comrades, then: a whole revolutionary battalion armed with nylon shopping bags.

The woman went back to the bench, and Fowler scribbled a while longer. He had no intention of actually doing the interviews Ellen wanted. Experience from the hotel business provided him with some likely statistics. Production was off this amount, shipments were delayed by so much, the situation was expected to continue for thus-and-such amount of time. In a stroke he considered particularly inspired, he attributed these statements to the Jewish-Mexican manufacturers whose names he'd read in the old woman's clippings. Gave it an air of authenticity.

The crane operator from the Omaha job crossed to Fowler's side of the street in pursuit of a lunch spot. Fowler followed to ask questions about how many sewing machines had been recovered, how much fabric, and where it was all being taken. The burly laborer was glad to cooperate, particularly after learning that his quotes would appear in *Newsweek*. He told Fowler how entire apparel factories were being reconstructed in another part of the city. The government approved because it wanted all manufacturing eventually removed from the central part of the city.

As it happened, the new locations were more efficiently laid out and more convenient to the highways. "Everything the Jews touch turns to money," said the PEMEX worker. Fowler had to agree, though he couldn't include that in his story. *Women's Wear* catered to fashion executives, and Fowler believed that in the United States, too, Jews controlled that industry.

The crane operator left Fowler in the restaurant, nursing a Nescafé that had been tepid to begin with and writing out his story in longhand. He was through by three, well in time to meet the deadline.

There was a crowd on the street, gathered around a PEMEX tanker truck. From half a block away, Fowler watched soldiers jump out of the cab and bark at the crowd until it fell into formation. The people, mostly women and children, carried receptacles—metal buckets, pink-and-blue plastic tubs, milk bottles. They'd come to get potable water.

A group of men in business garb strolled past the truck, dispersing into single file to edge past the bucket bearers. They regrouped into three abreast as they approached Fowler. Two dark men, obviously Mexican, flanked a foreigner so pale he looked peeled in contrast.

The man in the middle was Jim Rigg. The three swept by, close to Fowler on the narrow sidewalk. So close that Fowler could see Rigg's moist, pinkish eyes. They didn't seem to fix on him, or on anything in particular. Rigg was drunk. In enough control to work. But drunk.

At the corner of San Antonio Abad and Avenida de Taller, the area's major intersection, good-byes were said. Rigg lurched a few inches off the curb and stood peering into the distance while the Mexicans continued on to the Metro station. Fowler watched it all from the shadow of a wall. It would be a taxi for the boss, a one-peso subway ride for the managers.

Rigg twisted his head from one side to the other, looking for taxis. At last, one came. Fowler exhaled a huge pent-up breath.

A subway train swept over the elevated tracks. Fowler waited until it left before he went to the station. There was no way to know what those unfocused eyes had seen, what that slack mouth had said to the Mexicans.

The next train arrived within minutes. It slid in softly on rubber wheels, but as Fowler boarded it, his heart clanged like iron against iron. He told himself there was no reason to assume that the leaflets had appeared at the Lara. Even if they had, he could image Rigg, no reader, receiving one and pushing it aside. Would a wealthy industrialist bother calling the number?

Then Fowler remembered the amount of the reward. Too generous for Mexicans. Just about right for Americans. They might have thought of that. As he got off the Metro at the Allende station, he felt vulnerable, exposed. He'd been better off dead.

Ellen took a long time squinting at the writing in his notebook.

"I suppose substance matters more than style in the trade books," she said. "You really don't have a lede graf to speak of."

"Suppose you put that in yourself and dock me for the time," suggested Fowler, who'd come prepared for something like that. He pleaded a need to rise early for his European flight.

Ellen didn't like it. She said she'd shave twenty dollars off. Both her reaction and the discount were more than he'd expected.

"How about forking over the paycheck now, boss?" He had planned to punctuate this with his sexiest wink, but it didn't come. Everything was off cue.

It got worse. He was expected to "input" the story on one of the press club's machines. That meant typing, and Fowler could not type. It would have taken him all night to transmit the short piece he'd written. The effort would have exposed him.

In the end, he made excuses. Something about secretaries, wives, others who'd always done the "clerical side of the work" for him. He became breathless with nervousness, almost stopping midway.

Ellen dug into the pocket of her pants and pulled out 20,000 pesos, about forty dollars. The gesture struck him as masculine; he saw now how completely unattractive she was. "I'm going to have to do some fact checking on these quotes," she said, in a way that assured him she would simply dump the whole thing in a trash can.

"What's this for?" asked Fowler, when the notes were securely in his grip. But he knew the answer: For forty dollars, he had gone to San Antonio Abad and exposed himself to Rigg.

"Kill fee," said Ellen.

Fowler left the press club, compressing the bills Ellen had given him into a tight little roll that he put inside his waistband. He adjusted it several times so that it wouldn't press against his stomach, which had begun pulsing and aching on his return subway ride. Nerves, he thought, until he remembered the lukewarm coffee in the luncheonette on San Antonio Abad and the soldiers. They'd been delivering potable water.

Forty dollars wasn't much, but that and the remainder of his Citizens National check was enough for a start. He'd begin a new life in another city. The north might be best. Hermosillo maybe, or Juárez, some place that was still growing despite the economic crisis. He could easily afford food and rent for two months, maybe much longer. Things were cheaper in the provinces. He could have a private car take him part of the way, then switch to a bus. But the buses made few stops, and the toilets on board were unreliable. Fowler was beginning to shake with pain. Hermosillo would have to wait until tomorrow.

In central Mexico City, to walk east is to wade further into despair. That's how Fowler went now, exchanging the limestone buildings of Mata for crumbling brick. It was still daylight when he arrived at the streets with the plain, bald names—"Barbers," "Tailors" "Painters" "Tobacconists." The sidewalks hissed with contraband: pirated audiocassettes with typewritten labels, digital watches stuffed with more features than anyone could imagine a use for, "Garbi" and "Barby" dolls lying naked on their handsewn outfits, wooden lasts for underground shoemaking free of business taxes. Several small children were queued up for an arcade video game on the sidewalk outside a candy store. Fowler paused, clutching his abdomen, as a girl dropped a coin in. She drummed impatient fingers on the screen until an English-language message appeared: *If you are playing this outside the country of Japan, you are breaking the law.*

The neighborhood was one of the city's oldest, full of the infections and adhesions that accumulate with age. Things that would have been decorative and historically interesting anywhere else—door knockers shaped like elephant heads, for instance—were merely macabre here. The door of a machinist's shop was surrounded by flatiron soles; crowning the design was a cartoon of a woman fashioned from radiator parts. It was a trade sign and something else. Honest craftsmanship was a joke here. The real money came from the black market.

This was Tepito. Fowler had not intended to end up in this place, where people too dim-witted for commercial crime relied on the standard variety. Old men wouldn't walk down these streets at night without their sons at their side. But Fowler had exhausted his welcome at the other unofficial shelters, and Garibaldi Plaza had exhausted him. He'd heard of the big Tepito self-help center. Word of it had spread to the other tent cities. It was said to provide medical care.

People directed him to the churchyard on Vidal Alcoser. People were clustered on folding chairs outside the closed gate. No new registrations right now, he was told. All the comrades were meeting inside, from Tlatelolco, Guerrero, Garibaldi, Morelos, Santo Domingo. It was a historical moment. A citywide coalition was being formed.

Fowler collapsed in groans next to the row of folding chairs, under a sign that advised, DO NOT DEFECATE IN THE STREET. Something fell lightly on his shoulders. He looked up to see a young woman crouching over him, her long hair cascading onto him. She pulled him up, and took him by the hand to the churchyard gate. It took several thrusts of her small, determined foot before the thin, rusted chain gave way. She led him silently past the mass of people smoking and arguing in the church basement to a door opened just wide enough to expose a rusted, wonderful toilet.

# 17

WILLIAM BERMUDEZ WAS getting to know his American businessman. What better way, the French policeman had suggested, than to visit the scenes of his youth? Bermudez's American businessman had entered puberty in Lomas de Plateros, a silent, white world in the southwestern hills of Mexico City. There had been no earthquake here. Life went on as usual, a life of electronic security gates, guard dogs, fancy cars behind bars, *supermercados* with shelves ostentatiously decked with white bread and toilet paper. In other words, it was just like the places where the richest, palest people lived in Puerto Rico.

The high school had been difficult to find; there'd been no pedestrians to ask directions of. Finally a gardener had delivered instructions through iron railings, directing Bermudez to a bunkerlike structure where the administration office was about to close for the day. An assistant principal examined Bermudez's badge and pretended to understand the English of the Texas arrest warrant. He disappeared into an inner office, rematerializing with a list decked with seals and written in Gothic script.

The assistant principal stood waiting while Bermudez copied the names and addresses into his notebook. They had white bread out here, but no Xerox machine.

Evidently the calligrapher had run into some Gothic trouble with the unfamiliar *w* in Fowler. Bermudez skipped that name, copying everything above and below. He wondered which members of the Escuela Preparatoria Leopoldo

Zea, class of '67, had liked Brian Fowler. He wondered if any had liked him well enough to give him money and shelter him eighteen years after graduation.

None of the pay phones were working, and it took several more gardeners for Bermudez to find the public long-distance kiosk. It operated out of a restaurant. The woman who manned the phones and served the tables told him to take a seat. In a moment, she said, she'd give him an outside line for local calls, 200 pesos for the first three minutes. Just as soon as she gave some customers their plastic basket of tortillas.

There wasn't any long-distance business these days, she said. She also said she had no time to help him look through the phone book—big as the Manhattan white pages—and identify the Lomas de Plateros addresses.

But then Bermudez started addressing her as "mi amor," and the more my-loves he tossed at her, the more time she found she had. In fact, when a clutch of customers trooped in to eat, she called her sister out from the kitchen so she could stick by the phone booths and keep helping Bermudez. She seemed to like thinking about something besides the soup of the day.

Bermudez decided to tell her what he was after. She frowned at the list of graduates from Leopoldo Zea Preparatory School and spun out some annotations.

"This one is very rich," she'd say. Or, "Oh, yes, this lady. She married a doctor in San Ángel. Very stuck up."

The waitress-operator was a big help. She singled out the students who had stayed in town. She knew the names of their fathers. Otherwise, it would have been like looking for a José Rodriguez in the Bronx.

An hour and a half later, Bermudez had an appointment with the one Zea alum still living in the neighborhood (a bachelor, the woman told him authoritatively). A bunch of other grads hadn't strayed far, but it was getting too late. He'd get to them tomorrow.

The gardeners had knocked off for the day, so Bermudez

left his rented car near the restaurant and took a cab to the
first address. He regretted it as soon as the driver started
winding up into the hills. Felipe Maldonado—*"Engineer
Maldonado,"* a maid had corrected when he called—lived
behind tall gates in a pink stone villa on about two acres,
relentlessly landscaped. There weren't likely to be many taxi
stands around here for the return trip.

Once past the intercom on the gate and the distant
snarling of dogs, Bermudez was admitted to the villa by a
maid. He got a cool drink and a brief look at Engineer
Maldonado. The engineer appeared in a half-buttoned white
shirt, clicking a cuff link into place. He extended a hand to
Bermudez.

"Welcome," he said. "You'll excuse me, please. I'm still
dressing."

Bermudez had risen for the handshake. He towered a few
inches over Maldonado, but the engineer made up the difference in smarmy self-confidence. His skin was as light as an
Anglo's, and he had an air of owning the world. He was friendly,
though, with a warm smile for Bermudez, and an even warmer
one for the maid—something was probably going on.

"No need to dress," Bermudez said, but Engineer Maldonado was gone. Into the room trooped his mother and
father, saying they were happy to meet the policeman from
New York. They sat for a while, chatting about *Cats, 42nd
Street,* and some other Broadway shows that they'd seen and
Bermudez hadn't. The subject of national origin was
brought up subtly. Puerto Rico was mentioned, and there
was a pause.

"So!" The engineer reappeared in a cloud of cologne. He
had his suit jacket on now, three-button double-vent gabar-
dine, too conservative for Bermudez's taste, but perfect for
royalty. "You'll accompany me to a party," he informed
Bermudez. "It's all arranged with the host."

"I—"

"Oh, don't worry about dress. New York is casual. We
know that. How's the Palladium these days? Still insane?"

"If you don't mind, I need to ask you a few questions. Ten minutes. I'm afraid I've got to move fast on this investigation." No need to mention that the trail was already colder than the frozen margaritas that Bermudez had refused and the Maldonado parents were now imbibing.

"Yes, an investigation! Imagine, Papa! About Brian Fowler. You remember Brian from the *prepa*?"

A mist descended over the father's eyes. "There were so many Americans here in those days. Before the crisis."

The engineer had his hand on Bermudez's back now and was steering him to the door. "Come. It's going to be a great party."

"Will there be other people there from your *prepa*?"

"Some," said the engineer. "Some have been very successful. Others . . ." He paused, searching for the correct aristocratic insult. "Others, I've lost touch with." He smiled, satisfied with that.

"Let's go," said Bermudez, though he wondered if Fowler might not be more likely to hit up the outcasts for a loan.

Maldonado had a sports car, of course, new and fancy but American rather than the anticipated Porsche. Maybe that's what the father mean by "the crisis."

"What do you want to listen to?" Maldonado was tearing down an axis road that Bermudez couldn't identify. He fanned out a handful of cassette tapes. "I've got everything. You choose. Julian Lennon, The Ray Coniff Singers. You name it."

"You're joking," said Bermudez, who'd been hoping for *cumbias, boleros, sones.*

Maldonado downshifted and turned into an entrance ramp for the beltway that ran around Mexico City. "Did you think we were hicks who only listen to Mexican music? Put a tape in. How about The Carpenters?"

They were too early. The sumptuous stucco house still smelled of DDT and disinfectant, and there were big air pockets between the guests, none of whom hailed from dear old Leopoldo Zea, according to Maldonado. Bermudez fielded a few questions about Manhattan and sequestered himself in a wingback chair in the living room. There was a window to the side of the chair, and he squinted out into the night. He wasn't sure what part of town he was in, but it was sure far from his rented car.

He wandered over to another window, bored. Had it been possible to shuffle feet on a shag rug, he would have been shuffling.

"There you are!" Maldonado shoved a drink in Bermudez's hand, and Bermudez discarded it on a table. It was getting to be a routine between them. Then the doorbell chimed, and a crowd of people poured in. They must have been traveling in a convoy.

The air kisses and backslapping *abrazos* became thunderous, and the DDT smell was routed by perfume and aftershave lotion. Bermudez strolled around, uncertain how to work the room. Maldonado had disappeared permanently, just when he needed him, and this wasn't the cop's kind of scene.

He noticed some people flowing into a den off the living room and followed them. There was a group assembled in front of a television set. That public-service announcement was playing again, the one he'd seen on his hotel room TV a dozen times since arriving. It flashed pictures of a nurse, a construction worker, a soldier, a Red Cross worker, all of them cheerfully brandishing the tools they'd used in earthquake rescue efforts. They were actors, totally unlike Abel, Gauthier, and the woman who typed out lists of names at the common grave. The whole thing was fake, faker than the fakest dishwashing detergent commercial on American TV.

"*Gracias a ti*," rumbled the male announcer over each shot of a "worker."

"You're welcome," shrilled one of the men seated in front of the screen. His companions collapsed in giggles.

"I'm sick and tired of this earthquake," someone else said. "Such a bad image for our country."

"Best thing that could have happened," argued a third

voice. "The government's finally going to move some agencies out of the city, ease the congestion."

One of the others: "Today they said SecTur is moving to Veracruz."

Another: "Fantastic."

A news report appeared on the television. Soldiers and volunteers were combing through the wreckage of a home where family members swore they'd heard the cries of their missing child, Óscar. A microphone was held up to a volunteer who said every possible cranny had been searched. Cut to an ancient grandmother, who insisted that little Óscar was crying pitifully.

"A mass hallucination of the ignorant," pronounced one of the party guests. "Why does Televisa keep showing these maudlin *telenovelas*?"

Maldonado loomed up again. No drink this time, but there was a man behind one of his shoulders and a woman behind the other, both peeping excitedly at Bermudez. Bermudez slipped down further into his chair, exhausted. He was going to be trotted out for display again, the *Neoyorquino*. They'd ask him about drug addiction, salsa, the Limelight Club, and football. The television had been turned off, but now a Debbie Boone record was playing, and the people with the bowls of potato chips were due to come around again soon. Bermudez held his head in his hands.

"These people went to the *prepa* with me," said Maldonado. "They know Brian."

Bermudez was on his feet.

"So what kind of guy was he?" said Maldonado, playing cop, parroting the questions Bermudez had asked on the high-speed chase to the party.

"It's been a long time," said the man.

"Was he friendly—"

Bermudez pushed his way past Maldonado. "I'll handle this, thank you. Was he particularly friendly with anyone at school, anyone still living in Mexico?"

"No," said the woman, wrinkling her nose. "He was only

friends with the American students. He took an American girl to the graduation dance." Bermudez noticed that this woman was wearing a huge white artificial flower in her hair. It looked odd next to her decidedly thirtyish face. As if she were still waiting for Fowler to ask her to the prom.

They corroborated what Maldonado had said on the way over. All of Fowler's American friends were gone, returned to the States when their fathers were transferred, as his had been. The old classmates expressed surprise that Fowler had ever returned to Mexico. He hadn't seemed fond of them or their country.

What a joke, then, if he died here, thought Bermudez, remembering the Hotel Toronto.

"He never even learned to play soccer," said the man in a tone of amazement.

Bermudez's own elementary school memories crowded in: playground confusions during a game of Mother-May-I, puzzlement over puns, cryptic references to cartoon characters. "It might have been tough for Fowler to blend in," he mused aloud, "not really speaking the language."

"Oh, he spoke it well," said Maldonado.

"Not at first," said the woman, "but he was here three years. He did very well in Spanish Literature class. I remember someone who used to cheat from his papers." She jabbed Maldonado in the ribs and giggled. "Children learn languages very fast, you know. I started my children on French very early."

Either because school-day memories triggered regression or because the people at this party were very silly to begin with, the three old classmates began babbling to one another in beginner's-textbook French.

Bermudez moved away, stunned. It was the wife, Monica Fowler, who'd steered him wrong.

What were her exact words? Not, "No, he doesn't speak Spanish," but rather, "He doesn't speak it to *me*." She said he'd been helpful with a gardener and a maid, and Bermudez had run the wrong way with the ball.

It had never occurred to him that Fowler spoke fluent Spanish. To be sure, there were a few Irish priests in his neighborhood who labored away at the language, delivering their sermons in an oddly constructed Spanish. But Bermudez had never met an Anglo who could speak it naturally.

Fluent Spanish would gave an American the keys to the city. Brian Fowler's Mexico wasn't the small circumscribed world of Fodor guides and American Express offices that Bermudez had imagined. The cop had to sort this out, retrace Fowler's possible steps in this new light. . . .

Maldonado was tapping his arm, offering him potato chips. Why didn't they just leave the bowls on the damned tables?

"Any chance of leaving soon?" asked Bermudez. He was tired of this shindig, and there was nothing more to be gained from staying. These people knew nothing about Fowler's present whereabouts. "I'm not being paid to go to parties."

"Yes, I'm very curious about this." Maldonado selected a potato chip for himself. He held it between two fastidious fingertips, examining it. "Exactly who has hired you to look for Brian Fowler?"

Maybe it was because Maldonado's suit must have cost five times as much as Bermudez's best one. Maybe it was because he'd never seen *Cats* and he didn't go to the Palladium. For whatever reason, Bermudez stood in the middle of a crowd and told Maldonado what he hadn't told Gauthier—what he hadn't even told his own brother. He said he was working for Connie Oland.

A buzz traveled through the room. Bermudez was offered multiple bowls of pretzels and potato chips by people who took a good stare at him. The woman wearing the big white flower, the one who'd attended school with Maldonado and Fowler, came up to Bermudez again. This time she was dragging another woman by the hand.

The second woman must have been a new arrival, because Bermudez hadn't noticed any Americans here before. And she was obviously American, a classic New York type. The Park Avenue matron.

"I understand you're an American private eye?" said the newcomer. He was right. The accent was pure Park Avenue. He wondered if little kids from Brooklyn or Queens could become bilingual in that.

"Right."

"And you're employed by Connie Oland. *The* Connie Oland?"

He nodded.

"Well, *I* am a reporter, and I *adore* Connie Oland. Could we have a little chat tomorrow at my club?"

Bermudez thought about it. A newspaper, what the hell? Maybe this was the best way to get the word out and find out whether Fowler had been seen alive after September 19. That was still the number one issue. Spanish wouldn't have done a corpse any good.

"At my club then. I'll just jot down the address here. One o'clock."

She handed her card to him. Doris Pike, *Mexico City News*. They were to meet at the Mexican Press Club. 6-A Mata Street.

$\triangledown$

# 18

FOWLER WATCHED THE woman who had saved him boiling
water in a corner of the room. She squatted on the floor,
careful to avoid the spots where rain had dripped during the
night. Fowler lay on a blanket savoring the stillness in his
stomach. It had stopped moving and cramping some time in
the night, after the third pill.

The room was furnished with pallets holding cartons of
eggs stacked ceiling-high against the damaged walls. The
rain had dampened the canvas thrown over the eggs. Some
of them were probably ruined, but there were still enough
good ones to feed scores of families in the barrios where eggs
had been scarce for more than a week. Those families would
get these eggs if they could pay for them. Every day the eggs
sat here the price went up.

The sun had come out about an hour ago. There were no
signs of it here, but the roof had stopped leaking, and
children were shouting outside in a courtyard. The woman,
who had the odd name Itzel—she claimed it was Aztec—said
the bodyguards didn't like the children to come in here from
the street encampments. But it was impossible to prevent
them without using physical force, and Itzel wouldn't allow
physical force to be used on very small children. For those
older than seven she had no objections. She and her brother
Silvio had started thieving at age eight or so.

The electronic buzzer on the microwave oven sounded,
and Itzel rose to unplug the appliance from the extension
cord drawing juice from the socket of an overhead light bulb.

"Leave it plugged in," said Fowler. "There's an off button somewhere on the control pad." He spoke lazily, not bothering to get off his blanket and show her the button. She wouldn't want him to, he knew; she liked taking care of him, she'd come early in the morning to see how he was. He watched her flop back in front of the microwave and tuck her long brown legs under her skirt.

A small wrinkle appeared on her forehead as she tried to puzzle out the controls. Maybe when she was older, that's where a crease would appear. It was hard to imagine now. Her twenty-two-year-old face clung smoothly but not too tightly over her wide brow and high cheekbones. Fowler looked at her and felt lazier still, almost luxurious.

He jerked up to sitting position. "Don't touch the part of the plastic that's in contact with the water."

She swore, whether at him or the microwave oven it was impossible to determine. Like a Connecticut *Yanqui* in King Arthur's court, Fowler had come here from the future to explain to Itzel and her brother why they couldn't use metal in the microwave. Now Itzel had a nice collection of microwave cookware. Working with relish, accustomed to wielding a knife, she had spent the morning slicing bowls and plates out of some of the big plastic canteens that were stacked nearly as high as the eggs, holding water.

It was good water, Itzel insisted when Fowler asked her to boil it. Hadn't it come from an army truck? Fowler agreed that it would be fine for him after just a little boiling. It was standard Mexico City water from intact pipes, the type that was in short supply now. Fowler thought of the women he'd seen on San Antonio Abad, waiting in the street with their sad assortment of pitchers and bottles. All the canteens in this room were uniform. Hoarders knew enough to use the jumbo size.

The door opened, and Silvio came in with one of the bodyguards.

"We got the oven to work," Itzel reported. "Look. It works with the plastic pot."

Silvio frowned at the water, his face clenched tight as a fist. "Good." He directed this remark to Fowler, who had stood up when Silvio entered. You didn't lie down when Silvio was around. You wanted your muscles tensed in case of sudden blows. "You saved someone's life, you know that? I thought that guy in Nuevo Laredo sold me two dozen fucked-up stoves. I was going to go back there and knock his fucking head off."

Silvio punctuated this by pulling his headband tighter around his longish hair. He walked over to where his sister sat, admiring the bowl of boiled water.

"Okay." He pointed a booted toe at the microwave. "Put it away. We're gonna sell the whole batch today."

"Get your foot away." She slapped it. "You're going to knock the water over." She gripped the plastic receptacle carefully by its top edge and walked with it toward Fowler's corner, apparently thinking he wanted to drink the water hot. The bodyguard barked a laugh at this obvious display of affection. In a swift, skilled movement that gave no advance warning, Itzel turned and splashed the water in his porcine face, then ducked to evade his lunge. Silvio came between them.

"Stay out of this, Gabacho." Fowler gladly cut short the tentative movements he'd made in Itzel's direction. He had invented a new name yesterday. Daniel, probably, he wasn't sure. The illness had made him forget. It didn't matter now. They had fixed on El Gabacho, a shade more insulting than El Gringo.

"You. No spitting," Silvio warned his sister. Peace had been restored now. The bodyguard left with a glare, moving back to his post in the courtyard.

Before the earthquake, Itzel said, a dozen families had lived in this squat brick structure, sharing the toilets and sink in the parched inner yard. Now the families were on the street outside, and the building had been taken over by the *pillines*, youth so lawless that they transgressed even Tepito's extremely lax rules of behavior. On the street, people had attached banners to their tents, protesting the failure of the government and the landlords to repair their damaged homes. They didn't dare protest the *pillines*.

Itzel said there was more water and eggs in the other apartments. Some of the eggs were rotting because the trucks didn't come to take them out for sale. The trucks were busy moving people who'd lost their homes. You could get any price you wanted in the moving business these days, she said. Silvio was also looking into an arrangement with funeral homes; people were desperate for funerals. Itzel sighed as she talked about it. In her view, Silvio had overextended the capabilities of their modest band of "colleagues."

But Fowler liked Silvio's vision, particularly because there was a role in it for him. That's why El Gabacho had been allowed to sleep in a Silvio-controlled building. Even through his dysentery haze, Fowler noticed the brother's initial annoyance at seeing him, annoyance that escalated into curses and punches at the wall when Silvio learned more of the circumstances. Itzel had been sent to the Tepito Cultural Center to case out the joint, as it were. Silvio and associates were contemplating a raid on the blankets and supplies stored in the churchyard.

That Itzel had already broken the lock on the gate to let Fowler in was considered a tactical error. The cultural center workers would notice, of course, and they might decide to replace it with a good lock. On the other hand, Fowler's illness had caused Itzel to ask for medicine and discover where it was kept. Silvio approved; there was a big market for medicine. He could deal with the lock, he said. After a little conversation with Fowler, he decided he could deal with him, too.

"You all fixed up?" he asked Fowler. "Ready to make the run?"

Fowler pointed to his stomach. "Still a little queasy. Give me a day or two."

Itzel was wiggling her feet into the red high heels she had shaken off earlier. Silvio shifted possessive eyes from her to

Fowler. Fowler could practically see the thoughts passing through his Iron Age skull, painfully slowly, like words on a broken-down teleprompter.

"Better be ready soon," he told Fowler. "We don't have time to let you hang around here eating our food and having a good time."

"I'm sure," said Fowler, who had neither eaten nor had the good time Silvio was imagining. He had already determined that there was no percentage in arguing with Silvio. The best strategy was to seem calm. Silvio didn't know any more about calmness than he knew about Americans, and that was amazingly little. He seemed only dimly aware that it was unusual for an American to be in Tepito.

Itzel began putting the microwave oven back into its carton, preparing to move it back to the apartment next door, where there were dozens more, all believed until now to be defective because of the way they acted on metal. It wouldn't have been unusual to receive defective machines, she said. The colleague in Nuevo Laredo had delivered junk before. All the Walkmans, the radios, and the televisions had to be examined before they moved out on the street and potentially engendered complaints or even warfare.

It would be better, Silvio said, to take El Gabacho, who said he needed work, on the next trip north. Though Silvio had only the sketchiest notions of nationality or language, he knew that U.S. citizens could cross unchallenged into Mexico with suitcases full of electronics. In one trip, El Gabacho could accomplish what took a Mexican courier loads of time and wads of bribe money.

Itzel was leaving now with her heavy bundle, saying good-bye to Fowler only with her eyes so that Silvio couldn't see. He acted more like her lover than a brother. In fact, it was hard to believe that the two were related by blood— Silvio, with his scarred face set on a thick neck and body, and slender Itzel with an almost Egyptian pointed nose placed over sensual Mexican lips. Her waist-length hair, the first part of her to touch Fowler—more would follow later, he felt sure—was also unusual, loosely curled in open spirals. She confided that it was a permanent, from an American drugstore kit. She'd asked him to buy another for her when he went to Texas.

Silvio left. Fowler stayed on the blanket, restive because all his strength had returned. But he couldn't let them see that; he needed more time for what he had to plan and do.

In the early afternoon, the door moved. Fowler had hoped that Itzel would bring him lunch, but instead the bodyguard came in with a plate of pig's-head tacos and a bottle of soda. Fowler greedily drank the soda, glad there was something to replace the lost water of the morning. He played with the tacos, eating nothing. They would have set the cramps off again.

The bodyguard sat and ate with him. He gave his name, but Fowler already knew he was called El Feo—the Ugly One. Obviously an intellectual type, he'd brought some reading matter with him. It was the picture magazine called *Alarma!* that Mexicans seemed to favor for long bus trips, even though its principal photographic subject was the vehicular accident. Pictures of crime victims, preferably mutilated, rounded out the assortment. El Feo perused it thoughtfully as he ate his own lunch and Fowler's leftovers. Dessert was a cigarette, one of those malodorous domestic brands. He left ashes and garbage behind as a souvenir.

The faking of illness allowed Fowler the full day to plot his moves. The situation was a lucky break. For the first time since he'd seen the leaflets, the feeling of panic had left him. It was really gone now, not just in the background, where he'd pushed it to get through his dealings at the press club. There would be no leaflets here. Even if there were, he'd be protected by the code: Nobody reported on anybody but the landlords.

The medication had cured Fowler's stomach. He could leave for the provinces now. He had Ellen's forty dollars curled into his waistband, and a little left over from before. But there was a reason why one-quarter of Mexico's population lived in the clogged, polluted capital. In the provinces, there was no work. You had to be all set before you went.

Silvio, to be sure, had offered him an insulting sum for his labors, presumably much less than the Nuevo Laredo man got, or there would be no incentive to change middlemen. But Fowler could think of several ways to make the trip worthwhile, even if it did involve one dangerous day in Texas.

It would be risky, but it would be a start. Soon after he came back, he'd have capital. And, as Silvio had already discovered in his crude way, there were more ways than ever to get returns on your capital in Mexico. Hoarding and gouging were primitive, but more sophisticated things, too, would be born in the earthquake.

A story was being told in the protest banners hung on the tents in Tepito's modern-day Hooverville. The people on the streets feared that their homes would never be repaired, that the landlords would use the opportunity to demolish the tenements, where rents had been frozen years ago. "Now come the real estate speculators!" warned the paint on the bed sheets. A few years of cooling off in the provinces, and Fowler would return here. Tepito fringed the business district; it long had been a hotbed of government opposition. Now the quake had done what the ruling party could not. Tepito would finally be razed. Fowler wanted to be around when it was cashed in.

Some modest profits from contraband would give him a good start. It would be simple, really, this run to Laredo. Someone else would do the driving. It was a simple matter for an American to pass back and forth over the border carrying luggage. All you needed to get into Mexico was a driver's license. And all you needed to leave was a tourist card.

The stomach medicine must have made him drowsy the night before. Otherwise, he couldn't imagine how he had managed to sleep. The earth was still heaving from time to time—seventy aftershocks since the second earthquake, it was said—and the walls of this room had already shifted out of place. Fowler had been lying in the dark, but now he rose and switched on the light. Cockroaches scurried over the egg pallets and the garbage El Feo had left on the floor.

When Itzel came, her shadow extended far from the door that she had opened softly, almost to the corner where Fowler sat watching her. It was very late; she'd be missed at home. He was surprised when she came to him, seating herself in front of him wordlessly. Her limbs were wonderfully long, and now he could finally let his eyes rest on the areas between them.

He was gentle at first, unsure whether resistance would arise at the last minute. He turned the light off at her request and wrapped her arms around his back when she seemed prepared to lie limply in surrender. After a while, her submissiveness aroused him. He turned the light back on despite her protest, and he tore at her with his teeth and hands, hoping later to see the bruises. This drew neither passion nor protests from her. He kept it up until he was as bored as she seemed.

When it was over, she pulled her clothes on hastily and lay down next to him again. Reluctantly, he put his pants back on. The room felt close and hot. Still, he thought he could get some sleep now.

"You'd better get back now," he said. "Silvio will be looking for you."

"Oh, him. He gets drunk and falls asleep in front of the television set. He hears nothing at night."

Fowler crossed his arms on his chest and closed his eyes. The light bothered him, but if he turned it off, she might interpret it as an invitation to stay.

"They had that thing on the news again," she said. "About the little boy Óscar."

"I don't know this kid," said Fowler. He was irritated. It was going to be hard to sleep.

"The one who the family hears under the rubble, but no one can find him. Do you think there are still survivors?"

"Don't worry about the little boy," mumbled Fowler.

"There are too many little boys in this country already."

"No, I'm worried about Silvio's plan. He wants some of the guys to start charging money for rescues. He says it's easier to charge now, because the foreign rescuers are leaving, and the volunteers are going back to their jobs. But I think it's a waste of time. Almost everyone is dead, right? How long can they stay under there?"

She seemed wide-awake, more animated than she'd been during the act of sex. She picked up a copy of *Alarma!* that El Feo had left behind and leafed through it for a while, clucking her tongue enthusiastically over the gore, nudging Fowler from time to time so he could share her delight.

"I'm going to sleep now." He didn't bother about her feelings this time. He wondered why he ever had.

She sniffed the air. "The eggs are getting rotten. You'll have to get up early. We're moving everything out of here. The eggs are going out for sale, and everything else is going to the Palacio Negro."

Palacio Negro—the Black Palace. Not recognizing the name, he asked if there was a place there for him to sleep.

She shrugged. "You go in there, you won't find your way out again. That's the oldest part of Tepito, off Labradores." She sketched zigzags in the air. "Like a maze. We're going to set up headquarters in there. It's safer. There's a rival gang that's after our stuff. They'd get lost in there."

"You can lead me in and out."

"You've got to leave for the north tomorrow night. They want to go as soon as they finish moving. You're not sick anymore. I'm going to tell Silvio."

He got up as soon as he heard the door close behind her and crossed to the light bulb. Poised to pull the chain, he paused. His eye was caught by the copy of *Alarma!* left open near his blanket. He picked it up for a closer look.

Mario would have hated this. The parts of his face not obscured by blood gave no hints of his good looks. So, his coworkers, even the relative who was always nagging him to get back to work, hadn't bothered to cover him with a blanket. Or perhaps they had, but the photographer, arriving with the police, had paid them off. Fowler felt contempt for the relative. Imagine, allowing that.

The caption below the photo blamed the "senseless killing" on "a thief." The police, of course, wouldn't investigate further. Mario's family had neither the money nor influence to get them to do so.

It would be more difficult with an American, Fowler reminded himself. The embassy might start trouble. He clicked the light bulb off and lay down on his blanket. Within moments, he felt sleep coming. His body was satiated, and he had no real reason to worry. His plan was good.

▽

# 19

THE RAIN HAD drummed all night against the plywood covering Bermudez's window, sending him into a sleep of contentment. As a small child he had slept in a room with a tin roof that made pinging noises when the rains came. It was a long time ago, in Puerto Rico, at the home of his grandmother. He awoke thinking of her pleasantly, until he remembered the lie about her illness he'd told the lieutenant. A fear seized him. What if it came true? He realized now that he had chosen the lie because of its likelihood. She was old, she was from a part of the world where people didn't live long. If she were taken sick after his return to the police department, what excuse could he give to go see her?

The phone on his nightstand was ringing. He reached for it automatically, realizing only as he grasped the receiver what a momentous occasion this was. After days of checking for the messages that never came to the hotel desk, he had at last had a response to his leaflet.

"Hello." The word was out before he remembered he should have used Spanish. There were several clicks on the line, and it went dead.

He kept the door open during his mournful shower, ready to leap at the phone again. Ravenous for breakfast, he sat watching the television until noon. Cartoons. A public-service announcement from the government advising parents to put coats on their children now that the weather was colder. News: the search for little Óscar was still on. The *Gracias a ti* spot again.

Don't bother thanking me, Bermudez told the TV as he chose between the two ties he'd brought. I'm just on my way to waste some time talking at the Mexican Press Club.

He had pulled the door behind him when he heard the phone ring again. He patted all his pants pockets before remembering he'd put the key in his jacket. The phone cut off in mid-ring as he raced toward it. Bermudez imagined the caller with the leaflet in his hand, balling it up and tossing it away again after this second attempt. He had expected crank calls, false leads, but these had been the first calls of all.

Only a few of the leaflets were remaining, piled on the bureau. Bermudez picked one up. The English, that was the problem—he never should have translated them into English. The American tourists were all gone now, and Mexicans would be put off by it. Bermudez slipped one into his pocket.

After this pointless interview with the Pike woman, he'd have them reprinted, change the phone number while he was at it. He didn't need to stay in this mangled Hotel Marquesa. Plenty of the hotels he'd leafletted were in better shape than this one. Gauthier's wasn't fancy, but it was practically in mint condition. Maybe he'd change to that one, save Connie a little money.

"She really does have a great deal of money, doesn't she? Any luscious little details you can give me—the car, the fur coat, the jewelry maybe? How about the house in Malibu? Have you been there?"

Bermudez thought he saw a sympathetic look in the waiter's eyes as the drinks were placed on the table before him. A vodka and tonic for Doris Pike, who had arrived looking like she already had a few under her belt, but just a Coke for him. He never drank on the job. But was he really on the job?

Doris Pike took a hearty sip from the highball glass and sighed. "Even the drinks seem weaker these days. Everything's just *wrong* since the . . . thing happened. I can't even say it really. You can't imagine how traumatic. And how deathly sick of it we all are. I won't even write it in my column anymore. I call it 'the E-word.' So much better, don't you think? Approach it with a little humor?"

The waiter asked if they wanted anything else. Doris Pike made a wave of dismissal. Bermudez said no thanks.

"Now, about Miss Oland. I understand she delayed a big Universal project—something about a woman race-car driver, I believe?—to make that thing she just finished in New York. Universal was livid, I understand. Cost them hundreds of thousands."

Connie was in California now. Yesterday she'd sent Bermudez a telegram so long that the Western Union operator must have developed carpal-tunnel syndrome typing it out.

Just keeping tabs on her employee, he figured. But then why all the personal stuff about how she was doing her own stunts for the race-car picture and how it was scaring her sometimes? Why the part at the end—THINGING ABOT YOUR TOUCH AND OUR GOOD LOVING THAT SEEMED SO WRITE, as the telegraph office had transcribed it.

It didn't hurt to keep the carrot in view, he supposed.

Or it meant something maybe. Maybe.

"I can only speak about my investigation here," he told Doris Pike. "We're trying to bring a man to justice."

The columnist frowned and waved her hand above her glass. She might have been swatting at a fly, or at Bermudez.

"Isn't this what they call a 'small film,' this *Typewriter Girl* thing? I know Schubel always gets nice notices for his films in the *Times* and all that, but does anyone really see them?"

"Schubel?"

"The director, my dear. The one Connie Oland is . . . shall we say, spending time with?"

Bermudez put his hand in his Coke to pick out the ice. You couldn't eat the ice here, it was dangerous. "I don't know anything about that."

"You sound personally concerned, darling. My, my, Connie certainly spreads her charms around, doesn't she?"

Bermudez had learned a lot of things in the Movie and TV Unit. His commanding officer and some of the older guys had come in from the old Tactical Patrol Force. They'd been the people responsible for averting violence during the protests of the sixties. If a street tough approached Bermudez with a jeer, Bermudez knew how to keep his face immobile. If people crowding around a rock singer or soap opera star began trampling one another, he knew how to restore order.

But when an old lady repeated an idle piece of celebrity gossip, he lost control completely.

He regained it a moment later, sitting quietly until the blood seeped back into his neck.

Your average star-struck old lady wouldn't have noticed a thing, it all happened so fast. But it wasn't by chance that this old lady was lunching at the press club. Bermudez could see what was going on. She might as well have whipped out her notebook.

"Did you say you were a policeman before you undertook this investigation?" He hadn't said, and she hadn't been interested until now. He didn't need to say anything. She'd seen that movement in his right shoulder.

"A lot of people think it's easy to write a lighthearted column. They think anyone could do it." She consoled herself for this insult with a swig of vodka and tonic. "Actually, I was a hard-news reporter for years before I worked my way into this. The *Daily News*. How's Liz Smith's column these days?"

"I usually read the *Post*," mumbled Bermudez.

Doris Pike nodded. "New York Police Department." He could see the imaginary notebook again. "I thought I heard those melodious tones of Brooklynese."

He thought how much better off he'd been with the people who thought he was from Veracruz. He could only pray that Liz Smith didn't have a subscription to this woman's newspaper.

"I think I'll ask for the check, if you don't mind. Now where is that Carlos? Probably inside, tending bar. They have such a terrible system here."

"Listen," said Bermudez. "Connie—Miss Oland—sent me to look for a man down here. In Mexico City. There was a court case in Texas about her grandfather, okay? This guy's mixed up in it. He's been missing since the earthquake." Bermudez remembered he had bought a copy of the leaflet. He drew it out of his pocket. Maybe she could run the photo. He had to salvage this somehow.

"The earthquake," repeated Doris Pike, almost yawning. "Just problem after problem. Oh, hello, Ellen." Some people had jostled against her chair on their way to a table. Bermudez showed her the leaflet, but instead she pulled her shawl closer around her. "It's getting awfully cold for this patio, isn't it? I wish Carlos would come with that check. I've really got to run."

Bermudez rose. There was no use prolonging this. He wondered if she had contacts at the Waldorf, if she could find out he'd stayed with Connie. The cops stationed in the private lobby of the Towers had seen him, had even winked congratulations on the second night. But there was a buddy code about leaking these things, and it seemed to work better than the buddy code about covering for partners who were in a building with armed drug dealers, maybe because keeping your mouth shut about sex didn't deprive cops of money.

Nothing had come out about it in the press while he was in the United States, but there'd been that bodyguard in the next room. Gossip columnists had a way of hooking up with people.

"I'll leave enough to cover it," he said, digging for his wallet. Doris Pike gushed thanks and left, moving faster than he would have thought she could. Making a beeline for the typewriter, he supposed.

The waiter came a minute later, but Bermudez had already thrown a generous number of bills on the table. He was through the French doors when the waiter caught his elbow.

"You forgot this," said the waiter.

It was the leaflet. Bermudez mumbled a thank you and took it, but the waiter kept hold of his elbow.

"There's someone sitting outside I think you should meet," said the waiter. "A very reliable person. A reporter for *Newsweek*."

"No way," said Bermudez, allowing himself to be gently steered back to the patio. "No more interviews."

Almost everybody eating at the press club had gripes about the service that afternoon, but Bermudez and Ellen got a steady supply of soda and beer. The waiter, Carlos, kept coming over and checking on their progress. He chipped in a few observations, too. Somehow he'd developed quite a bit of animosity toward Brian Fowler. Dixon, he and Ellen called him. Tom Dixon.

But it was the same man, that was certain. Even the fashion-reporter cover made sense; Bermudez knew what the wife did for a living. At some point, Bermudez had switched from Coke to Tecate—just a few because he had a lot of work before him today. But he had a little celebrating to do, too. He was no longer looking for a mortality statistic. He was looking for a living man with an urgent need for cash.

"He never mentioned anything to indicate where he was staying? You didn't talk about places in the city at all?"

Ellen shook her head. "I can't believe he duped me like that," she said, not for the first time. "I gave him an assignment without asking to look at his clips. Really dumb."

"Clips?"

"Clippings. Articles he'd published before. It never occurred to me anyone would want to pose as a *trade* reporter. You know another funny thing about him I should have noticed? He's on his first trip down here, supposedly, but he already speaks Spanish fluently. You mentioned that, didn't you, Carlos?"

Carlos had been pretending to hover over a nearby table, but this brought him back with a snap. "The Spanish? Yes, very good for an American."

"I'm an American," said Bermudez, almost involuntarily.

"Yes, but you are of *La Raza*," said Carlos.

"I've been down here four years, and I don't speak that well," said Ellen. "How did he learn it? Special classes for hotel executives?"

Bermudez was about to give her a thumbnail biography of the young Brian Fowler, but Carlos stepped on his lines.

"Executives!" he repeated. "That guy is an executive?"

"The manager of an expensive Texas hotel," said Ellen. "Bermudez filled me in while you were serving people. He might have caused the death of one of the hotel guests. That's why the police are looking for him."

"A murderer, that I can believe. But an American businessman, no."

"Oh, c'mon Carlos," chided Ellen. "You've been watching too much American TV. We don't all dress like people in 'Dynasty.' Look at me, for instance." She playfully flipped up the collar of her blue chambray shirt.

"*You* are clean. That guy looked like he slept in the street."

Ellen shrugged. "Kind of scruffy," she agreed.

As for Bermudez, he put down his beer can. He had some driving to do.

▽

# 20

Most New York cops could get around their precincts blindfolded and would only have to peek a little to navigate through one or two neighboring commands. But a cop in the Movie and TV Unit knows the city. Every candy store in Bay Ridge, every asphalt plant in College Point is a possible film location. They've even used Staten Island.

So though Bermudez had seen the low-rise apartment building only once, and that was by night, he was able to trace his way back there now. He did it by feel, pointing the rented Chevy along the boulevards and axial roads.

It looked different now that a lot of families had moved off the streets. The apartment number was the hard part. For that, you asked a neighbor. A woman finally came up to the door struggling with some big bags of vegetables. She didn't recognize the last name, or even the first one, but she knew which bell to ring for the accountant with the broken arm.

Abel wasn't home, but his wife said she expected him shortly. She invited Bermudez to make himself at home in an apartment that looked a lot like his mother's. Same little knickknacks all over the place, same kinds of religious pictures.

The wife excused herself to resume cooking dinner. Bermudez could see another female moving around in the kitchen. A servant, maybe; she and the wife didn't seem to have much to say to each other. Three little kids, two of whom he remembered from the sofa on the street, poked their heads in from another room. They stared at the visitor for a while, then ran away like shy little animals.

Abel came home, an attaché case in his good hand. No tie. The men down here didn't seem to wear them.

"So you're still down here," Abel said when the kids had been pulled off him and corralled elsewhere, and the wife had returned to the kitchen. "Still trying to find out if your man is breathing."

"He's breathing all right." Bermudez pulled out the leaflet. One of the corners was torn, a souvenir of Ellen's first grab for it. "This is my man," he told Abel. "He wasn't buried in the Hotel Toronto. I met some people who saw him two days ago. They say he looks like he's been sleeping in the streets."

"Like hundreds of others," said Abel. "Our experts checked this building out, or I'd still be there myself." He took a closer look at the leaflet. "Brian Fowler."

"He calls himself Tom Dixon now."

"This is a very large reward. Who is going to pay all this money?"

"My employer," said Bermudez, feeling eyes searching his face.

"Whoever it is must be very rich." This was said not with awe but rather with suspicion.

"If he was in Tepito, who might have seen him? That night you walked me through the streets we came upon a dispensing station you hadn't seen before. Have you discovered any others since then? How many do you think there are?"

"You are going to offer this reward here?"

"I'll pay the reward for information, of course, but I don't want to post the leaflets in Tepito. Fowler changed his name. He must know someone's after him. I don't want to drive him further underground."

"It's better you don't post the leaflets here," said Abel. "Tepitans will do almost anything for money, but not many will betray a person for it."

"He committed a crime. He's wanted by the police."

"Ah, yes, the police." Abel looked knowingly at Bermudez.

"Many people in Tepito have problems with the police. In fact, it's estimated that the police commit sixty percent of the crimes in Mexico."

Bermudez didn't press the question about the dispensing stations. The visit was over.

Darkness was dimming the smog as he walked back to his car. He thought he could find his way to that big shelter by the church, but he needed to go back to the hotel first. If he was going to question people, he needed to give them his phone number, and his phone number was about to change. He might as well move to the Lara tonight. It was closer to Tepito anyway.

There were no legal parking spaces near the door of the Marquesa. He got as close as he could. He was traveling light; in one trip he could have all his stuff in the trunk and be gone.

The desk clerk looked like he'd been expecting him.

"Could you get my bill ready?" said Bermudez. "I'm leaving tonight. I'll give you a number for forwarding my phone calls. I'd appreciate it if you could tell the other people on the desk staff about the phone calls. You have a pen?"

"These gentlemen are here to see you."

Bermudez looked around to see two Mexico City cops coming out of the men's room.

"I'm two flights up," he told them. "You want to take the elevator or the stairs?"

The desk clerk's face fell. He was going to miss the excitement.

"This is yours, correct?" said one of the cops when the door was closed. The leaflet he handed Bermudez had been folded into a tiny square. There were two creases over Fowler's face.

"We found this on the body of a young man," the cop continued. "His throat was slit in the alley outside the hotel where he worked."

The other cop showed Bermudez a picture of the boy. Oddly, it wasn't a police photograph. It was printed in a cheap magazine, about the size of a comic book.

Bermudez showed them his ID from the NYPD. They told him their names. One of the cops asked if he could have some water from the bottled supply on Bermudez's dresser. The other asked permission to smoke.

"You've questioned people at the hotel, I assume?" said Bermudez. "The family. Any suspects?"

The cops looked at each other, embarrassed.

"This was a boy from a very simple family—" began the one in the chair.

"We thought possibly the matter could pertain to this request for information," said the other, walking over to the nightstand ashtray to grind out his barely smoked cigarette. He was ready to do business.

They were here for the reward. Bermudez stood quietly, despising them.

"Even a poor boy might have enemies," he said. "You wouldn't know unless you had investigated, would you?"

"Perhaps, perhaps not," said the standing cop. "Wouldn't you like to know the name of the hotel where this happened?" You could practically hear his palm snap open.

"I don't think that's necessary," said Bermudez. "Thanks for stopping by."

The cops exchanged surprised glances. Then the one in the chair got up slowly.

The next part was going to be difficult, but Bermudez forged ahead anyway.

"Tell me something," he said. "A friend of mine here, a French policeman, told me you have to buy your own ammunition."

"Yes," said the one who had been smoking, the one who was obviously in charge. "It is a great financial burden—"

"And your pistols?"

"No, those are given to us."

"But if you were to lose your pistol, you would have to pay to have it replaced? But it could be replaced, am I right?"

The price was settled on quickly. As soon as the door closed behind them, Bermudez leaped for the phone. His fingers shook as he dialed the hotel whose name he had seen in the magazine, in the caption under the photo of the dead boy.

"Mr. Dixon, please," he said.

"I'm afraid Mr. Dixon is no longer here," said the voice on the other line. "He left a couple of days ago."

Bermudez flung his clothes into his suitcase, packing some shirts around the revolver. The cigarette stub still glowed in the ashtray. He doused it with some of the water the partner had been drinking.

He was glad to get away from here and the memory of those two. His hatred for them was even worse than his hatred for bent New York cops. Everyone knew what went on down here. What happened in Mexico made life a battle for William Bermudez of Red Hook. They were the same color as him. *La Raza*, the waiter at the press club had said—Ernesto jive. He shook his head. Some *raza*.

The waiter. He had a reward coming to him. Why hadn't he asked? Probably some sort of Mexican etiquette; he was waiting for Bermudez to make the move. Wearily, he put his bags down and picked up the phone again.

"You have a waiter there," he said when they answered at the press club. "A bartender, actually. Carlos is the first name. When does he come on in the morning?"

He was still there.

Yes, he said when he came to the phone. He had thought about the reward, thought hard. "There is a committee to help the people harmed by the earthquake," he said. "Nothing to do with the government, an independent group of people from the neighborhoods. They have an account at Banco de Mexico. I can give you the number."

It was about eleven o'clock. Bermudez drove to the Hotel Lara, just northwest of Tepito, where Brian Fowler might be bedding down in the street right now. A killer lying side by side with Bermudez's people, *La Raza*.

$\triangledown$

# 21

A GUN COULD probably be bought in Tepito without too much difficulty, Fowler knew. A silencer might be harder. But possible.

There was no use tantalizing himself with such thoughts. On the other hand, it was hard to stop doing it when El Feo's bull-like body had been in his line of sight all morning. The day was cool, but it was hot work moving the pallets of eggs, the water containers, and the cartons of microwave ovens and stereo equipment. Silvio and his men long ago had stripped to the waist. Fowler groaned behind them, hefting eggs onto trucks. transferring boxes to the Palacio Negro, where El Feo showed the way through the maze. Yesterday, his holster and gun had been an ominous lump beneath his jacket. Now exposed next to the rolls of his waist, they seemed almost luminous.

They had left Fowler alone to stack cartons in the new storeroom. Already the piles were three-deep, thick fortress walls of cardboard and rope. Soon there'd be no space in the center of the room. The ceiling was impractically low for warehousing. Nonetheless, Silvio was pleased with his choice.

"Still here?" said Silvio when he arrived. He pushed two boxes into the room. Rack stereo systems, Fowler saw from the lettering on the carton. Emerson, a cheap brand. Not that anyone down here would know. It was amazing the prices you could get for this stuff down here, twice what anyone would pay in the States.

"I made a bet with El Feo. He said you'd be gone. I said, no." Silvio laughed uproariously at his little joke, which he'd told several times this morning. He loved how he'd stuck Fowler up here, like a fly in a web. The storeroom was in the most confusing part of an utterly confusing network of dwellings, accessed by a series of steep, narrow staircases, some of which had to be descended before others were ascended. In a Middle Eastern souk it would have been the innermost stall.

Even longtime inhabitants of this building couldn't find this room, Silvio boasted. Only a handful of inhabitants remained; most had padlocked their apartments and moved onto the street without Silvio's prodding. Tepito's earthquake mortalities had been concentrated here, in the Black Palace.

Of all the tenements in the district, it rose highest. Sections of the top level were gone. Brick and dust still clogged the twisting passages, making them even more cheerless than usual. The light in the Black Palace was scanty, particularly in the spiraling interior corridors. They'd been built around a series of small patios—a Mediterranean design entirely unsuited for the rain and smog of Mexico City.

El Feo wasn't in sight, but Fowler knew he was somewhere beyond the door in the dim hallway. Silvio wasn't making a move without his henchman, who'd undoubtedly been responsible for transporting the rack systems. They were heavy items for squirish Silvio; he made only a ceremonial pretense of doing his fair share of the work.

El Feo and another man stuck their heads in.

"We're through now," Silvio told Fowler. He pointed to El Feo's companion. "He'll watch it while we're up north."

Fowler followed the two men out. Down two flights, turn left at the landing, up three more flights, through the room that became an atrium when the quake sheared its roof off, forty paces down an angled hallway . . .

"You say something?" El Feo turned around with a look that could turn someone into a pillar of stone.

Fowler realized he'd been chanting aloud. Softly, but aloud.

He stumbled, believably, he hoped. "I said, don't go so fast."

Silvio laughed.

A door opened, revealing an old man with a face like a sucked orange.

"*Pillines!*" he cried. "You're up to no good."

El Feo and Silvio paid him no mind. Perhaps they took it as a simple statement of fact.

Out on the Labradores they parted—Silvio and El Feo to sell eggs and water from a truck that had barged through the tent-filled streets to wait chugging outside the Palacio Negro, Fowler to spend the day as he pleased.

"We meet here at eight," Silvio told him. Again, he named the fee he would pay for Fowler's assistance in smuggling. Somehow between yesterday and today the amount had dropped slightly.

"I'm hungry. I need money to eat today," said Fowler.

Silvio grudgingly counted out a few coins, not even enough to buy the *comida corriente* at a fly-specked table in a market. "It's an advance," he warned. "I'll deduct it."

Directly over Fowler's head, an angry spot was trying to burn through the smog. High noon. He had barely enough time.

His clothes stank of sweat. He had kept his shirt on, fearful that the bills stuck in his pants waistband might become visible without it. A few blocks away on Tenochtitlán he found a one-eyed woman selling used clothes. He sifted through the pile for men's jackets, holding them to his nose while the vendor's bad eye seemed to glare at him through its wounded iris.

"You could use a new shirt, too," she said. "And here, look, these pants would fit you."

He peeled one of the notes off his waistband roll to pay for the jacket. The woman performed the customary ritual of folding it neatly and lowering it gently into an old plastic bag. Neiman Marcus would not have done it better. It was a pity that the jacket was already wrinkled beyond the powers of any pressing machine.

Fowler was steered to a shop labeled Sastrería by a young boy who not only gave him instructions but insisted on skipping alongside him as he walked there. The child made Fowler nervous. He would have to find his way to his final shopping destination alone. It wasn't good to be watched.

The tailor handled the jacket as if he were wishing for tongs. "First to the laundry," he said.

"I have no time," said Fowler. He offered a good price. The tailor pulled off a long piece of thread, stiffening his face as he licked the end. The jacket smelled terrible. Eventually it would air out. For now, Fowler wanted it to look unmistakably used.

The boy who'd given him directions was waiting outside the tailor shop.

Fowler gave him some of Silvio's coins. "Go away," he said. Later, he'd have to find food, clean food, somewhere outside Tepito. It was quite true that he was hungry.

Because he didn't want to ask directions, it took him a while to locate his next stop. It wasn't a stationery shop per se, but a candy store that sold string by the foot, paper by the sheet. Fowler bought some good thick manila paper and a black Magic Marker. The storekeeper had no change, so there was a maddening delay while she went to beg some from neighboring merchants.

Fowler went to pick up the jacket, pausing outside the shop before he entered. His boy guide hadn't returned. The tailor was done.

"A very difficult job to do in a rush," he protested as Fowler turned the garment inside out to inspect it. "The lining is fraying." But he had done his work well. It would hold.

Browsing the stalls set up in Plaza Fray Bartolomé de las Casas, Fowler looked much like the other shoppers. His hair and complexion were lighter, but he was as dirty and wrinkled as any of them. Like many of the men, he spent a long time admiring the contraband electronics set out on blankets, between pyramids of oranges and piles of mosquito netting. He devoted particular attention to the digital watches and other small items, picking them up and asking their price, until the vendors—mostly young men in jeans and T-shirts—grew impatient. They could tell from the looks of him that he wasn't going to be buying.

There were fewer people crowded around the youths selling jackknives and switchblades. In Tepito, these excited no interest; they were staples, like salt and tomatoes. Fowler made his selection quickly. From a neighboring peddler he bought a used book, slim but large and with a heavy cover. This he slipped into one of the pockets the tailor had sewn into the lining of the jacket, the one on the left side. It would provide a counterweight for his next purchase and help the jacket hang naturally.

Fowler could see now how clever it was to frame a shop entrance with flatiron soleplates. It was the closest these people got to advertising. Fowler returned to the street that had first brought him into Tepito and passed through the door he remembered, between the rows of soleplates and under the woman sculpted of radiator parts.

There was a long wait until the hammering stopped in a back room.

"What diameter?" the man in the greasy apron wanted to know.

Fowler made a circle with his thumb and forefinger. "Heavy," he said. "The heaviest you've got."

Out on the street, his new purchase tucked into one inside pocket and the book in the other, Fowler took another look at the radiator woman. Was it only two days ago that he'd passed by here for the first time, sick and looking only for cover? Now there was more, so much more, within reach.

The Metro to San Antonio Abad was packed. Workers going home for their midday meal. I took too long, Fowler thought. It might be too late.

But he took heart when he reached the wide boulevard and saw the events of several days ago being played back.

Nothing had been edited out: The families of the seamstresses still sat on their bench, cranes snorted above the
flattened buildings, soldiers dispensed water to a queue of
bucket bearers. Fowler could imagine no lovelier scene than
the one taking place on this gritty industrial street under a
toxic sky.

Yet he purposely ruined this fine reproduction. Instead of
planting himself in front of the luncheonette where he'd
enjoyed that fateful cup of infected coffee two days before,
he strolled the street making inquiries.

Jaime Togs turned out to be one of several tenants in a
building of modest size, touched lightly by the earthquake, it
seemed, though there may have been more damage inside.
Judging by the number of names scrawled on the door, Rigg's
company was stuffed into tight quarters. Fowler was somewhat
surprised. The blitzed Omaha clothing factory had led him to
expect something grander, an entire Jaime Togs Building.

Fowler checked the side streets. They'd been badly damaged; almost no one was left on them. One in particular was
extremely quiet.

It was three o'clock, about one hour into the dinner break.
Stationed across the street, Fowler watched what little
activity took place around the building that housed Jaime
Togs. A woman carrying an enormous round basket covered
with a cloth went in, probably to sell *tortas* to whoever might
still be laboring at the machines. Two men in twin white
overshirts emerged and stood chatting by the door for a
moment before parting. Clerks, most likely. Or a manager
and a salesman.

Then Rigg was there, again with a Mexican on either side
of him. As before, the three walked in the direction of the
Metro station—slowly, because Rigg was setting the pace.
Across the street, Fowler shadowed them.

But something was different today. All three stopped for
a chat at the big intersection. Nearly abreast of them, Fowler
slowed down. He couldn't approach now while the Mexicans
were there.

They were all going to share a taxi, that was clear. Lost in conversation, the trio stayed on the curb. No one had yet been elected to take charge of the hailing. They weren't missing anything: These were poor hunting grounds for cabs, and none passed. Eventually, however, one would come.

Miserable in his heavy jacket, Fowler weighed his options. He could approach now, but to be seen by the two Mexicans would change everything. On the other hand, he couldn't let Rigg leave like this. Silvio was depending on him to do a border transaction, and Fowler was going to show him just how much his trust was worth.

A white Volkswagen Beetle was speeding toward the intersection. One of Rigg's companions broke off from the conversation and raised his hand. Fowler swallowed and stepped off the curb. He would have to show himself now.

The Volkswagen whipped past. It was full.

The Mexicans looked around for another taxi. Seeing none, they touched Rigg on the arm, on the shoulder, and made their way to the Metro station. Enough of helping the boss.

Dizzy with relief, Fowler set off across the street. A wave of vehicles had been unleashed by a green light somewhere down the road. Fowler darted between them, ignoring the car horns.

"Rigg!" he yelled when only one line of cars separated him from the other side. "Jim!"

For a moment, Rigg seemed to look in Fowler's direction. Then a taxi rounded the corner from Avenida de Taller. It stopped. Rigg opened the door.

"Rigg, you old bastard!"

He was crouching to get in.

"It's me! Fowler!" The disclosure seemed to echo over the street, louder than the horn that sounded one long, final protest as Fowler dashed toward the taxi.

"Fowler?" The rheumy eyes took in the jacket, the unkempt hair.

"Go," Fowler told the cabbie. "I'll take him."

"*Señor?*" There was no answer. Rigg stood wobbling in the street. The cabbie reached back and slammed the door. More honking as the taxi plunged into the stream of traffic.

"Come on. I've got a car now. I'll give you a ride."

Rigg still seemed unsettled, but he obeyed.

"Your plant's around here, isn't it? Down this way, right?" It was important to keep up the patter.

"Weren't you gone somewhere? Guadalajara?"

"Acapulco. Just got back. Where you going—the Lara? I'll leave you off."

They were back near the factory now. It was time to cross.

"God, you look awful. You know, somebody in the hotel said someone's looking for—"

"Awful, huh?" Fowler laughed, but the laugh sounded false, and the traffic wouldn't let up. He wanted to cross Rigg over now, keep up the momentum. To pause was to consider. "I was beach bumming. Around Salina Cruz. Puerto Ángel, down there. Hammocks, beer, women. Ever do that? It was great. Terrific."

"How'dja happen to wind up over here?"

Fowler pivoted. He located the building where Rigg had his company and pointed it out, pretending to shoot at it. "Hey, that's your place, isn't it? I saw the sign. Hymie Togs. You're the Hymie."

Rigg chuckled, relaxed. "That's me. Hymie. *J-A-I-M-E.*"

It was time to cross the street.

Fowler said he was parked on a side street. They walked and walked.

"How much farther?" asked Rigg, panting with exertion. Fowler had meant to stroll, but his feet were keeping time with the beat of his pulse.

Finally they'd reached a parked car, a white Ford Escort. It was new enough, with a dashboard and rearview mirror free of religious paraphernalia. It would do. "This is it," Fowler announced. "Get in. It's open."

Rigg tried the handle. "You must've lock—"

The tailor had made the inside pocket of fine cloth. The piece of pipe slid out of it easily, and with one smooth motion, Fowler brought it down on the back of Rigg's head.

He had to roll him over to finish up with the knife. That might not have even been necessary. Blood was oozing from the man's lips, and a gurgling noise arose from his throat. Fowler lingered longer than he should have, stabbing hard, trying to make the gurgling stop. But for a long time he could hear it over the *whummph, whummph* of the knife.

Next came the business about where to leave the sign. He had thought of skewering it onto the body with the knife, but there was too much blood. Fowler had to be fastidious about his clothes and hands. He was experienced at that sort of thing; more than once he'd had to assist at a hotel cleanup wearing a business suit. With loathing, he licked the red spots on his palms.

In the end, he shoved the sign under one of Rigg's legs. Most of the message was obscured that way, but there was no time to think up anything better.

Fowler carefully wiped the pipe and the knife handle with an inside corner of his jacket before sliding his hand under the dead man's rump. For a moment, his heart stopped. But it was only that the wallet was expensive leather, very thin. He hadn't felt it at first.

A dozen blocks away was a main road where cabs were more plentiful than on San Antonio Abad. Only after Fowler was settled into the backseat did he allow himself to open the wallet.

The plastic protectors held some photos of kids—grandchildren, maybe—a membership card to a Harlingen business association, a Texas driver's license. One MasterCard, issued on a New York bank. An American Express card would have been better, but Rigg probably knew there wasn't much use for it down here. Fowler considered the photo on the license. A problem, but probably a surmountable problem.

Breath held, he spread the bill compartment open. He hadn't expected much cash, and there wasn't much. A thin piece of folded paper was tucked behind the peso notes. He drew it out slowly, almost savoring the suspense. It was a MasterCard receipt.

There was only one slot behind the plastic card holders. Fowler's fingers trembled as they dug. A tissue-thin paper came out. Even before he opened it, he could read the red lettering on the inside. It was a Mexican tourist card.

The cabbie was slowing down.

"This it?" he asked.

It was indeed. The international telegraph office. Rigg often forgot to pick up his weekly money wire. Since all you needed to collect it was a tourist card, Fowler was going to take care of it for him.

There was plenty of time to do it before meeting Silvio and El Feo back in Tepito, where Fowler would climb into their truck complaining of hunger and pennilessness and wearing the shabby new jacket, which they would think he'd owned before, and which still had plenty of use left in it.

It would be a shame to let Rigg's last money wire go to waste. For surely it would be the last one: News of his death was going to travel fast. Someone would come for that Ford Escort.

There was going to be no doubt about who committed the murder. The sign on the body said: DEATH TO THE JEW FACTORY OWNERS WHO SUCK THE BLOOD OF THE POOR.

Rigg wasn't a Jewish name, but you couldn't expect Mexicans to know that. Fowler silently congratulated himself, though he had to credit Rigg for giving him the idea.

The visit to the telegraph office was quick and fruitful. Fowler made it back to Tepito early. El Feo and Silvio weren't back yet.

He decided to wait inside the Palacio Negro. His breathing was coming shallowly for some reason. The effort of finding his way back to the storeroom required intense concentration, and before long he had calmed down. Down two flights, left at the landing, up three more flights, through the room that had lost its roof—he stopped short of the point where the storeroom guard could see him.

A slight tremor shook the building during his second pass, and pieces of brick sprinkled down on him. Fowler became confused and took a few wrong turns. When at last he found the exit, he ran out into the middle of the street and stood there, panting. Some of the tent people stared.

Moments later, Silvio and El Feo drove up and opened a door for him. As he got in, he thought he heard someone calling him: "Mr. Fowler, Mr. Fowler."

"What's spooking you, Gabacho?" Silvio demanded.

"Nothing," said Fowler. He had heard nothing. There was only one person in Mexico City who knew him by the name of Fowler, and that was Rigg.

▽

## 22

Sᴏᴍᴇᴡʜᴇʀᴇ ᴀ ʙɪᴛ south of San Luis Potosí, El Feo felt it was time to make conversation.

"I heard you've got machines to wash dishes up there."

Fowler, who was dozing, roused himself. He assumed the question had been addressed to him. Silvio was out of earshot, still at the wheel, next to the seat El Feo had abandoned to stretch out in the back. Silvio refused all offers of relief; he said it was peaceful to drive at night. For six hours, Fowler had sat across from El Feo, his back propped against a bare metal wall, hearing nothing but the clattering of the van and the crumpling of beer cans as Silvio dispatched them at regular points during his peaceful ride.

"Is it true, Gabacho, about these machines?"

El Feo kept surprising him. For one thing, the man managed to sleep prone on the bucking floor of this ancient delivery van, too big for the purpose of this journey but the smallest vehicle in the contrabandists' fleet. Its shock absorbers had long since failed, a state of affairs that became particularly noticeable during Silvio's sudden accelerations over bad pavement.

Now El Feo was amazing him again with this conversational gambit—a wild departure from his custom of treating Fowler like a fellow insensible object.

Fowler confirmed the existence of dishwashers.

"But the plates . . . don't they get all broken when they whirl around in there?" El Feo sucked hard on his cigarette, as if the nicotine would help him puzzle this one out.

Fowler's legs were getting numb. He uncrossed them and stretched them out. Maybe he'd keep them that way for the 150 miles to Matehuala, then cross them again for the two and a half hours to Saltillo. It was important to think of amusements. Already he'd spent several hours mentally retracing the path through the Palacio Negro from the entrance to the storeroom. He had it down pat now. Doing it more would only lead to confusion.

"Nothing's broken in the U.S.," he told El Feo, yawning. "Haven't you heard? The streets are paved with gold."

"Don't get any ideas about staying on the other side. We've got someone to keep an eye on you."

A typical Mexican waste of resources, in the American's opinion. It would waste Silvio's time to line the guy up, and it would waste Fowler's time to buy him off.

It would also waste funds from the supply in Fowler's waistband, but that didn't bother him too much. There was plenty to spare now. Rigg had been awfully forgetful about picking up cash from the telegraph office.

At dawn Silvio asked El Feo to take over the controls. He didn't like daytime driving, and the beer was all gone. Compared to El Feo, Silvio was as delicate as the heroine of the princess-and-the-pea story. Before lying down, he spent a long time groping around in the dim light for the extra clothes he and Feo had brought. These he spread on the floor of the van as a cushion.

He seemed annoyed that Fowler had nothing to contribute to this effort. "You gotta get a new outfit in Laredo," he warned.

"The hell I am," said Fowler. "Not on what you're paying me."

"You're supposed to look respectable when you cross back over the border."

"I look plenty respectable."

"You? You're starting to stink."

"There won't be any trouble. I stink different from you. I stink American."

Silvio had his padding all arranged now. He lay down and pulled his headband over his eyes.

"You're some sad *gabacho*, Gabacho," he told Fowler. "Imagine. I can give you a better job in Tepito than you can get in the States."

A minute later he was snoring. He and El Feo had it all figured out. The same way they figured out dishwashers.

They reached Nuevo Laredo at one in the afternoon. El Feo came around and opened the rear door. Silvio slid out first, then Fowler followed, lame until the kinks worked out of his legs.

El Feo and Silvio, on the other hand, sprang into action. They knew their way around here. The van had been parked next to a desiccated town green, a cruel parody of the *zócalos* or *jardines* that graced the centers of Mexican cities farther to the south. Silvio strode away purposefully, while El Feo ushered Fowler to a park bench.

They sat there wordlessly. Cicadas sang in the sweltering heat. Across from the square was the big Mexican National Railways Station. Fowler knew a few Americans who'd taken trains from Laredo to Mexico City, just for the kick of traveling in the old Pullman cars. They said it would have been fun if the air-conditioning had been working. A couple of Pullmans were sitting out on the tracks now. The train left at night, so they had all day to bake in the sun.

A truck labeled with the address of a Matamoros business kept circling the square. One of its back doors was unsecured. It flapped open and shut at regular intervals, always at the same points in its orbit. Fowler had plenty of time to make a study of it.

Silvio came back with a newspaper and a smug look on his face. He sent El Feo off to buy some suitcases and settled next to Fowler on the bench.

"Get them in a store," Silvio yelled after El Feo. "None of that shit at the market."

The newspaper was in English, from the U.S. side. Silvio had already found the pictures he wanted.

"The cameras are good, but don't get too many of them. Too expensive. Concentrate on these tape recorders and radios with the earphones. Everybody wants them."

Fowler followed Silvio's finger as it traveled over the electronics ads pointing out small Japanese-made items. Silvio produced a pocket calculator and started adding up prices.

"Get some of these calculators too. Like this one," he held up his own for a show-and-tell lesson. It was a bulky Texas Instruments scientific model, seventies vintage, the kind that no one really bought anymore.

"Oh, shit," said Silvio, flipping through the newspapers. "No calculators on sale. Forget it."

"I'll just look for a good price," said Fowler.

"Oh, no, you don't. We figure out the whole shopping list right here. I figure out the whole bill right to the last peso. If anything's missing from my order, you better have the change for it. Nobody's going to shaft me and get away with it."

But he really wanted the calculators. He kept flipping through the ads, searching for a picture of one. Three electronics stores had sales going. One was evidently an independent local store. Its ad was the smallest. The others were chains familiar to Fowler. One was known for its slogan: "Nobody undersells us."

El Feo appeared with the suitcases. They were vinyl, hopelessly cheap looking. It didn't really matter. Of the people who crossed the border on foot, only Americans had suitcases. The Mexicans used cardboard boxes.

Silvio spent the next half hour scribbling his order with a pencil stub in the newspaper margins.

"No boom boxes," Fowler protested. "I'll break my back carrying all that shit."

There was even a contingency list in case supplies ran short.

"Seven percent sales tax," Fowler said. "Add it in."

Silvio looked dubious.

"*IVA*," he translated. There was a national value-added

tax in Mexico, not that any establishments in Tepito charged it or paid it.

Grudgingly, Silvio ran it through his calculator.

El Feo ran to make a phone call.

"We got someone to welcome you to the U.S.," Silvio told Fowler. "Just in case you get homesick and decide to stay. El Feo's describing the suitcases to him so he'll know it's you."

The money was in the van's glove compartment. Some of Silvio's buddies had already changed it into dollars at what was supposedly a good rate.

The order came to almost $5,000. Silvio counted the bills out three or four times.

"That's the closest I can get it," he said at last. "Four dollars and eighty-five cents over. That'll come out of your salary."

"Fuck yourself," said Fowler.

Halfway across the international bridge, near the signs advising people to jettison their illegal drugs *now*, Fowler took off his jacket and threw it into one of the empty suitcases. Sweat and heat had actually removed some of the wrinkles.

"Your tourist card, please." He was at the Mexican checkpoint. The guard glanced at the flimsy piece of paper.

"Okay," he said when Fowler showed no signs of moving. "Go ahead." But Fowler waited one more second, watching the guard stamp the card and place it in a pile. It was gone now, this thing he'd killed a man for.

The U.S. Border Patrol wasn't interested in him. Some Mexicans had arrived before him, and their belongings and identification documents were getting the full treatment. Someone asked Fowler the usual questions about drugs and plants. No one opened his empty suitcases.

The welcome wagon was right outside the door. It turned out to be a kid, dark, about eighteen years old.

"Hi there," he said. No accent. Fowler had already figured out that he must be second generation. An illegal never would have come this near the border patrol.

Fowler stood close to him. "Get away from me," he said quietly, "or I'll call the police and say you tried to mug me."

The kid hesitated for a split second before his Adidases made tracks. There was no need for baksheesh after all. The kid was Mexican-American. He knew how the justice system worked here.

Since Silvio would never have believed how much cabs cost on this side, Fowler hadn't bothered to ask him for the fare. It took nearly fifteen dollars to get to the first mall, but Fowler didn't mind. Just a cost of doing business.

America. The difference was evident immediately. Laredo, a forgettable Texas town, suddenly seemed like a super-modern metropolis—something out of science fiction. The ride to the mall had taken Fowler past industrial parks, office towers, slick billboards advising people to "Drive Friendly." And now the taxi was dropping him off in front of stores that fairly gleamed with standardization.

Fowler was back in his own country, his native state.

His first act was to walk into a drugstore and buy a pair of sunglasses, the most opaque ones he could find.

He also bought a small notebook and a pen. These he took into the independent electronics store, which was in this mall. The sale had not attracted much customer traffic, a fact that didn't surprise Fowler, since the sale prices were unimpressive. He asked to see some items that were not on sale. This took a while because most of them were located behind glass. He bought nothing, but he took a lot of notes.

The two major chains were in another mall about five miles away. Fowler phoned for a taxi and read through the ads again while he waited for it to come.

The first chain outlet sold electronics on its street level, major appliances in the basement. Fowler began with the electronics, repeating most of what he'd done in the independent store. Because it was getting late, he asked to see fewer items.

Next, he walked downstairs and spent a little while

examining the explanatory tags on the refrigerators and ranges.

"GE," he told the salesman who had offered to help him. "I don't even need to see the others. I always go with GE."

The salesman wrote up his selections on a clipboard. One top-of-the-line refrigerator, complete with a dispenser that delivered water and ice through the door. The range he picked out was a more modest model. A logical set of choices for a bachelor.

"Just moving into town?" the salesman asked, writing up the slip.

Fowler followed his eyes to the suitcases. "Right."

"How will you be paying for that?"

Fowler pulled out his MasterCard.

The salesman's back stayed turned for a long time. Fowler watched the numbers light up on the credit-checking machine.

"I'm afraid this will put you over your credit limit, Mr. Rigg." His voice was lowered, discreet, a funeral director's voice. "Perhaps we can put one of the purchases on another card?"

"What if I just take the refrigerator?"

The back turned, and buttons were pressed again.

The smile gave Fowler his answer. There was enough in the credit line for the refrigerator, a little over $1,000.

"Actually," said Fowler, "I've changed my mind."

There was a drugstore midway between the two electronics chain stores. Fowler got the home perm solution for Itzel and something extra for himself. He ate at the mall food court. Most of the food stands featured sanitized Tex-Mex food. With some difficulty, Fowler located a croissant sandwich and tortellini salad.

The second electronics store demanded that customers check their bags at the door. Fowler was glad to get rid of the suitcases. They made him look unprofessional. What he was about to do required all his professional skills.

The first step was to locate a young sales clerk in good physical condition. He found his man—sandy haired, broad shouldered—under the sign suspended from the ceiling that said, "Nobody undersells us."

Fowler asked for the three dozen personal tape players Silvio had told him to buy from the independent store.

"Sorry it took so long," the clerk said, straightening his tie. "We had to dig real far back in the storeroom."

"You said these are fifty-nine ninety-nine each?" said Fowler.

"That's right."

"Something just occurred to me. See this ad? This other place has them for ten dollars less. That's the same model number, isn't it?"

"No problem," said the clerk, not bothering to look at the ad. Undoubtedly, he was familiar with it already. "We'll meet their price. Nobody undersells us."

Fowler followed the same pattern with some of the other products he'd been told to buy elsewhere. By this time, his stack of purchases was covering a counter.

"Let me pay for that so you can bag it for me," he offered, pulling out his money roll. The clerk seemed relieved. He was a smart kid. He'd been beginning to wonder.

Now it was time to make some gain. Fowler read some of the items and quantities off his list. He made sure to start with his biggest-quantity orders.

"What did you say you want for that? Well, I don't know. I've seen it in San Antonio for a lot less. Twenty dollars less, I think."

"We can give you fifteen off."

Soon a manager came over. He took over the sales duties while the clerk made the storeroom runs.

"Didn't I see that on a TV home shopping show for a lot less?" said Fowler. Solidly established as a volume customer, he was growing almost reckless.

The manager shook his head. "I doubt it. That's one of our special sales items. All I can knock off on that is ten percent."

Next, Fowler led them over to the photo section and asked

for a dozen 35-millimeter autofocus cameras. The manager wouldn't budge on price, claiming problems with the supplier.

"All right," said Fowler. "Hey, put those on my Master-Card, will you?"

It went through, as he knew it would. He was probably just a whisker under the credit limit.

Now it was time for the little glass cases. The store had a generous supply of feature-loaded digital watches on hand. The credit-card-sized calculators were more of a problem.

"We could only find forty of these," apologized the manager. "Maybe next week."

They called a cab for him and helped him carry his bags out to it. He redeemed his suitcases. No one was surprised to see them. Electronics stores on the U.S.-Mexico border were familiar with a certain type of customer.

The driver agreed to let the car idle in the parking lot with the meter going while Fowler tore packaging apart and stowed his purchases in the luggage. It was dark now. By the light of the car's coach lamp, Fowler pulled his jacket on. Careful to avoid lumps, he spread the watches and calculator along the inner pockets.

The cabbie said he knew of a gun store that stayed open late. Fowler had him lug one of the suitcases inside the door while he took the other. Then he asked the driver to wait for him.

"You could've left the bags in the cab," the man pointed out.

"Oh, yeah. That's right," said Fowler.

"I wouldn't have took 'em." The cabbie, deeply offended, flung himself out of the store. Fowler watched through the plate-glass window as the man huffed back to the cab. A door slammed in the darkness outside, and the engine started up, but there was no sound beyond that. He was going to wait.

There was only enough time for a quick browse through the low-end autoloaders. Fowler chose a Raven P-25, California-made, a cheap little Saturday night special. It was all he felt he could spend, particularly since the ankle holster turned out to be so expensive.

The man on the other side of the counter shoved a federal license application at him: Alcohol, Tobacco and Firearms Form 44-73. That was all you needed to fill out in Texas.

Fowler wrote in Rigg's Texas address and date of birth.

The form asked if he was an illegal alien, whether he was an unlawful user of drugs, whether he had been adjudicated to be mentally deficient. His pen ran down the "no" boxes.

Are you under indictment for a felony that carries a prison sentence of more than a year? Fowler checked no.

Are you a fugitive from justice?

Fowler was eager to leave now. He flipped his wallet open and displayed Rigg's Texas driver's license. The salesman dutifully copied down the operator's number. It was a photo license, but that didn't seem to matter. At any rate, nobody asked Fowler to take off his sunglasses.

That was all, except for a bunch of boxes of hollow-point cartridges. A .25-caliber pistol wasn't much good against humans without hollow points. Even then, you had to be careful to aim for the face.

Fowler managed to push the suitcases out the door. Then the cabbie came over and helped him the rest of the way.

"I lost some time on the meter when I carried these in for you," he said. He sounded pissed, but politely pissed; he knew what kind of shopping Fowler had just been doing.

The cabbie took him to a McDonald's drive-in window, then breezed over the international bridge. Fowler lumbered out with his bags and watched the taxi execute a neat U-turn and speed back to the other shore of the Rio Grande. He let out a long breath. The American side was to his back now.

The Mexican border official handed Fowler a tissue-thin square of paper printed with red lettering. By now, he'd memorized Rigg's name and date of birth. Under the question asking about mode of transportation in Mexico, Fowler circled the little pictogram of a train. It was customary for Americans to catch the night train from Nuevo Laredo to Mexico City.

Again, Rigg's driver's license number was copied down

laboriously. This time, Fowler had the sunglasses off. The Mexican official wouldn't question his likeness to the photo on the license. He and Rigg were both blond.

"How long will you stay?" asked the official.

"Six months." They never allowed more than that.

There was some business with rubber stamps, and it was over. Fowler was documented.

The Mexican didn't ask to see the contents of his luggage. However, he did mark both suitcases with chalk, drawing the letter X over the sides in long, staining strokes. The authorities liked to be thorough.

Silvio and El Feo were waiting just beyond the checkpoint.

"You're late," said Silvio.

El Feo seemed to make a low, guttural noise in his throat. Or maybe it came from one of the pariah dogs that was nosing around an upturned garbage can nearby.

They checked the suitcases against the shopping list in the front seat of the van. They all had to jam in there together because there was no light in the back.

"You erase something from this list?" accused Silvio, examining his own scrawls. "I thought I told you to get more of these cameras. I should have made another copy of the list for myself."

He tore open the bag from the drugstore and pushed the home perm kit into Fowler's face.

"What's this?"

"A gift for Itzel. I spent my food money on it."

Silvio spat and grumbled some more, but Fowler could tell he was pleased with the haul. Careful to keep his ankle covered, Fowler crawled into the back while Silvio and El Feo stayed up front, recounting their day's adventures in a Nuevo Laredo whorehouse.

As for Fowler, he was pretty pleased, too. He'd netted about $2,000 in cash, a nice supplement to the grand he'd picked up at the telegraph office. And the calculators and watches in his jacket could be sold at a 100 percent markup. Fowler wasn't about to stand in the market peddling them himself, but he knew where he could find a middleman. There was that other contraband operation in Tepito, the gang that Silvio was so worried about.

It would have been nice to try out Rigg's credit-card cash-advance limit in a bank, but the photo license wouldn't have held up under a bank manager's hard stare. Anyhow, banks were dangerous places for people like Fowler. They had direct lines to the police. He'd done right not to take the risk.

Finally tired enough to lie flat, he felt the van swing onto the Pan-American highway and start the journey to the crushed capital of Mexico. Fowler smiled to himself. He was a bona fide tourist now, with money enough to have a really fine time.

## 23

THE CHAMBERMAID DID some hard thinking while cleaning William Bermudez's room at the Hotel Lara. It's not
right, she thought as she mopped the tile floor around his
bed. But he'll never notice, she thought, lifting Bermudez's
alarm clock and swiping the bureau top with her dust cloth.

She changed his bed, cleaned the sink of his stray hairs,
gave him new towels, and decided to steal from him.

She felt particularly bad about it because this guest was
very neat, not at all like that other American who used to
vomit in his room, not always in the bathroom either. She
wouldn't miss that one now that he was gone; still, it was
horrible the way it had happened.

The hotel was so full of excitement lately. First a guest
murdered by political extremists, and then—then something else she could only call a miracle.

The chambermaid, who wore her hair in long braids, never
would have expected any of this at the Lara. It seemed like
something that would happen at one of the grander hotels:
the Villa Real, for instance.

For the first time in her four years of employment, she felt
almost a thrill about working at the Lara. And for the first
time in her life, she was stealing.

The thing that she wanted was on top of a chest of
drawers, directly in front of a large mirror. When it was safely
in her apron pocket, she stopped to examine her reflection.
She saw no difference, except that her hair wasn't braided
as neatly as usual.

The guest's comb lay on the chest. It was an American-made comb of strong metal, perfect for taming dense, coarse hair. The chambermaid took it and set to work, undoing the plaits and combing with long, leisurely strokes. Today was a special day. She wanted to look beautiful, and to test her bravery. If the guest came back . . . well, she'd think of something. He was seldom in anyway.

At the moment, William Bermudez was interrogating ten-year-olds at a city park.

"Have you been there?" one of the kids wanted to know. "In the teacups, the big teacups that four people can sit in?" Another American had described them to him, not long ago. "I've seen it on TV. They spin you around, like this."

The next question had to wait until the kid stopped whirling around. Then it had to wait until everybody stopped giggling.

A killer named Brian Fowler was loose in this city, and Bermudez was talking to small boys about Disneyland. This park, as a matter of fact, was a lot like Disneyland. From what he gathered, hundreds of people had slept here in the early days after the quake. But by now the people with long-term housing problems had migrated to harder-core encampments, like the ones in Tepito. A city made of tarpaulins and tubing wouldn't have lasted here. This was a nice neighborhood, nicer than Bermudez's neighborhood in Brooklyn. It was full of people who wanted their park back.

As for his investigation, that was a lot like Disneyland too. Interviews with people at the hotel where the murdered kid worked turned up nothing. Well, practically nothing. Bermudez now knew that Fowler had changed his name, but not his appearance. He knew that Fowler was the kind of killer who could slash someone he'd talked and joked with.

Bermudez knew something about the victim too. The visit with his family had been awful. The mother choking with sobs and showing him pictures. Nice-looking kid, well liked, about the same age as Bermudez's brother, Edward.

Bermudez's leaflet had ended it all for him.

"If I come to the United States, will you take me to Disneylandia?"

Bermudez looked up. It was the boy who had spun around, the one they called Sócrates.

"Disneyland's a rip-off," Bermudez told the boy. "You've got nice places to visit in your own country. Don't nag your parents to take you there. They probably can't afford it."

One of the oldest of the staff here, a teenage girl, walked toward the steps where Bermudez and the little kids were sitting. She wore an apron, on which she was wiping her hands.

"I'm free now," she told Bermudez. "Dinner's cooked."

Sócrates clucked his tongue. "*Ay*, Susana, you're going to get in trouble."

"We're not supposed to cook here anymore," the girl explained for Bermudez's benefit. "The local authorities want everyone to move into the official shelters. Now what was it you wanted to see me about?"

He showed her the photo. The boys gathered around, practically pressing their noses on it.

"His name's Brian Fowler, or sometimes he goes by Tom Dixon. American, but he speaks Spanish fluently. He killed a man a few days ago."

"*Qué padre!*" approved one of the boys.

"I'm trying to track him down. Prevent it from happening again."

The girl shook her head. "I'm new here. Maybe if you could come back tomorrow, talk to someone who was here at the beginning, right after the temblor."

Sócrates, who'd been there from the beginning, recognized his old friend Mr. Dixon. He'd also recognized Mr. Dixon on that day he saw him in the church basement in Tepito, where representatives from all the neighborhood self-help groups were having a meeting. Sócrates had been there to represent Mexican youth.

It wasn't possible to say hi to Mr. Dixon because Sócrates

had to pay attention to the meeting. Anyway, Mr. Dixon left right after using the bathroom. There was a lady with him, his wife maybe, with curly hair. Sócrates remembered her very well.

But he said nothing. Mr. Dixon was going to take him around Disneylandia someday.

The drive back to the Lara had become familiar to Bermudez, but he seldom did it before dark. Days were spent moving from tent to tent in the streets and squares of Santa Catarina, Tlatelolco, Tepito, Santo Domingo, Garibaldi. In Garibaldi and Santo Domingo, Fowler had been seen, but not for days. Those who'd seen him were asked to call if he surfaced again. Each time Bermudez asked someone to do this, he wondered if he was marking a target.

Bermudez parked and walked to the hotel, feeling the heavy holster under his jacket slapping against his hipbone with each step. He hadn't eaten much in the past few days. He was a man in a hurry, growing streamlined like a bullet train.

From the Lara he could swing over to Santo Domingo and visit the old man who said he had slept next to Fowler. You couldn't trust these people to telephone. They had nothing. He gave them change for the phone, but they spent it on tortillas.

Still, he would have liked to check for messages at the desk. He couldn't even get close. An amazing hubbub was going on over there, every maid and bellboy grouped around someone or something. Maybe a birthday.

Bermudez took the stairs two at a time to Gauthier's room. He had come back to the hotel out of friendship, out of feeling. A person couldn't become a searching machine; there were higher things in life. Besides, this wouldn't take long.

Gauthier answered the knock. He was packing. The dog was sitting on the floor, chewing on a sock or something. Bermudez didn't know what shocked him more—Gauthier in plain clothes or seeing that dog playing.

"So this is it?" said Bermudez.

"Not exactly. They just told me the flight's postponed until tomorrow afternoon. Bad fog in Paris. But I started packing, so I'll finish." The Frenchman had a cigarette clenched in his lips. That surprised Bermudez too. None of the young guys on the NYPD smoked anymore. Gauthier did it stylishly, like he did everything else. Bermudez liked the cut of his plain white shirt, the way it tucked into his pants with a blouson effect. Once again, he envied the French policeman. He'd gotten his man. Dozens of them, in fact. More than forty rescues.

"Well, I probably won't see you again before you go," said Bermudez. "Anything I can do to help?" That would be a switch.

"Scratch Aurore behind the ears. She isn't looking forward to the flight, are you, girl?"

"They give her tranquilizers or something?"

"Exactly. That's what I keep telling her. She'll get a nice shot before we leave for the airport. It's going to be lovely, *cherie*, so much better than the flight in. She had to come here—how do you say it, straight?"

"Why's that?"

"We had to go on duty, directly. She found seven people in the first few hours."

Gauthier laid a pair of pants in the suitcase and zipped it up.

"So," he said, crossing to a labeled bottle that kept company with his purified water. "A farewell drink? Oh, no, of course. You are working."

"So to speak. Go ahead without me."

Gauthier measured a shot into his water glass. "Did you see that commotion downstairs?" he asked.

"I was going to call you from the desk before I came up, but I couldn't get near it."

"Thank the Germans for that." Gauthier took a drink and made a face, whether at the liquor or the Germans it was hard to tell. "There's a young man downstairs who was rescued by the Germans just days ago. One of their last rescues before they delivered all those bad speeches about the Mexicans and left in a puff."

"A huff," corrected Bermudez. "Why is the man here?"

"It seems his girlfriend works here. He should be in bed. He was very badly dehydrated. Survived because he was trapped under a leaky pipe. He caught some of the water in his mouth. A miracle, really. He should be dead now, you know. And it had to happen to the Germans."

"Hmmmph," said Bermudez. His mind was wandering off, planning his route. There had been that woman in Santa Catarina who thought she remembered an American. But the man she described was too short. . . .

"Where did you get that gun?"

Bermudez snapped out of his trance. His hand went to his jacket buttons. Closed. But cops were the same the world round; they could tell when someone was carrying.

Bermudez displayed it. "Mexican service piece. Purchased."

Gauthier shook his head. "Shameful, aren't they, these Mexican police? Although I do not make statements about it to the press, like my arrogant German colleagues, still I am shocked. They were here earlier, doing an investigation. A charade, of course."

"Here?" For a moment, Bermudez thought it might be those two he'd met before, trying to get the gun back.

"That business with the American. The political murder in the sewing district that all the papers are shouting about. He was a guest here. Yes, I was surprised also. He was new, I think. I had never seen him."

"Oh, yeah. That guy. I remember that."

Gauthier filled in some of the details anyway. A cop who knew when someone was packing a piece had no trouble knowing when someone was bullshitting. A long hunt on a cold trail hadn't left Bermudez much time for newspaper reading. And his encounter with the gossip columnist had kept him away from the newsstands. He didn't want to see that woman's write-up about Connie and that director.

Schubel, that was his name. Bermudez wasn't even sure how to spell it.

"Have you heard from your . . . er, employer lately?" Gauthier asked.

As a matter of fact, Bermudez hadn't. He had caved in and told Gauthier about Connie. Gauthier was a friend.

It was time to say good-bye. Bermudez even said good-bye to the dog. Ordinarily he had nothing but scorn for people who talked to dogs, but this was a police dog, it was different. His own room was one flight up. He took the stairs and came out on the part of the corridor farthest from his quarters. The chambermaid was out in the hall, fiddling with something on her cart. She was the one with superlong braids, the regular one, but she acted like she'd never seen him before. Startled.

He used his bathroom, then sat on the bed studying his Mexico City map, already ripped along the folds from hard use. Someone had told him about a community shelter in a barrio called San Camilito.

He toyed with the idea of going there, but in the end decided to spend the rest of the day in Tepito. He knew Fowler now. He'd started killing the gentlemen's way—by criminal negligence, remote control, the kind of murder slumlords committed. Before long he was slicing a kid in an alleyway. It was all the same thing. Fowler used to be a big-city, high-voltage executive. If he was still on the streets, he was somewhere in the great lawless mass of Tepito.

Bermudez needed his comb more than he needed the map. In the mirror he looked for the New York cop who used to stand next to the police line showing his good side to the female passersby and dreaming of a cushy job in Burbank. This time, while Bermudez was dreaming a boy had bled to death.

He'd been stupid to react when that gossip columnist made the crack about Connie and the director. The thing between him and Connie had never been real. It was just a mutual back-scratching association, his legwork exchanged for a nod to the right Hollywood people by her.

It didn't matter anymore. The thing between him and Fowler was real now.

Bermudez finished with his hair and went out to buzz the elevator. The doors opened, and a young woman wearing sunglasses and a scarf got out. Bermudez stepped aside to give her room, but instead she twined her arms around him.

"*Café con leche*," she said. It was Connie.

∇

# 24

THEY SHOULD HAVE made it back to Mexico City by early afternoon. But first Silvio had decided to stop in San Luis Potosí for an elaborate, lengthy breakfast. Then there'd been trouble about a tire blowing on the highway and the spare needing patching. By the time they reached the capital it was night.

They nosed into the city from the north through the usual congestion, but as they approached Tepito, something was different. Traffic locked into place. The streets were clogged with demonstrators.

Fowler was the only who could figure out what was going on.

"Anniversary of the Tlatelolco massacre," he said. There'd been protests every year since 1968, when it happened, the main event after a week of student unrest—helicopters dropping flares on a crowd of antigovernment demonstrators, secret police popping out from behind an Aztec monument with pistols blazing, protestors running into a nearby church for cover, soldiers following them in. Fowler had been at preparatory school in those days. It quieted things down, made the Mexico City Olympics go smoothly ten days late. Best thing that happened to Mexico, the chance to host the Olympics. Anyone in the hotel business could appreciate that.

"All right, all right," said El Feo as he hammered on the horn. "Fuck the government, but let us through."

Fowler had crawled forward from the back of the van to peer through the windshield. The marchers formed a solid wall; there was nothing for it but to sit and watch. The national university had turned out its usual hundreds of demonstrators. They marched by department, interspersed with the contingents from left-wing political parties. The unions marched in hard hats, the neighborhood organizations came with their children.

The signs were different this year. Slogans commemorating the massacre were far outnumbered by demands related to more recent events. Scores of banners screamed for a moratorium on payment of the external debt. But most of the red paint clamored for the reconstruction of quake-damaged housing.

One particularly wide banner, stretching nearly the width of the street, was carried by one of the barrio groups. The kids in charge of holding it had some trouble keeping it aloft. From time to time, it drooped dangerously close to the protestors' homemade torches—kerosene-soaked twists of newspaper that were dropped lit in the street whenever flames began licking fingers. "Nature shook us, but the government threw us out," said the banner.

Fowler kneeled in the van and thought about what a fine job Mother Nature had done. Natural selection at work, the way the earthquake had destroyed barrios while leaving the poshest districts intact. Here it was the late twentieth century, and these people were walking around with flaming torches like they'd just discovered fire.

A small gap formed between contingents, and El Feo barreled through. He took side streets in Tepito, keeping his horn going to give the tent people a few nanoseconds of warning. The plan was to park in front of the Palacio Negro on Labradores, but the block was jammed with people.

El Feo unrolled a window. "What's going on?" he asked a passerby, a man in a straw hat.

"We're meeting here to feed into the march," said the man. "We're going to be the last ones, the *damnificados* of Tepito. When we get to the Angel, all the other groups will split to let us through and applaud us." The Angel was the monument to Independence on Reforma, terminal point for most of the big demonstrations and the centerpiece of one of those traffic circles that created automotive nightmares.

"Should I ram into them?" El Feo asked Silvio. "If I move, they'll scatter."

"Nah. It's a moment of glory. Imagine, all those university types making way for Tepitans."

Silvio's attack of neighborhood allegiance meant that the suitcases had to be carried through the crowd into the Palacio Negro and the storeroom. More people had already packed themselves around the van. Silvio and El Feo could barely get their doors open.

"Sling the suitcases into the front," Silvio ordered Fowler. "We can't get through to the rear door."

Fowler did as ordered. Silvio took the bags and kept the passenger-side door open as Fowler crawled over the seats. He clutched the package from the pharmacy containing the hair-care products.

The odor of burning kerosene assaulted him as he pushed out of the van. The Tepitans were lighting up for the protest.

"They're starting to clear out," said Silvio. Perhaps it was his feeling of barrio pride that prompted him to help Fowler out of the van, encircling his waist in a brotherly embrace as he did so. El Feo stood by idly, squinting through the darkness at the crowd.

"What's this?" Silvio said, patting Fowler's jacket.

El Feo spun around, his instincts telling him that something was upsetting his master.

Fowler said nothing. He watched the other two. The crowd was dispersing. The three of them were barely aware of it now.

"Check his pockets," said Silvio.

Fowler stood passively as El Feo patted him down.

"No piece," El Feo reported, stepping back.

"I didn't say he had a piece," spat Silvio. "What's he carrying in there?"

El Feo grabbed a corner of Fowler's jacket and yanked it open, exposing the pockets on the inside. He pulled out a handful of the credit-card-sized calculators.

"It's slugs or something," he told Silvio.

Wild with impatience, Silvio snatched a paper torch from a passing child, who protested for a moment until his parents hurried him along. Silvio shook the calculators out of El Feo's thick palm and examined them under the flame. The aroma of burning kerosene became heavy, almost unbearable, and Silvio's eyes burned as fiercely as the cone of newspaper.

He walked toward Fowler, holding the torch like a weapon now. "Where did you get these?" he said slowly.

Even with the crowd thinned, there were people around them. The denizens of the tents had come out to resume their usual places on the street armchairs and couches. Some were just 100 feet from the three men who stood facing each other next to the van. Still, no one in Tepito would have taken much notice if Silvio had brought the flame against Fowler's face. Certainly no one would have found it remarkable if El Feo had pulled out his gun.

But it was too late for that. Fowler had already reached for his ankle. By the angry light of the kerosene torch, Silvio and El Feo saw the Raven P-25—small, but plenty close enough to blast right at their faces.

"Get in the van," Fowler said, opening the passenger side for them. "Keep your faces toward me. Silvio gets in first." He wanted to keep an eye on El Feo.

When they were in, Fowler stooped down and scooped up the drugstore bag that he'd dropped in the street. He stayed in a crouch. It was too dark to watch what El Feo was doing inside, and he didn't want to get in the path of any bullets that might fly out the window. He stayed close to the van until he was at its rear, then broke into a run.

The suitcases were still on the street. A man on the run couldn't take them.

But these were Fowler's last minutes as a fugitive and a vagrant. Before the hour was up, he was stepping out of the men's room at the train station in Guerrero, clean shaven except for the mustache he had grown over the past few days.

It was dark brown now to match his hair.

He took a cab to the Pink Zone and found a men's clothing boutique that was still open. Initially, they were reluctant to wait on him, but after he paid for his selections—an Italian-made shirt, a navy blue blazer and light flannel pants—their attitude changed completely. When he asked to wear his purchases immediately, salesmen sprang into action with scissors and brushes, snipping off price tags and removing lint.

He left his old clothes in the dressing room, except for the jacket. That he disposed of himself in a street trash can so that no one would notice the modifications. It was no longer needed. There was ample room for the calculators and watches in his new briefcase. The briefcase was made of native leather, not nearly as smooth and supple as Italian or Brazilian leather, but handsome all the same. A rich chocolate brown, it made a nice match for the small Samsonite suitcase that he'd packed with underwear and shirts still in the store's paper bags, because the bags gave the suitcase a bit of extra weight.

Dark brown was also the color of Fowler's new wallet, bulging with U.S. cash and equipped with neat slots and compartments for Rigg's tourist card and MasterCard.

The tourist card got a cursory inspection from the man behind the desk at the Villa Real, who copied down the number.

"And how will you be paying for this?"

Fowler fished out the MasterCard. As he did so, the clerk looked at him, at a brown-haired, well-dressed American with a thin mustache—bearing no resemblance to the portrait on a leaflet that may or may not have been distributed here. Bearing even less resemblance to the panicked, barefoot man who'd been turned away here a few hours after the earthquake.

A machine rolled over the MasterCard, and Fowler was asked to sign the billing slip. This would pay for his room, his sauna at the Villa Real health club, his late dinner at the

hotel restaurant famed for its chef, and all the other amenities that Fowler intended to enjoy before tomorrow, when
he would return to Tepito to unload his small electronics.

"Enjoy your stay, sir," the clerk said in English. It was all
English here, all deluxe. Seven hundred rooms and suites,
ten restaurants, five pools, tennis, putting green—Fowler
knew all about it, he was in the business.

He also knew they wouldn't realize that Rigg's MasterCard
was over its charge limit. Possibly, they'd look in the bad-num-
bers booklet to see if the card had been canceled—something
that wouldn't happen until a statement came in and Rigg's
family noticed the Laredo charges. But those little gadgets for
checking credit lines weren't found south of the border.

"Where's the nearest rental-car place?" he asked the clerk.

"We can arrange a rental right here, sir. Hertz, Avis,
whatever you prefer. We'll have them bring the car right to
the front door. What type of car would you like?"

"I'll take care of it in the morning." His first priority was
to get cleaned up. All he'd been able to accomplish over the
men's room sink in the train station was what his mother
used to call a whore's bath—some quick splashes over face,
hands, and armpits.

An invisible signal was given, and a bellboy moved forward
to take the key from the clerk and relieve Fowler of his bag.
Tomorrow, after Tepito, he'd be on the road again, driving
north to a smaller city, where someday every building project,
every political nomination, every public celebration would
depend on a nod from the big American businessman.

In the sauna, he'd think of a new name. Donald Something,
maybe. They could pronounce that. No, "Don Donald" would
sound silly. They were going to call him Don, the ultimate title
of respect. Cortez must have been called Don.

$\triangledown$

# 25

B ERMUDEZ DIDN'T SPEND the evening in Tepito after all;
he spent it in bed with Connie. Once they got up to go out
for dinner. She was alarmed at how skinny Bermudez was,
asked him if he'd been taking care of himself. He said he'd
been doing a lot of walking. She traced her fingers along his
calves and thighs to see if that was true. He asked if they
really had to go out for dinner.

They got up and dressed. She had short hair now, chin
length, for the part of the woman race-car driver in the new
movie. He noted how it turned in slightly at the curve of her
jaw and pointed to her lips. It seemed to be sending a signal
to her and he crushed his mouth against hers hard, and it
turned out it hadn't made much sense to get dressed.

Later she stood in front of his bureau tucking in her blouse
for the second time.

"I keep seeing him in my dreams," she said. She was
examining one of the Wanted leaflets. Bermudez had abandoned the idea of having them reprinted with his number at
the Lara, but a pile of them were still lying around. The room
was pretty messy, he noticed. The maid cleaned, but she
never seemed to rearrange his belongings. Didn't want to be
accused of stealing, he figured.

"The way he moved," Connie said, "I remember it from
the times I visited Grandpa. A certain arrogance he had, cock
of the walk. I knew he survived the earthquake; you didn't
even need to tell me. Things like that don't kill vampires."

"I'll find him," said Bermudez, and for that moment he believed it.

There weren't any nice places to eat around the Lara, and they didn't want to bother with a cab, so they settled on a taco place around the corner. Connie would only eat quesadillas, tortillas with melted cheese, anyway. Something to do with a diet.

The floor of the little dining area was unpainted concrete, and they sat on broken wooden chairs. A piece of oilcloth painted in a fruit pattern shielded the kitchen from them, but as the *señora* passed back and forth through it, serving them, she left it gaping open, and a boiling caldron containing an eyeless pig's head came into view. Bermudez hoped that Connie, whose back was to it, wouldn't turn around. Mexico had taught him what it meant to be Latino, but the bad old feelings crept in once in a while, and he wished he could sweep Mexico's deficiencies under a rug.

Actually, one of those deficiencies had brought her here. The phone lines to the United States were back up now, she said. After a couple of bad connections—probably the rings he'd heard that morning in his room—Connie had gotten through to the Marquesa three times. But she was given no information. The dopes at the desk had ignored Bermudez's instructions about referring his calls to the Lara. Finally, she'd gone to the Marquesa in person and wheedled his address out of someone.

She claimed she was happy to be here, that it was nice to visit a part of the world where she could eat in a restaurant without photographers crawling out of the woodwork. Not to mention autograph seekers, because, yes, she was back to signing autographs because you couldn't let things faze you.

Gauthier recognized her, though. Bumped into them in front of the hotel, and what did he do but ask for her autograph? Connie kneeled down to give Aurore a good petting that made Bermudez half jealous. Gauthier was pretty jealous himself, that was obvious, and maybe even a little surprised that the movie star story turned out to be true.

He flashed Bermudez a congratulatory smile while Connie was busy with the dog. Still, Bermudez would have preferred to be envied for his detective work. It was unspoken between him and Connie, but he'd failed her. He hadn't produced Fowler.

They exchanged good-byes once again. On the way up to the room, Bermudez told Connie about the rescue techniques with the dogs.

"I saw something about that on the news. Which reminds me, whatever happened to that little boy who keeps calling for help but no one can find him?"

"They have that on the U.S. news?"

"Óscar, that's his name, isn't it? Everyone's praying for him."

Connie was tired from the flight and fell asleep quickly, but in the night, Bermudez became a boy calling for help. He awoke in a sweat, fairly sure that he had cried out aloud, but Connie still slept soundly beside him.

His watch told him it was the next day already. Connie would have to leave soon; her absence was costing the producers tens of thousands per day. And Bermudez, he was costing her money, too, with this hotel room and his food bills, all for nothing.

He'd have to tell her today that he was the wrong man for the job. It was dangerous to pretend anymore. One man was dead, there could be others. Bermudez didn't know what he was doing. He was an ordinary cop, soft from his easy assignment in the Movie and TV unit. He couldn't keep the oilcloth pulled anymore. Connie had to face it. To collar Fowler might take some fireworks. She'd need someone like the guys in Emergency Services. To find him would take a talented detective. The NYPD was full of them. Broadbent, the cop from the 109th Precinct who'd solved the Salad Bar Murder, was just one example.

For some reason, the Salad Bar case had been at the back of Bermudez's mind all day. It started when he was in Gauthier's room, something about that other homicide. The American—the one who'd stayed here at the Lara. He'd been eliminated by political militants. Something about sewing factories.

Bermudez slipped out of bed and pulled his flashlight out of a bureau drawer. He used it to dial Gauthier's room number, shielding the beam so that it didn't awaken Connie.

It took about eight rings for Gauthier to answer; maybe he had taken tranquilizers along with the dog. He was pissed about being awakened until he heard the question. Then he stopped being a tired person and turned into a cop.

"Did a political group take responsibility for it?" Bermudez whispered.

"No. The only evidence was the sign."

It was the Salad Bar homicide all over again. A casualty of the ethnic wars between the blacks and the Koreans, only that wasn't what it was. It was a Korean-on-Korean murder with personal motives—a straightforward case except that the killer had been clever enough to use newspaper headlines to create a smoke screen.

"You said the guy was new here? Only stayed here a day or two?"

"I never said that, my friend. I said I myself never saw him."

But Gauthier hadn't spent much time indoors.

"His name. What was his name?"

"I don't know. I don't save the newspapers for souvenirs. Just tequila and chocolate, that's all I'm bringing home. Wonderful chocolate they have here. Oh, yes, and the liquor with the worm inside. I am bringing that too. Very curious."

Gauthier hung up.

Connie stirred in her sleep, probably because she could feel him vibrating like a tuning fork. The American had been stabbed and bludgeoned to death. The boy at the hotel had been cut. It was difficult for Americans to bring guns into Mexico and difficult to buy guns here if you were short of money.

"What are you doing?" Connie raised herself up against the bedboard. She switched on the nightstand lamp to find Bermudez pulling on clothes.

"I'm tracking down Fowler. Be right back."

He flew down the stairs and strode through the empty lobby. This wasn't the kind of question he wanted to ask by phone.

The night clerk was someone he didn't recognize, not that he'd been around enough to learn who everybody was. This fellow was so gaunt and pale that Bermudez placed him in his mid-thirties until he took a better look and shaved ten years off that estimate. The guy looked sick, too sick to be working, much less on third shift. There was someone helping him, though. The chambermaid who cleaned Bermudez's room stood next to the clerk, making notes on some papers. She must have been really racking up overtime.

"Can I help you?" said the clerk. The girl looked up and kind of jumped back when she saw Bermudez.

"There was a man here who was killed, an American—"

"Yes, Mr. Rigg. Very sad."

"I met him slightly, just a few minutes. I thought I might send condolences to his widow in the States. Never did catch his first name, though. You happen to know it?"

"James."

"Was he here long?"

"Oh, yes, for a very long time. He had a business in Monterrey and a branch here. Paco knows him well. If you need more information, you can ask Paco."

"Paco?"

"The bartender. Mr. Rigg spent many hours in the bar."

"Well, I don't think I need to talk to Paco. You've got the guest register right there. Can you tell me something? Was Mr. Rigg here before the earthquake?"

"I can tell you that without looking."

"It's kind of hard to explain, but I need to check the exact dates."

"But I remember very well," said the clerk. "This is my first night back since the earthquake, and I knew Mr. Rigg."

The clerk looked like he needed a different size in a uniform; he was swimming in the one he had on. It didn't seem to bother the chambermaid, though. She'd been looking at him with moon eyes the whole time he was talking. Meanwhile, she was giving Bermudez little frightened glances from time to time. Peculiar.

"Well, thanks very much. What's your name?"

"Mendoza. Juan Antonio Mendoza."

Bermudez had it figured out by the third flight up.

Connie was up and dressed. The curtains were open, and light was struggling in. She had all the lamps on anyway; somehow she knew there was work to do.

The lists of hotels were still around somewhere, the ones Bermudez had compiled from American Express and Fodor's and Arthur Frommer when he was leafletting. He banged drawers open and closed and rifled through his suitcase looking for them, cursing himself for neglecting to write down the names of the seedier hostelries he'd discovered on his own.

"What do we do?" asked Connie.

"I'm going to call every single hotel in this city. I think Fowler's in one of them."

"He is?"

"But he's James Rigg now."

"A made-up name?"

"A real man. RIP. A vampire victim."

Phoning went maddeningly slowly. Each time, Bermudez had to ask the desk for an outside line before dialing. Juan Antonio probably never expected to work so hard on his first night back.

After an hour or so of this, Connie suggested booking another room so that she could take some of the lists and hit the phones, too.

"But you don't speak Spanish. Some of these hotels have no English-speaking staff."

"Teach me what to say. I can tell if they respond *sí* or *no*."

She learned it after one repetition, rolling her r's splendidly. Bermudez went down to the lobby again to arrange for the room.

Juan Antonio and the girl had their heads bent over a
sheet of paper. When Bermudez approached, the girl
snatched it away and stuffed it in her pocket.

"What's going on?" asked Bermudez. Could they be spies
for Fowler, noting down all the numbers he was calling?

"Tell him," Juan Antonio commanded.

She kept her head bowed, mumbling from behind her
dangling braids. Bermudez heard something about being
sorry and never stealing before.

Juan Antonio had her pull the paper out. It was one of
Bermudez's worthless leaflets.

"I took it from your room," she mumbled. "It was the only
one left. Some of the other maids used to have them, but
they threw them away."

"I don't care about that, but what are you doing with it?"

"We've been calling the number here," said Juan Antonio,
pointing to Bermudez's former extension at the Marquesa.
"But the man who distributed these has checked out.
Yesterday, no one could tell us where he was. We were going
to try again. We try every time the shift changes."

"*I'm* the man you're looking for. I gave out these leaflets.
Don't you remember?"

But the chambermaid had been at a memorial service for
Juan Antonio that day. The stories came spilling out about
how Juan Antonio had rescued Fowler at the Hotel Toronto,
only to be trapped himself at another rescue site on the
following day when the second quake hit.

"The reward is still good?" asked the chambermaid. "Juan
Antonio has many medical bills. He was trapped for a long
time."

Bermudez hesitated.

"I saw him again, just the other day," said Juan Antonio.

Or you're saying that to get the reward, Bermudez
thought.

"In Tepito, in front of the Palacio Negro."

Now Bermudez was interested. The Palacio Negro, the Black
Palace on Labradores. He knew it well, as he knew all the

landmarks of Tepito. It was badly damaged; no one was in there, the neighbors told him. He'd been a fool to believe them.

But it had been three days since Juan Antonio had made the sighting. A van had come to pick Fowler up, he said.

"Did he see you?" Bermudez asked.

"No. I think he heard me calling, but the van came before I could catch up with him."

That was lucky for Juan Antonio. His neck was safe.

Three days ago, Rigg was murdered and Fowler was seen leaving Tepito. Bermudez needed another phone. The room across from his was vacant. He paid for it, and Juan Antonio handed him the key.

"Why are you looking for Mr. Fowler?" he asked.

"You saved a bad man," said Bermudez.

The business day was starting. Men in suits were rushing through the lobby. Bermudez set Connie up with a list in the new room. But it got harder and harder to get outside lines. Other guests were using them too.

Bermudez was approaching the end of his list. The Maria Cristina Hotel.

"Yes, Mr. Rigg is here. Shall I ring him for you?"

Bermudez let a long breath out. But there was something about the pronunciation.

"Is that *R-I-G-G*, Rigg?"

"No, sir. *W-R-I-G-H-T*."

He hung up and held his head in his hands. It took him a moment to notice that Connie was standing in the doorway.

"The Villa Real," she said quietly.

He thought of asking whether she was sure. He thought of calling to double-check.

But all the confirmation he needed was there in her face. She'd found her grandfather's killer. They went out to the car.

$\triangledown$

# 26

THE ROUTE TO the Villa Real was the route to the common grave, all the way down Reforma, just a little to the north of the Diana statue, across the street from the northern cap of Chapultepec Park. It was all done up in pre-Columbian style, as if hoping to be mistaken for a Toltec monument. All the Audis with Texas plates being loaded and unloaded at the entrance gave it away, though.

Bermudez pulled up as close as he could and jumped out of the Chevy. He was surprised when Connie remained seated.

He opened his door halfway and leaned in. "You don't want to come?" he asked her. He didn't want her to be there if it got ugly, but he thought she'd want the chance.

"I can't," she said. "I forgot my damned sunglasses. There are too many Americans in there. It would slow everything down."

"Okay." He could tell it was costing her.

She reached out to squeeze his hand. "You'll recognize him all right?"

He nodded. There was the photo on the leaflets and the others he'd seen in the wife's album in Dallas. He carried them around in his head the way a grandmother toted a brag book.

"It could be hours," he warned her.

"I'll wait."

"Don't watch me walk away. Act natural."

"Natural?" She was used to more precise direction.

"Bored."

A small neat wrinkle appeared between her eyebrows. "But it would be natural to watch you," she said, the actress in her rebelling. Nonetheless, she dutifully complied, turning to face the windshield as he closed the door.

He caught a last look at her in profile as he closed the door. The muscles around her eyes were relaxed now, more relaxed than usual. She was wearing her famous face like a mask. If she could have torn it off and followed him she would have. He knew that.

Her acting instincts were right. There was no reason why she shouldn't watch him go, at least no reason related to police work. He just didn't want her to see him like that, getting smaller and smaller in the distance. He wasn't sure what would happen inside.

He'd parked behind about fifteen other cars on the circular driveway. His car blended right in. Any car here with Mexican plates also had a rental-car company sticker. The Villa Real might have been designed to look like something dredged up on an archaeological dig, but it wasn't for the natives.

Inside, the indigenous people lost ground to the conquerors. Aside from a few sketches of crouching jaguars on the fake stone walls, the whole lobby could have been flown in from Atlantic City. In the atrium was a swimming pool with a couple of middle-aged guys splashing down it on orange paddleboards. A glass-enclosed elevator was sliding down a nearby column, giving everybody a nice view of the swimmers' bald heads. Bermudez figured that the architect must have had different vistas in mind when he laid the place out.

A quick scan satisfied him that Fowler wasn't here. He headed for the reception area. The potted plants lining the carpet fluttered as he passed.

There wasn't just one reception desk, there was a sea of them, with a line before every one. A woman ahead of him had a lengthy grievance about the texture of her bed linens.

Finally, it was Bermudez's turn. They gave him the room number for James Rigg.

"Shall I ring him for you?" asked the clerk. When it came to the staff, the Toltec theme went completely out the window. Bermudez had never seen so many European-looking Mexicans gathered in a single place. They must have used the same standards for hiring that the Cotton Club used for its chorus line.

"No, thanks. I'll use the house phone."

There was a clutch of them against a wall. Bermudez grabbed the phone in the middle so he could keep his eyes moving right and left.

Fowler answered after three rings. Bermudez's body suddenly felt superalert, as if the electrical impulse of the telephone wire had jumped through it. "Excuse me, sir." Bermudez said in his most servile voice. "Is this the room that ordered the champagne?"

Fowler said no and hung up. Bermudez's hand was trembling with anticipation as he put his own receiver back in its cradle. The hunt was drawing to a close.

Fowler's room was on the twelfth floor. Bermudez asked a bellhop if there were any elevators besides the fishbowl job. The crowd piling up on that one told him it was going to be a local. The boy steered him toward a row of standard-issue ones.

Only one other passenger joined him, everyone else apparently preferring the scenic route. Bermudez was whisked nonstop to twelve. He took a moment when he got out to study the little fire-safety floor plan mounted behind Plexiglas next to the elevator call buttons. It pointed out Stairway A and Stairway B and advised guests to use them in case of emergency. Fingerprints clouded the Plexiglas. The little map had probably attracted a lot of readership ever since the quake.

A sign indicated rooms 1202-1220. Fowler was 1218. That put him at the far end.

The Mexican service pistol had felt natural until now. It weighed a little more than Bermudez's Ruger, but he'd become accustomed to that, like a change of wristwatch. Now, though, it hung on him like dead weight. As the thick carpeting squished beneath his feet, he was reminded of another hallway. In that one he'd walked with his partner in back of him, the smell of rotting garbage all around them and fear in their mouths. There'd been a different knock on a different door. He'd been the one to kick it in, but not the one to catch the bullet.

A door opened and a woman came out. She walked by him, expensive and noisy in her silk clothing, and the sound reassured Bermudez, removing his feet from the pocked linoleum of the Washington Heights tenement and putting them back on the thick pile of the hotel carpet and the soft, protective padding beneath. Everything was different now. Surprise would work for him this time instead of defeating him. He'd wouldn't knock. He'd wait.

Number 1218 was in front of him now. He checked up and down the hall. No door was opening, and there was no one in sight except a dark man in sunglasses intently waiting in front of the single elevator door located a few yards past 1220. Bermudez placed his ear to the door and listened. It was quiet. Naptime for killers, maybe.

To his left, he heard the elevator coming to a stop. He straightened and started doubling back in the direction he'd come from. Someone might be getting off at this floor, and Bermudez couldn't be seen lurking; he didn't want to be questioned outside the thin walls and cheap door of 1218. Instinctively, he cast a glance backward. Sure enough, a young couple were stepping out of the elevator, and the dark-haired man had backed up slightly to let them off. The female member of the pair had a good figure in a tight pair of jeans, and the dark-haired man looked idly after her before submitting himself to the elevator's closing jaws.

The corridor was subtly lit, but not so subtly that Bermudez hadn't seen Brian Fowler's face behind the shades and under the dyed hair.

There were more people coming out of doors now, with Bermudez hurtling past them. Stairway A was the closer one, in a recess near the elevator Bermudez had ridden, the conventional one. Fowler was in the observation model.

Bermudez pounded down the stairs, taking them two or three at a time. He was a jaguar now, the real thing, not one of those stiff drawings on the lobby walls. Reaching the bottom of the last flight, he sprang at the fire door and emerged, a wild thing among the muted colors and muffled sounds of the atrium.

Like a biathlon contestant switching off from cross-country skiing to target shooting, Bermudez had only seconds to calm his heartbeat. He had to be calm now. Calmness was obligatory. Except for the determined faces lined up before the registration desks, the people in the lobby were languid in their pointlessness. Bermudez strolled forward to mingle.

The two men were still paddling in the pool. High above them, the glass-enclosed elevator glided down its column, then halted to take on more human cargo. Bermudez folded his arms and looked up at it, just one more tourist admiring the marriage of mechanics and frivolity. The elevator car slid closer—it was about four floors up now—and the passengers came into view. Only the ones nearest the glass were distinguishable, and at first they seemed lighted in high contrast—almost silhouettes—but soon Bermudez could make out a tall man leaning against the railing that encircled the cage. He seemed to be surveying the scene below. In fact, he appeared to be looking in Bermudez's direction.

Bermudez kept his gaze fixed on Fowler, inviting him to look back, luxuriating in Fowler's ignorance of him. He would have smiled at his quarry, but the feelings coursing through him weren't the type to produce a smile, even though they were something like the beginning of hilarity. At any rate, he doubted that Fowler was the type to smile back at a stranger. They'd get acquainted soon enough. In just a few moments, Bermudez would move toward the other side of the column and station himself near the elevator doors. It wasn't necessary quite yet. He wanted a little more time to drink in the look.

A familiar fragrance wafted toward Bermudez from behind,

but it had lost its usual magnetic quality to become a scent of danger. Bermudez spun around. Connie was at his back.

"I couldn't stand waiting." She pointed to the sunglasses perched on her nose. "The gift shop had—"

She broke off to follow the rise of Bermudez's chin. They were both looking up now, and Fowler was looking back at them. Two sets of sunglasses canceled out each other, and Fowler's gaze leaped onto Connie's face. Distance and dark lenses couldn't disguise the features, the hair, the body he'd studied through a dozen movies. With only two more floors to go, the elevator stopped, and there was a commotion in the transparent elevator, bodies suddenly squeezing up against the glass sides like tomatoes in an overfilled jar as the tall man shoved his way to the door.

As if the action overhead had somehow radiated downward, the lobby, too, was churned into confusion as Bermudez raced to the stairway door. Stairway B, the emergency-exit maps called it. The gun was in his hand now, ready for peril on the stairs, but there was nothing. He opened the fire door to the third floor slowly, flattened against it, prepared to use it as a shield. A vacuum cleaner hummed in the distance.

A moment later Bermudez was sprinting down the corridor toward Stairway A. He'd had a fifty-fifty chance, and he'd blown it. Entering the stairwell, he heard a faint click and recognized its meaning: The door at the lobby level was shutting. He came down the flights in long bounds—jumping them, practically—but already it was too late. By the time the heavy door had swung closed, Fowler was already making progress through the lobby. Listening to the door was like looking at a star that had exploded light years ago.

Bermudez erupted into the lobby just in time to see the figure fleeing. Shooting was out of the question; people were everywhere, even the swimmers had come out of the pool, their paddles held straight up like exclamation points.

He ran, dimly aware of Connie beside him. The hotel guests had shrunk back against the walls to make a path for

Fowler, and they hurtled through it. But suddenly there was a group of women forming a wall ahead of them.

"Miss Oland! Miss Oland! May I have your autograph—"

Precious time was lost as Connie and Bermudez divided and dodged. They flew through the entrance as a green American car—compact, ugly, probably a Ford—squealed into action and lurched into the driveway. Bermudez extended his revolver and took aim at the tires, but an elderly couple chose that precise moment to dodder out of the hotel and into his line of fire.

"Let's follow," Connie gasped. "We can do it."

There was no alternative. They tore down the line of parked cars, both of them arriving simultaneously at the driver's side of Bermudez's rented Chevy.

"Me," Connie insisted, climbing in. And Bermudez, remembering the stunt work she'd been doing, relented. She blasted off while he was still pulling his door closed and careened over the curve of the driveway on two wheels.

They'd seen the direction Fowler had chosen onto Reforma. The traffic was fairly light on this stretch near the park. It didn't take Bermudez long to spot the Ford. It took Connie even less time to close up the distance between them.

"I'll make it up to you," she said, her eyes riveted ahead. "I was stupid, coming into the hotel like that."

"Drive," said Bermudez.

The easy stretch was behind them now. She lost some ground as they hit the heavily trafficked part, but Fowler's car was still in view. The tricky parts were the circles around the statues, the dreaded *glorietas* where six lanes of traffic merged into a mad whirl. It was worse than Manhattan's Columbus Circle—more like what you'd get if you plunked Brooklyn's Grand Army Plaza in the middle of Avenue of the Americas.

At the Diana statue, angry communal taxi vans tried to cut in ahead of her. She held her ground, cutting them off, forcing them aside. When they came out of the curve, Fowler's car was receding into the distance. But still visible.

The Chevy homed in on the Ford. They were equally matched, two boxy rental vehicles absurdly unsuited for a chase.

Bermudez found himself counting the *glorietas* ahead under his breath like a track contestant readying for hurdles. Yet to come were the Angel, Cuauhtémoc, Cristóbal Colón, Simón Bolívar—even San Martín if Fowler stuck to Reforma that far. At each *glorieta*, he had an opportunity to lose them: He could veer off down any of the streets that formed the spokes of the circle.

Cuauhtémoc was a breeze, but at the Revolución newspaper vendors were hawking tabloids in the middle of the road. The odor of the burned brake linings gathered inside the Chevy like poison as Connie recovered from a spin and set the car on course again. Cristóbal Colón passed in a blur of nearly swiped sides and deafening horn blasts.

They watched the green Ford streak down Reforma past Cristóbal Colón. At Simón Bolívar, as they gained on it, it feigned an exit onto an eastern spoke. Connie was duped for a minute, but screeched back into place.

The trouble came on the straightaway. Three buses locked into place, side by side, ahead of Connie and behind Fowler. "Damn. I can't see him anymore," she said. When the barrier of steel and diesel exhaust broke up, he was gone.

"Keep going," said Bermudez. He remembered now what lay off the road to the right: the sewer to which the rat would inevitably return. "He's traveling east down a side street. We'll go to the next circle and branch off to the right. It's quicker."

So there was one more *glorieta*, San Martín, then a right onto Rayón and into the part of Tepito where the streets were named for mechanics and shoemakers: people who worked the kind of bone-hard jobs Fowler had never done in his life.

Connie was daunted by the tents in the middle of the streets, but Burmudez urged her forward, hammering on the horn when she wouldn't, forcing children and chickens to run for cover. They bumped down the streets to Labradores.

It was easier there. People had already scattered for the green Ford that was parked at a crazy angle among their street hibachis and sidewalk sofas. A crowd of the curious was flypapered to it, gawking at the flung-open door and the running engine. Perhaps they took it for a piece of contraband placed on display, its ignition left on as proof of its working condition.

There was more staring as the Chevy pulled up and two people spilled out. "The Black Palace," said Bermudez, as if that would explain everything to Connie. But she asked nothing, simply following him as he pulled open the rotted doors with the hand that wasn't holding the gun.

Deciding what to do next was harder. A front courtyard dissolved into a web of passages. Bermudez chose one at random, pushing Connie behind him. Before long, the passage branched off into a fork. Bermudez stood still, listening to the absolute silence.

"We've got to go out again," he said. She nodded.

Back where they'd come in, he selected a skinny, shrewd-looking teenager with a head full of cowlicks from the crowd of gawkers.

"You know this building?" Bermudez asked.

The kid shrugged. Bermudez took that for a yes.

"Any other doors to it besides this one?"

"No."

Bermudez took a look at the first-floor windows. They were small and high, but not so small and high that a man couldn't escape through them.

The kid seemed to read his mind. There was a brain under those cowlicks. "Can't get to the windows," he said. "Everybody moved out, locked their apartments."

"But there are hall windows," Bermudez prompted. The hall he'd stumbled down had been dim, but not totally obscure.

The cowlicks shook from side to side. The boy traced little figure eights with his finger. "Lots of little patios," he said. "Everything winds around and around inside."

Bermudez decided to believe him. He walked to the Chevy, glancing back at the entrance every few moments, and pulled a map out of the glove compartment.

"Here's the Hotel Lara," he told Connie. "You're going there. Get Gauthier." He told her the room number. "And the dog. Bring them here."

Without a question, she got behind the wheel again.

"And hurry," he said. "They're about to leave for France."

She took off. From his station by the entrance, Bermudez watched a lame man scuttle out of the Chevy's path, working his crutches like an Olympic rower. Connie was no longer shy about the pedestrians.

# 27

Fowler squatted on the stone floor behind one of the Palacio Negro's staircases and wheezed. The race through the hotel had winded him badly, and there'd been no time to recover until now. He held his gun against his knee; it vibrated like a membrane as he struggled for breath. He did not want to sit, because at any time they might come after him, and he'd have to scramble up. He could have leaned against the dank wall behind him, but he didn't want the feel of masonry against his body. Ever since he'd seen Connie Oland from the elevator, the sensations had been coming back—the choking dust and the compression, the encasement in plaster and dust.

It depressed him to be back in Tepito. He'd already been here once today, early in the morning, but that had been different. He came to sell the small electronics to those other thieves, Silvio's rivals. He'd been a man out of a time machine, dazzling them with gadgets that had been invented years ago. Even now, between shallow breaths he managed a laugh, thinking of the price he'd gotten. And they had treated him with diffidence. He was no longer the pathetic Gabacho, the object of Silvio's derision. He had expensive clothes now. He'd spent an hour on a tanning bed.

A spider ran under the arch of his foot. He tried to scrape it dead, but it eluded him. A wheeze rattled in his chest, startling him by its loudness. Had it only been two days ago that he'd stood in this same building? He'd struggled for breath then, too, but opportunity had been waiting for him—the van outside, the trip to the border, the brass ring that he'd caught with so much daring and cleverness.

Now he was back to this, back in the gutter. The crummy rental car that was meant to transport him to a new life (it was a one-way rental; he still had to practice certain economies) had taken him instead to the slum. The automatic in his hand was cheap. Like an open container of baking soda in a dirty refrigerator, his new clothes were gathering the smells of damp unilluminated rock. He was being buried alive again.

A cough released a large plug of phlegm, and Fowler's genie came unbottled. He stood erect, respirating normally, taking inventory. His pursuers had tracked him to the building; the commotion on the street outside had told him that. But either they'd lost him already or—more likely—they were waiting for reinforcements.

He'd be outnumbered, but inside the labyrinth numbers meant less. He was the local populace in a guerrilla war; he knew the territory. Though he could not have described his present position by compass points, he knew where he was on the route to the storeroom. The incantation he'd used to amuse himself on the long trip up the Pan-American Highway was now his key to salvation; down two flights, turn left at the landing, up three more flights. . . . Whatever happened, he resolved to stay on the course he was sure of, the course that would lead him back to the entrance while his persecutors stumbled and dithered like stragglers in a hall of mirrors.

Or if they managed to find him, he would pick them off one by one. There was no way they could approach without his hearing them. He'd taken the early ground. There were stairways and turnings to fire around. Or when the time came, he could blast the padlock off one of these empty apartments, slip inside. No sense doing it now, when the shot would only reveal his position. It might be unnecessary anyway, and he needed to conserve ammunition.

A pulse thumped through a vein in his neck. The

ammunition had been left in the car. All he had were the six
hollow-point cartridges loaded in his pistol.

How many of the enemy would there be? He'd seen only the
one man. The actress didn't count. More must be coming;
otherwise, why the waiting game? It had been a while since
he'd passed a window. He was deep in the entrails of the
building now, the only illumination coming from the gray
sky over the odd small patios that punctuated the structure's
interior. Nervous, Fowler started pacing back and forth. He
caught himself moving down an unknown passageway and
stopped.

It was vital to stay on course. The beaten path from the
entrance to the storeroom.

The storeroom. Silvio and El Feo would be out on the
street selling their new booty. But they'd left a man behind
to guard the storeroom. Thoughts flickered through the
circuit board of Fowler's mind. The man and he had met.
He'd reintroduce himself, friendly, betting that Silvio—no
raconteur—had told the guard nothing about finding the
hidden calculators on Fowler and being surprised by Fowler's
gun. As for the gun, Fowler was shifting it now, holding it
inside his jacket. The guard would have his own surprise
soon enough.

*Buenos*, Fowler would say. They sent me to relieve you.

And Fowler would have himself a new weapon with new
rounds. Anything would be an improvement over the Saturday night special he was carrying, suitable only for sticking
up convenience stores.

Moving through the palace's spirals, he completed the
incantation. Up three more flights, past the room with the
sheared-off roof, forty paces down an angled hallway . . . The
last few paces put him next to an exterior wall where the
earthquake had torn out a window-sized opening. Fowler
was near his destination now, but he could not resist the
chance to surveil the ground for enemy forces. He flattened
himself next to the jagged-edged hole, careful not to show
himself, and peered out. But an abutment on the building

wall one floor below—a narrow ledge serving some cryptic purpose—blocked his view.

Footsteps. Near him. Fowler twirled around, the gun held awkwardly under his coat. If he was not quite ready with his weapon, he was right on cue with his smile, prepared for a friendly encounter with the guard.

But the figure who'd come out of the storeroom and around the bend in the hall was squatter and bulkier than the guard. Seeing Fowler, he froze. The daylight struggling in from the tear in the wall showed Fowler a moron face, popeyed with surprise.

El Feo.

Fowler began to slid his gun out from beneath his jacket. His target was too distant for a .25-caliber pistol, but there was no time to get closer. Or was there? Why hadn't El Feo gone for his own gun?

"Who's that?" El Feo brayed. "What the hell are you doing here?"

Fowler had it all computed before he took the swift short steps into better range. The imbecile hadn't recognized him. Fowler's dyed brown hair had failed to foil Connie Oland's minions, but it must have fouled up El Feo's rudimentary cognitive system: no blond hair, no El Gabacho. The mistake gave Fowler the extra moments he needed to move forward and take aim at the center of the body.

There was a yowl almost as loud as the report, and a crash as El Feo hit the floor. A mess of red gel speckled the wall behind the fallen man: the hollow-point bullet had torn part of the taurine body to fragments. But the pieces remaining had enough life to scream. Fowler waded through blankets of sound waves to stand over his bull, ready to deliver the final stroke. The cloth over the right shoulder was a sponge full of blood, and the face was an agonized gargoyle. But the left hand, as if with a mind of its own, had managed to draw the gun.

Fowler retreated and dived to the floor as the blasts erupted. Two, four, six wildcat shots thudded into walls and ceilings. They came nowhere near Fowler, but they wounded him nonetheless: He knew that El Feo's gun was spent. It could not be added to his arsenal.

Apparently the gushing faucet of flesh had enough mind left in it to realize that, too, because now El Feo's body was rising, Frankensteinian, energized by some invisible jolt of electricity. Paperweight eyes fixed on Fowler. The right arm hung limply on its string of a shoulder, but the left one was extended, murderous, as El Feo staggered forward.

Fowler put down his gun and waited. Bullets were precious now; this wasn't worth the price. He'd been a manager, he knew about budgeting. He stood patiently next to the rip in the wall, and when the apparition that had once been El Feo came close enough, he grabbed it and hurled it through the opening.

There were no more screams. The same structural feature that had blocked Fowler's view also prevented the body from falling all the way down, but it landed facedown on the abutment with an unmistakably terminal thud.

Fowler stood for a moment admiring his handiwork. It was then that he remembered the box of extra ammunition that El Feo habitually carried. He thought he could see it outlined on a back pants pocket. It was one floor below. Inaccessible.

El Feo's pistol rested several yards down the corridor near a minor tributary of blood. Fowler didn't bother bending down for it. This episode had eaten up time. The other pursuers, if there were any others, must be here now, calculating his position more accurately with every gunshot. He had netted absolutely nothing from this. Score: minus one bullet.

Well, one thing had gone right. He'd learned that his gun's trajectory was screwed up. That bullet should have gone into El Feo's chest. He'd have to adjust for that in the future.

The future was coming soon. He thought he heard noises now, far off.

▽

# 28

GAUTHIER SPRANG OUT of the car before the dog did. That should have told Bermudez right away that something was wrong.

The Frenchman, solemn, crossed the apron of road in front of the Palacio Negro. Boredom and impatience had pruned the crowd since Connie's departure. Tired of the procession of foreigners, the Tepitan street squatters had returned to their daily drudgery. Lard hissed viciously from a sidewalk hot plate as the man and the dog approached Bermudez. Connie trailed, her head bowed slightly like a mourner's.

Gauthier clasped Bermudez's shoulder. "We will do what we can, old man," he said, though it was he who suddenly sounded old. "But Aurore has already had her tranquilizer shot."

The three of them looked at the dog, teetering on the sidewalk. Gauthier reached down to stroke her, then pulled her by the collar toward the door. Bermudez was reminded of demonstrators going limp in handcuffs. This whole thing had somehow become damned silly.

But once the threshold of the hulking building was crossed, everything changed. Gauthier left his English at the door, rapping out a series of French commands that rang through the courtyard. The dog stiffened. The pair were no longer man and dog, but two police operatives.

Bermudez, his gun in his hand, turned to the others.

"He could be armed," he said. "It's very likely." A man

who'd moved from the slums to the Villa Real undoubtedly had upgraded from slasher to shooter.

Gauthier nodded. "We'll be all right," he said, giving the dog a pat. Bermudez wasn't awfully worried about him. Mexican customs regulations might have stripped him of his sidearm, but Gauthier was still a cop.

Connie was another story. Bermudez locked his eyes on hers. "He's killed two people," he said.

"Three," she corrected him, her chin jutting out like a blunt instrument. "You forgot my grandfather."

It was her unwillingness to forget that had brought them here, that had trapped Fowler in the coils of this building. Bermudez knew he had no right to tell Connie to leave.

At any rate, confidence was surging through him, and he felt as if he had the power to wrap his companions in an invincible shield. This time Bermudez wasn't going to stand and bear witness while someone else got clipped.

He turned again to Gauthier. The Frenchman leaned over the dog. There was a pause as the dog chose a direction. The playful, domesticated canine qualities that attracted children to her were shed, and the dog, surrendering to sense and instinct, became almost formidable. Mysterious messages were received and processed, and she broke into a trot.

The three humans followed the animal down clammy hallways, up half-ruined staircases, and through the brooding light of small patios, halting when she did, awaiting her decision.

During one of these pauses Bermudez was seized by dizziness. Ashamed, he clutched at a wall, and brickwork cracked and crumbled under his fingers. Through a fine terra-cotta mist he saw Gauthier kneeling on the ground, protective arm around the dog. Connie had remained standing, but when the bucking stopped and Bermudez went to her, he could see how the vivid colors of her face had been bleached light by fear.

Still, her first question was about the dog.

"Aurore?" said Gauthier. "It is nothing to her. She's been through a dozen aftershocks."

"Aftershocks," repeated Connie, for whom it had been the first. "Excuse me," she said, brushing hair away from her face. "I guess it's just that I live in California. I thought—"

Bermudez, still vigilant, backed up to clasp her hand. They waited a few moments. There were post-aftershocks still thumping through their breasts.

The dog was the first of them to recover. Businesslike, she dodged the fresh wreckage on the ground and resumed her lope through the maze. Wordlessly, the three fell into single file behind her, Bermudez leading. In every passage, they kept to the center, as if guided by a pair of invisible dividers. No one wanted to be near the unpredictable walls.

The dog slowed its trot and came to a dead stop. Even before Gauthier's murmured explanation, Bermudez knew what this meant. They were close to human life now. There was something here in this blank corridor lined with padlocked doors, identical to all the corridors they'd passed before. The three stood quiet as the dog moved forward to sniff at the doors.

"There!" whispered Gauthier.

Bermudez separated from the other two. Closer to the door, he could see that the padlock was fastened, but uselessly, on one loop of the doorjamb.

Gauthier gestured, and the dog fell back. Silently, Bermudez approached the door. It was time to go in. If he'd had a partner with him, one of them would hold a gun high, the other would go in low.

No partner this time. He would go in high. In most of the photographs Fowler had been standing.

But the man inside the room was cross-legged on the floor.

"Thieves!" he screamed when he saw Bermudez's gun. His mouth flew open in a long shriek, and a sparse set of ancient teeth were displayed.

Otherwise the room was empty. Bermudez took it all in:

the basin of water in the corner, the crippled chair, the straw mattress under the man, the scraps of petrified tortilla. This was someone's home. The man was a holdout in the abandoned building.

Bermudez slid his gun home into his holster and knelt next to the violated tenant, trying to explain. He wanted both to soothe and warn. There was a murderer loose, the man should know.

But the man was deaf or would not listen. Transparent hands flew in the air as he cursed and swore. And Gauthier, who had digested all this from outside the door, was signaling urgently for Bermudez.

Bermudez came out, closing the door behind him.

"What is it?"

"This," said Gauthier, pointing to the dog lying at his feet. She seemed to be sleeping, but fitfully, growling and shaking her head as dogs do when they dream of a chase. Her ears twitched, muzzily aware of a sound her human companions couldn't hear—the crack of gunshots muffled by the building's nautilus—like chambers.

"All right," said Bermudez. "We'll go on without her." Connie was at his elbow now. Nobody made a move. They knew it was useless without the dog.

Fowler listened for them as his fingers trembled over rope knots in the storeroom. Dozens of boxes lay strewn around him: egg containers oozed with broken yolk, cartons of stereo rack systems and microwave ovens had been kicked and hurled aside. Only a few of the boxes in Silvio's trove had been secured with rope, and it had taken precious time for Fowler to find them. Sweat slipped between skin and twine as he labored over the last knot.

It was good, stupid Mexican rope—awkwardly thick and unwieldy for its original purpose of securing cartons, but just right for lowering a 180-pound man out a window. Knotted together, there was just enough length to make it down one floor. That was good enough for reaching the ammunition on El Feo's body.

Fowler knew how to do it. He had rock-climbed on vacations in the New Hampshire hills. Silvio's haul included a monstrous air conditioner, almost immovable in its gray shipping box. Fowler, the rope draped around his neck, coaxed the box toward him, allowing the lighter cartons stacked above it to avalanche. The air-conditioner box would anchor the rope for the climb down.

Soon his breath was spent. In the corridor, Fowler lowered the box and crouched behind to push it. Reaching the place where the hall bent at a forty-five-degree angle, he stopped to rest. A few more shoves took him around the corner where his attack on El Feo had left its mark; at one point the box slid over a patch of blood and fishtailed like a car in a skid. A shiver passed over Fowler. He did not like to bend down and crawl in the muck.

But it was necessary. They were coming for him. There might be two, three of them, maybe a dozen. He needed rounds for El Feo's .38.

Then he would win. He knew he would. They couldn't be far away now. Either they'd give up, or they'd come up here. He would hear the approach and await them, hidden. Then he'd pick them off one by one.

He felt better when he reached the hole in the wall. Rock climbing was one of his skills, like scuba diving and sailing. Fowler was a man of parts. He secured the rope with a nautical knot, jammed the box up against the portion of wall beneath the hole, and prepared to let himself down. Some of his friends were enthusiasts of a climbing sport called bouldering. You did that without ropes, but you needed special equipment. In certain circles, it was considered superior to rock climbing.

Fowler remembered following trends like that. He promised himself he would catch up with them again. They were the things that really mattered.

His hands, already blistered by the physical labor of the past few days, chafed painfully against the rope on the slide down. There was one heart-stopping moment as a chunk of brick flew off the bottom edge of the hole; Fowler paused, suspended, half expecting the air-conditioning box to burst through the wall and take him down with it. But the crumbling stopped, and soon he was finding a foothold on the ledge where El Feo lay.

It was tricky business to lean over the body without losing his foothold; trickier still not to touch the exposed flesh and blood. It seemed more revolting in the open air. Fowler tasted bile swelling up from his stomach as he reached into El Feo's pants pocket for the ammo.

Cigarettes. It was a package of cigarettes. Fowler grasped the rope and prepared to haul himself back up. Gravity seemed to have intensified to Uranian levels. It looked like a long way up.

The dog rose heavily to its feet and wobbled.

"I don't know," said Gauthier. "The drug was very strong." He stroked Aurore's back. "You've had enough, you poor girl—"

As if insulted by these patronizing remarks, the dog shook off the hand and straightened. Her head was up now.

She was off, and with a purpose to her gait. Bermudez and the others bounded after her.

They were at the foot of a long staircase. Without an instant's hesitation, the dog began ascending. Breathless, the people followed.

"Earthquake damage," said Gauthier when they reached the top to find themselves in the room with a sliced-off ceiling. Nature had added one more patio to the tangle of manmade ones inside the Black Palace.

They passed another unexpected yawn of light as the dog raced past a hole ripped into the wall and the bulky carton placed in front of it. She was more interested in the intact section of wall beyond that. Her nose worked it like a vacuum cleaner until she paused at one spot.

Bermudez approached to take look. He felt it with his fingers.

"Blood," he announced to the others. "Fresh."

The dog continued sniffing, her nostrils greedy for the elixir. If the other drug had worn off, this one seemed to be taking its place.

"What do you suppose this box is doing here?" asked Connie. "Fedders," she read off the carton. She bent down to examine the rope around it and her eyes followed the rope's path out the jagged window.

From the doorway of the storeroom, where he'd retreated at their approach, Fowler listened to them. If only they had proceeded a bit farther down the hallway, past the angle that blocked them from his view, he could have shot at them from here. Waiting was one option, but he decided to make his move now, while they were talking. Silently, he moved toward the turning in the hallway, the Raven P-25 in his hand.

Someone else was moving toward the elbow in the hallway from the other side. Bermudez had sized up the situation: blood on the walls, a rope out the window, a body on a ledge. Carnage and cleverness: Fowler's signature.

Fowler heard the footsteps. He was prepared. He flattened himself against the wall, peered around it, and aimed for the chest, remembering to correct for the gun's failings.

But it was a cheap gun—sixty bucks so that money could be put toward bigger things—and even with the correction, it missed its mark. However, the hollow-point bullet meant to compensate for twenty-five calibers of chintziness made an impressive rip in the wall.

Maybe it was that, or maybe it was the aftershock. Or maybe it was years of landlord negligence that brought down the piece of roof above Fowler and knocked him to the ground.

Bermudez was around the corner now. He wasn't sure what he saw through the dust. Fowler might have been retrieving his gun and rising to his feet. Or he might have been lying unconscious—helpless, already vanquished—in the debris.

Many times afterward Bermudez tried to see it more clearly, the shadow in the cloud. Not then. Then he just blasted away.

A few yards away, a dog who'd been trained to save people howled piteously.